GOD GAME

Before I could move from my place in the dining room, or even begin to figure things out, the film cut to another hill. A medium-sized man, with broad shoulders and fair hair, wearing some sort of weird red armour, was peering at a distant view, surrounded by an array of dubious characters like the old goat Linco we had just left behind on the hill.

"Victory will be ours by sunset, Lord Lenrau," a thin, bald old man, an anorexic Lt. Kojak, shouted triumphantly.

Lenrau was no linebacker for the L.A. Raiders either. He, too, was probably in his early thirties, compact, tense, square-jawed, a quarterback maybe who was not quite tall enough to make it in the pros. His intelligent blue eyes were dull with pain and, I thought even then, a hint of being recalled from somewhere else.

"Only the lord of death will triumph today," he murmured wearily.

I liked him at once.

Then another shift, this time to a field of battle in which men and women were fighting with spears and ray guns, killing and mutilating one another more bloodily that I had ever seen in a film, even worse than those news shots of war about which the anchor person cautions beforehand that they are unsuitable for children.

The gore on my screen was unsuitable for anyone.

GOD GAME

Andrew M. Greeley

ARROW BOOKS

Permission to quote from the following is gratefully acknowledged:

"Author's Note," from *No.44, The Mysterious Stranger*, by Mark Twain, edited by John Tuckey and Robert Hirst, copyright © 1983 by The Regents of The University of California. Reprinted by permission from the University of California Press.

Mantissa by John Fowles, published by Little, Brown and Company. Copyright © 1982 by J. R. Fowles.

The Counterfeiters by Andre Gide. Copyright 1927 and renewed 1955 by Alfred A. Knopf, Inc. Reprinted by permission of the publisher.

Point Counterpoint by Aldous Huxley, published by Harper & Row Publishers Inc. Copyright 1928 by Aldous Huxley. Copyright renewed 1956 by Aldous Huxley.

At Swim — Two Birds by Flann O'Brien, copyright © Brian Nolan 1951, 1966. Reprinted by permission of Brandt & Brandt Literary Agents, Inc.

Arrow Books Limited
62-65 Chandos Place, London WC2N 4NW

An imprint of Century Hutchinson Limited

London Melbourne Sydney Auckland
Johannesburg and agencies throughout
the world

First published by Century 1986
Arrow edition 1987

© Andrew M. Greeley 1986

Printed and bound in Great Britain by
Anchor Brendon Limited, Tiptree, Essex

ISBN 0 09 948580 X

For Nathan and Elisa and the princesses

The secular scripture tells us that we are the creators. Other scriptures tell us that we are actors in a drama of divine creation and redemption. Even Alice is troubled by the thought that her dream may not have been hers but the Red King's. Identity and self-recognition begin when we realize that this is not an either-or question, when the great twins of divine creation and human recreation have merged into one, and we can see that the same shape is upon both.

—*Northrop Frye*

Grace builds on nature.

—*St. Thomas Aquinas*

God draws straight with crooked lines.
—*Portuguese proverb, quoted by Paul Claudel*

1 State
of the
Art

It was Nathan's fault that I became God.

It is, as I would learn, hell to be God.

Nathan, to begin with, is as close to a genius as anyone I ever expect to know. If this story has any moral at all, it is that you should stay away from geniuses.

His genius is part brilliance of imagination, part consuming passion for perfection. Maybe five years ago, I took Nathan for a ride on my O'Day 22' day cruiser in a five-mile wind (about all I risk) on Lake Michigan. He instantly recognized a new challenge—"strategic decision making" were his exact words. Now he races (with great success) a Petersen 42' racing machine to Mackinac every summer and I still drift around in my five-mile-an-hour winds.

A trim (fitness is a recent enthusiasm), long-haired, medium-height, Jewish political scientist from Detroit (they all don't grow up in Brooklyn) with a hint of scriptural fervor in his brown eyes, Nathan is a full professor (thus an academic immortal). It was in his other role, however, as impresario of software, that he made me God.

When he was a graduate student, at the age of twenty-three, Nathan took off nine months to work up a data-analysis package in order to write his dissertation. He's not a programmer but rather an interfacer, a software consumer who can talk Cobol or Pascal or whatever languages the programmers think in these days and tell them what we folks who don't know a bit from a byte need in the way of data-analysis packages. So his system is in tens of thousands of installations around the world.

Nice side benefit from writing a dissertation, huh?

He's also a fiction addict, which enables him to interface between the programmers and the fiction addicts of the world. That's how my troubles started.

I'm one of Nathan's prime guinea pigs. He tries out his new systems on me because, though he has never quite said it, I think he figures that if a bumbler like me can make something work, any client can.

So when by his own modest admission he had prepared the "state of the art in interactive fiction" last summer, it was natural that he would drive down from New Buffalo to my house at Grand Beach and try it out on me. He claims that he didn't anticipate what happened, so he is therefore not responsible. I'm not sure I believe him.

One God, after all, is enough. Arguably more than enough.

"Interactive fiction," he announced proudly, holding up a thick PC program package labeled *Duke and Duchess*; on the cover was a Boris Vallejo drawing of a lissome princess (reasonably well clad for a Boris princess) and a middle-linebacker kind of knight in a loincloth with a huge sword that he was waving at a terrifying dragon that obviously had evil designs on the princess.

"Data-analysis business slipping?" I asked skeptically.

Nathan's intense brown eyes sparkled. "No way. But I thought that with our graphics package it would be easy to add a sophisticated parser and create the state of the market for interactive fiction. We have a slow game for those with a PCxt or a clone and a fast game for those who have a machine with an Intel 286 chip like your Compaq."

"Oh," I said, "good packaging too. Do you have a dragon in the game?"

"No."

"No dragon?"

"No dragon. It's just a symbol of a swords and sorcery game.... What we can do now is like looking at the bison on the walls of the Lascaux Cave in France and being asked to imagine the *Mona Lisa*."

"Yeah? I want a dragon."

"In a few years," Nathan is strictly hard sell, "we'll have two spinning laser disks controlled by an even more powerful microprocessor, ten times bigger than the 286. It will be like doing your own cartoons. The disks, just like the ones on the CD players, will hold as much data as thirty-two published books, hundreds, maybe thousands of story lines."

"Great." I took off my sunglasses and put down my Elmore Leonard book. "Suppose I don't want to pick up rocks or kill trolls?"

"We are light-years beyond *Adventure*," he said patiently. "We have five thousand scenes on these eight disks...."

"That's why the package is so big."

"... With limited animation. The parser has a vocabulary of four thousand words; you can give it real instructions within certain limitations. They're all explained in the manual which I wrote myself, so you know it's good."

"I can kill animated trolls now."

"No way." Nathan was pacing restlessly up and down my sundeck. "This isn't a souped-up puzzle game. It's a real story. Even with our randomizer, the novelist has control of the action."

"Randomizer?"

"Sure, we can't permit rigid response patterns. It would ruin the fun of the game if we didn't leave some uncertainties. Nonetheless, within certain limits of variability the author controls the outcome."

Those words "random" and "variability" implied great problems for me. Stupidly I didn't challenge them. "He can make the dragon get the buxom princess?"

"Arguably." He paused in his pacing and jabbed his finger at me. "At least fifty possible story lines that can develop at the author's choice."

"That few?"

"We don't want to be excessive in our estimate."

"Estimate?" I glanced at the lake. The cloud on the horizon was, as the Scripture says, no bigger than a man's hand. I wished my teenaged waterski playmates would show up so we could ski before the storm which was promised for the evening.

"No one has played it enough times yet," he dismissed the problem with a wave of his hand, "to know how many lines exactly."

That should have been my tipoff. If the bunch of programmers who were ingenious enough to put together an elaborate decision-making package, an absurdly large parser, and an incredible number of graphics images, had still not been able to figure out all the eventualities in their little toy, then it had the capacity to run amok and do things they had never thought about. Guess who was supposed to find out? But it was too nice a hot, humid summer day for me to be that suspicious.

"So I'm supposed to get a big kick out of playing a game

with my 286?" I reached for the portable phone, and dialed the precinct captain in charge of waterskiing.

"You're not fighting the machine." Nathan sighed, not quite a West-of-Ireland, advent-of-a-serious-asthma-attack sigh, but nonetheless a noisy notice of *weltschmertz*. "This is interactive fiction. The machine facilitates your development of the plot by forcing you to exercise your decision-making abilities at key turning points. It's structuring your story for you."

"Yeah?"

"It gives you total control of your story line and characters. It makes you God in this particular story. God with color graphics if you plug your machine into a color TV set."

I think that statement is sufficient indication that Nathan knew the risks in *Duke and Duchess*. He denies it, but what else would you expect?

"Any storyteller," I said, forcing myself out of the lounge chair, "is God to his characters. He doesn't need a machine or ten PC disks to be that. As for God, Her program is not on the market."

"Stop to think about it," Nathan had enthused. "How many of your stories have *N* options for beginnings and endings? You can totally transform a plot with just a few keystrokes."

"All stories have *N* options." I drained my iced-tea glass. "Even the stories of our lives. The storyteller is God, He can do any ending He wants or redo the beginning if He feels like it. Characters get in the way, of course..."

"What kind of God is it," Nathan demanded, "who lets His creatures get in the way of His stories?"

"Our lives," I responded, turning theological as I love to do with Nathan, because even though he claims not to believe in God he is basically a rabbi who happens to practice political science and computer software. He is far more a God-haunted character than I am (you don't have to be very religious at all to be a priest). "Our lives are stories that God tells. We write them together with God. Coauthors. Our free will and His grace in cooperation and conflict. We like to read stories because we're all storytellers ourselves."

It was a quote from my friend Shags, but he wouldn't mind my using it in quasi-rabbinic discussion with Nathan.

"So now you can do it with a couple of keystrokes." Nathan smiled ecstatically. Then, as an afterthought, "Maybe God has a program like ours in which He does His coauthoring with keystrokes. Hey, while we're on the subject of God, what happens when His version of our story—assuming that He is, which I don't necessarily grant—and our version of our story conflict? Who wins? God, I suppose?"

"If you're a Dominican, yes." I went back to the hoary old debate between the Molinists and the Suarezians. "If you're a Jesuit, not necessarily. It's the classic struggle between grace and free will."

"And if you're a sociologist?" Nathan displayed that shrewd smile which occasionally creeps over his expressive lips when he thinks he's backed me into a corner (an event which I think is rare, but which he would tell you happens often; however, I'm writing this story, so I'm God for Nathan in it, so I decree for the purpose of the world I have created in this story that Nathan is almost always one down to me. If he doesn't like it, let him write his own story!).

"Well," I replied cautiously, "maybe you become a Whiteheadian, after Alfred North Whitehead, and decide that She is the Great Improviser, a highly skilled player by ear, a pragmatic empiricist who adjusts to what we do so that the end is one She wants."

"Sounds like hard work..."

"If She's addicted to storytelling, as most good storytellers are, She probably enjoys it. Anyway, whoever said that it was easy to be God?"

I would learn in the next few weeks that being God is indeed hard work, so frustrating and painful in fact that I'm sure God would quit if S/He could.

"Not me."

"Or," I continued, "you might try an explanation from William James: God is the great model fitter. He keeps trying different paradigms till She finds one that works."

"Anyway," Nathan continued enthusiastically, "if you want to be a great improviser or a master model fitter, it's as simple as a keystroke or a plain declarative instruction with this game. Pick an ending and work your way towards it."

Nathan was exaggerating as I would later discover. You could pick an ending all right, but once you'd launched the story and set your characters in motion, you could encounter a hell of a lot of difficulty in working your way towards an ending, even more in writing a story without his parser and decision tree and animation. Indeed, after the first game, I must have played it twenty more times (with a different Alpha 10 disk, for reasons which will be obvious later on) and couldn't come up with the same ending I did the first time—not that it really mattered at that point.

I suspect that the problem is—and it hasn't hurt the sales of the game, by the way—that the double-decision-tree algorithm Nathan's warlocks have built into the game is more logical (what else do you expect from a zero/one technology?) than noncomputer storytelling requires. An interactive fiction game, even a brilliant one like Nathan's (and I'll admit, damn it, that it's brilliant, a little too brilliant for me, to tell the truth) permits a writer to tell only those stories that will pass the scrutiny of another computer. Like Mr. Spock in *Star Trek*, *Duke and Duchess* won't let you get away with anything that is "not logical." Fortunately for us storytellers who are determined to produce the ending we want, our listeners or readers are less hung up on logic or even plausibility than a PCAJ is. If they were all Mr. Spocks, few stories would ever be finished.

Does God labor under the restraints of a computer game, or can S/He play it like we human storytellers? I'm not really sure. Maybe you can decide for yourself as you go on with this story.

But if all human storytellers were held to the logic of Nathan's algorithm, the fiction market would dry up.

Then we'd all be in trouble. Stories, you see, are not options. Professor Nathan Scott says somewhere that the little kid's plea, "Momma, tell me a story," is really a desperate plea for meaning. The astonishing, amazing, and confusing phenomena which impinge on the child's consciousness seem inexplicable, chaotic, terrifying. Momma's story puts some order into the confusion, some cosmos into the chaos. Religion in its raw and elemental manifestation plays a "momma" function: it tells stories which suggest that there is order in the confusion, meaning in the terror, cosmos in the chaos. Religion, in short, is a cosmos-creating activity or it isn't worth a damn and isn't even religion.

So is storytelling, even if you're a disciple of Jacques Derrida and are into the deconstruction of stories (one of the most unenjoyable ways of achieving academic tenure that I can imagine). It is as essential for the human condition as is oxygen.

Look, let's suppose you meet a stranger, maybe on an airplane, and you become friendly enough to ask the stranger who she is. Almost certainly she'll tell you where she's from, what she's doing now, and what the trajectory is for her future. She's an Annapolis grad who has served on a nuclear submarine for three years (I know women don't serve on combat craft, but it's only a story) and is now returning to her home in Rockford, Illinois, where she hopes with some luck to marry her childhood sweetheart who is a successful young lawyer and who, unaccountably, has been in love with her for fifteen years and until recently wanted to marry her. Just when he seemed to have given up, she changed her mind and decided that Rockford, with maybe graduate work in creative writing somewhere and a family of kids plus a weekend in Chicago every month or two, was a perfectly acceptable life. Now she had to win him away from a possible rival, which she thought she could do.

OK? Maybe a little bit more elaborate and appealing than a lot of stories you hear on an airplane, but you get the idea. Beginning, middle, trajectory; or to say the same thing in different ways, beginning, conflict, hope. As Berney Geis would put it, you begin with violence, you end on a note of hope, and you have one, better two, likable Jewish characters and one very strong woman.

(All such ingredients are to be found in this tale by the way, and as an extra bonus, a lot of strong women.)

Now suppose that you and the young woman have a bit of the drink taken, several glasses of Baileys Irish Cream, let us say, and she shows some signs of nervousness: maybe she's missed her opportunity, maybe she's lost her love because she recognized him for what he really was too late. You ask her what her life means. She hesitates, because that's a very personal question, but she's already revealed a lot of herself and you don't act like she's a damn fool. So she tries to tell you. Their sub, a black, football-field-long engine of mass destruction, had experienced a malfunction on the bottom of the Arctic Ocean. For several hours it seemed that the redundancy systems had all gone out and that they would all either freeze to death or drown in the icy waters of the ocean. She had not been afraid particularly.

She continued to monitor her gauges and screens. The cold reminded her of the midnight Mass in her parish church when she was seventeen, and of the light of the crib shining in the darkness of the church. Light in the darkness, the priest said, which the darkness would never put out. She remembered thinking that Martin, her young man with whom she was then in a state of adolescent crush, was a light in the darkness of her discouragement with school and conflicts in her family. She had left home and him because later she thought he was dull. But something seemed to change in him when he graduated from law school and entered his own practice, defying his father's insistence that he join the family firm. His last letters, before he seemed to give up on her, had been witty and a little mad and very passionate; but she had not thought of him as light in the darkness, Jesus revealing himself in her life, until the lights went out in the sub, and the dim auxiliary power lights flickered on. She didn't exactly pray, but she did promise herself, and maybe Someone Else, that she would return to Martin and tell him that he had always been her light. Just then the power came back on and the sub was functional again.

As she tells you her story of light and darkness, her own eyes, dull from worry and weariness, regain brightness and enthusiasm. Her hope is renewed. Martin, lucky man, hasn't a chance of escaping from her.

The struggle between light and darkness and the triumph, contested but indomitable, of light over darkness, a "structuring" symbol which her heritage has inherited and partially reshaped from Persian religion, has become the critical symbol (the "privileged symbol" Paul Ricoeur calls it) of what her life means, the core of her religion, the cosmos-making story in her existence.

A cliché narrative? Not to her and presumably not to

Martin either. And not to a storyteller worth his salt or to readers for whom the storyteller can make her adventure come alive.

To her it is a great adventure, scary, anxiety-producing, romantic, challenging. It's a story in which she is the narrator, the protagonist, the center of the action, sometimes the only attractive character, other times a sinner seeking redemption, a pilgrim from light to darkness.

Thus are we all storytellers, narrating the story of our own lives and finding in our religion, whatever its overarching symbols, the cosmos-making themes that give final purpose to our existence.

Even if we insist that life has no meaning, if like Jacques Monod we think it is all chance, we still explain who we are by telling stories.

Fiction doesn't imitate life. Life imitates fiction.

Sometimes life imitates fiction imitating life.

So Nathan and his elves were meddling in matters that they did not understand, and to be perfectly fair, could not be expected to understand. They didn't realize that sometimes fiction can take control of life.

Neither did I, as far as that goes.

I didn't argue all that out with Nathan on the sundeck. Later, however, after we'd watched the tapes and tried to figure out what the hell had happened, we agonized for hours, like two Talmudists, about these themes. Particularly about who Ranora was. I accused Nathan of wanting to hire her as a programmer. He accused me of wanting her as an adoring teenaged daughter—which was, I thought, a complete misreading of 'Nora's character. But more about that extraordinary peppermint-candy young woman later.

"It's perfectly possible," Nathan raved on that first day on my sundeck, "to postulate a double ending of the game, which will be equiprobable. Like in *The French Lieutenant's Woman*."

"There are four endings, counting the two by Meryl Streep in the film, and three of them are not probable at all. Besides, it's an abdication of a storyteller's responsibility not to make his own choice of an ending."

"Absolutely no obligation," Nathan insisted.

"Flann O'Brien or Brian O'Nolan," I continued to disregard his comments, "starts *At Swim Two Birds* with three beginnings, all equally improbable, and finishes with three endings which are not merely improbable but quite mad. That's fun, classic fun, but it really isn't storytelling."

"Fine." Nathan suppressed a yawn. "Try that, too, if you want. Our program can do anything a storyteller can do. Only better."

As things turned out, it could do one thing that a storyteller couldn't do. Not only could it influence people who are created in the writer's imagination and eventually the reader's, it could influence real people.

At least we think they are real people.

God only knows.

"God with complete control." Nathan followed me down the steps towards the babble of teenaged male and female voices (Michele, of course, in charge) talking the argot which is common to the species.

That was simply untrue, though whether Nathan's mistake was in algorithm or theology is a puzzle I haven't straightened out yet.

Anyway, after the punks and punkesses thoroughly humiliated me on the lake, we returned to Grand Beach as the black storm clouds began piling up on the Chicago side of the lake and marching inexorably towards us. A lover of summer storms, I noted with satisfaction that it looked like a humdinger.

I'd better say a word or two about Michele since she plays an important part in the story. Well, maybe she doesn't. You'll have to judge that for yourself.

At first impression, she is like a thousand pretty Irish Catholic teenaged women I have known—brown-eyed, brown-haired (slightly red tint inherited from the maternal side of the clan), with a raincloud-exorcising smile, articulate, intelligent, strong willed (an understatement), and talented (in her case singing and acting). Unlike most of them she will not, as another one put it once, "peak out" at seventeen. Also unlike many of the others, she is a superb athlete, more because of grace and balance than because of strength and determination. Twice her "Irish Twin" brother, Bob, failed after a dozen tries to master a new ski. Both times Michele popped up on the first effort, much to her sibling's dismay. Neither time did she lord it over him, so, poor guy, he was reduced to bragging about her accomplishment when we returned to the village.

Her relationship with the "twin" (thirteen months younger) gives a clue about a striking difference between Michele and most of her species at the same age. Perhaps because she spent so much time as a child taking care of another member of the family who was desperately ill, she is extraordinarily sensitive to others' suffering and discreetly concerned and caring in her attitudes and behavior towards them. Sometimes, I think, almost too "responsible."

Not, however, about unimportant things. Like returning phone calls.

Does this character description explain what happens at the end of the God Game story?

As I say, you'll have to make up your own mind about that.

After I dropped Michele off at home, I had to deliver the other skiers to their respective stations before I could try Nathan's game. John Larkin to the "Pav," as the local clubhouse eatery is called (short for "Pavilion," if you please) to cook hamburgers and spin his own SF tales about an imaginary trip to Brazil, and Heidi to the beach where she plays the lifeguard role with precinct-captain skills on which we Irish apparently don't have a monopoly.

After I had left the teens at their posts, I decided that it was time for a bite to eat. I ate a banana and opened the instruction book for *Duke and Duchess*. It was, I'll admit, a clever package. The narrative context was elementary. Two principalities, partly medieval but partly futuristic (the *Star Wars* milieu) which had been feuding for centuries. One was presided over by a Duke, the other by a Duchess; each had been raised from childhood to hate the other and the other's principality. They were surrounded by evil viziers (Come on, Nathan, they're not Turks!), high priests, witches, wizards, mad scientists, and others with vested interests in either war or peace. The characters of the two protagonists were undefined. *You will create their personalities,* the manual announced enthusiastically, *by imposing decisions on them.*

There was nowhere in the manual, and I must insist on this, any mention of an "ilel."

A basic plot structure, a familiar story line, jazzed up by fantasy mummery. You can make one of them bad and the other good. The bad or the good then will win the conflict depending on your narrative vision. Or you can go the irony route and make them both bad. Or you can choose the tragedy line and make them both good but sufficiently flawed that they still destroy one another. Or you can opt for comedy and make them both good and sufficiently wise and/or flexible that they overcome the obstacles and create peace between the two principalities. Only if they do succeed, it must be against heroic odds and just barely at the last minute.

OK. Standard plot, standard dilemma from the human condition: Can we overcome our own prejudices and the prejudices of those around us sufficiently to live in harmony, and perhaps love, with those who are different from us?

The medieval/futuristic setting, the computer mumbo jumbo, the parser and the graphics, the ingenious double-decision tree (the essence of the algorithm that Nathan's resident gnomes had dreamed up) were merely gimmicks. Nonetheless, they might be interesting gimmicks to teach students of any age the craft of storytelling. Given the undisciplined and self-indulgent tripe that passed for serious fiction in the little magazines, that might not be all bad.

Yet there was a naïveté in Nathan's enthusiastic prose. Your characters do not emerge as the *tabula rasa* which liberal social science likes to think is the human personality at the beginning of life. Characters spring into existence like Venus from the sea, fully grown and with biases and prejudices, weaknesses and strengths, fragility and courage, hopes and frustrations like anyone else you meet in the course of life. The storyteller, an artist in bricolage, has to make do with what his preconscious has given him in the way of character fragments. How could Nathan's medicine men deal with that? I suspected that the characters of the Duke and the Duchess were a given in the algorithm, possibly projections of the unconscious and preconscious biases of the medicine men, oops, medicine persons. So it really wouldn't be my story.

I made a note to tell Nathan that he had to permit his authors to build in their own character/personality program for the various leads in the tale. This could be done by a menu-driven program, pop up a series of questions, multiple choice, which forced the "author" to think through the kinds of people his characters were. Neat idea. It would knock Nathan's algorithm into a cocked hat. But with all the available .RAM space in an AT and its clones, his magi should be able to program for "precharacterization," and that would make the game even more fun and a better teaching device. It would also enhance the marketing pitch: "Create your own persons!"

(As those of you who have played the revised game know, that is precisely what the magi, programming and marketing, did. They even built a Ranora into the game when I decided that the real version of that strange little imp would enjoy enormously becoming part of the game.)

Oddly enough, the people I had to deal with when the game finally began rolling, including Ranora, were persons I might have created if I had a menu-driven program, characters who lurk in ready-made, "off the shelf" bits and pieces in my own preconscious.

I glanced again at the Boris cover painting. Someone on Nathan's staff must be a science fiction buff. If the Duke, a certain Lenrau, was dumb enough to choose the dragon over the Duchess, known appealingly as B'Mella, he needed psychiatric help, poor man.

My theology goes in the comic direction, anyway. Tragedy is horrendously real, I believe, but only penultimate. Every storyteller is a theologian and every story is about God, one way or another, despite what the local Cardinal of your choice might try to tell you.

The first thing to do was to connect my Compaq 286 (so called because it is based on an Intel 80286 chip)—a portable clone of the PC/AT—into my TV. No easy task for one as electronically illiterate as I am, because the cables and connections behind my Zenith wide screen make a mare's nest look neat and orderly. The only way I could force the hookup to work was to run it through my satellite receiver box, which would soon prove to be the cause, or maybe only the occasion, of my God problem.

We don't have cable at Grand Beach, you see, so I have this massive green mesh disk pointing at the sky, listening (as I used to tell people jokingly) for communications from outer space or from God. Actually, it is mostly useful for bringing in the Bravo channel every night of the year. Without thinking about it, I programmed the system to save not only the input from Nathan's floppies but also from my first game.

Another note for Nathan: If you can't condense this monster and if the laser-driven disks are not ready yet, you have to tell the user how much space he's going to need on the cover of the package.

I finally loaded the monster, ordered the machine to execute the program, and waited for my big screen to light up in rather anemic pink and green with the title:

The Duke and the Duchess
A Medieval/Futuristic Fantasy Romance.

Good for you, Nathan; you've touched every base. No, on second thought, you don't have the word "mystery" in the title.

I'll admit that I should have read the manual more carefully; but who reads manuals carefully save for the magi, gnomes, and medicine persons who think in Pascal?

I did grasp the distinction between "commands" and "utilities." The former were simple propositional statements, followed by the required <cr> that the parser deciphered for you. No longer were you required to send commands in Fortran or Fortran-like statements such as SMASH TROLL. You could tell the program LET'S GET RID OF THIS DAMN TROLL <cr> and it would reply primly, I DO NOT

KNOW DAMN. Then you'd instruct it EVIL <cr> and it would kill off the benighted troll.

The utilities were programmatic instructions, almost always self-explanatory, like SUSPEND GAME, STATUS, TERMINATE GAME, BEGIN GAME, DUKE, DUCHESS, D&D (for both the Duke and Duchess, apparently in random order), PAUSE. They were linked to function keys; Nathan and his elves even provided a card you could insert over the Compaq's function keys so that you didn't have to remember that F3 was STATUS and F10 was TERMINATE GAME.

Also you could assign in process a shift/function key to a particular character—like Malvau or N'Rasia—who wasn't listed in the manual but to whom you wanted to give a name and a role in the story and then, should that character's subplot move backstage, you could reprogram the shift/function key.

Clever.

So I told the machine that I wanted the game to start.

I made another mental note: call it "story" not "game," and pushed the STATUS key, perversely thinking of it as F3.

The screen erupted in a kind of sickly red with black flashing letters that said WAR!, kind of an overdone and garish version of the *Airplane* and *Submarine* games.

Keep those two in mind when you're reading this report. Nathan's crowd had obviously studied them very closely because they were both winners in the crazy software market and had figured, not unreasonably, that if they could develop a product that the reviewers—who have almost as much impact on software purchases as do New York drama critics on the theatre—would compare to either game but say it was "more advanced" but still "user friendly," they would have a super winner.

User friendly it is, until your electronics mare's nest goes out of control. Still, the blurb I let Nathan use over

my name tells the truth, in spades: "The most compelling
game I have ever played. The most fascinating story I have
ever heard."

Tell me about it.

Anyway, after a lot of color pyrotechnics, the graphics
changed to a bunch of little blips like the graphics on a TRS
model 100 banging off one another. The machine made a
lot of shrill screeching noises, a poor imitation in my judgment for the sound of war and no competition for the rushing
wind, the roaring lake, the crackling lightning and booming
thunder outside. I was tempted to turn off *Duke and Duchess*
and watch the far more interesting show the real God was
putting on.

Which is exactly what I should have done.

I pushed the D&D function key to get a look at B'Mella
and Lenrau. The Duchess was a blob of blue on a beige
background and a concatenation of high-pitched screeches
on the Zenith. The Duke was red on black and less-high-
pitched beeps. The caves of Lascaux, huh, Nathan?

Then lightning struck my house.

More specifically, it struck my satellite dish and sent
a glow of blue light dancing through my house. No time for
an act of contrition either.

The lights went out, the big screen turned black, then
blank, and the rain beat furiously against the roof.

"Wow," I said with dismaying lack of originality. I crept
over to the dining-room window and looked out at the dish.
It hung like a wilting flower, now focused on none of the
satellites. No Brazilian movie with Sonia Braga on Bravo
tonight.

Then the lights came back on. Instead of Nathan's game
there was a movie on the screen. So maybe the dish was
not completely hors de combat. A slender, attractive woman,
a somewhat younger and darker Faye Dunaway (or, if you

want, Kathleen Turner at the present) probably in her late twenties or early thirties, stood on a shallow hill against an ominous gray sky. "Carnage," she said grimly.

"We are routing them," a suspicious-looking old goat with a scraggly black beard whispered in her ear.

"Linco, if this continues," she closed her eyes, "everyone will be dead."

"More of them will be dead, Lady B'Mella," said the old goat, who was wearing a cloak covered with stars, "than of us."

B'Mella? What the hell?

She didn't look like Boris's pneumatic blonde. Rather, she was tall and slender and elegant, a brown-eyed, brown-skinned, long-haired, dark lady from the fringes of the land of night. She was wearing a loose and thin blue gown which hinted at loveliness instead of revealing it. However, the most striking thing about B'Mella, if that was really her name, was the drawn, haunted expression on her finely carved face, a woman who in a brief span of life had seen uncounted horrors but was still vulnerable to being hurt by more horror. I think I fell in love with her at once.

Before I could move from my place in the dining room, or even begin to figure things out, the film cut to another hill. A medium-sized man, with broad shoulders and fair hair, wearing some sort of weird red armor, was peering at a distant view, surrounded by an array of dubious characters like the old goat Linco we had just left behind on the hill.

"Victory will be ours by sunset, Lord Lenrau," a thin, bald old man, an anorexic Lt. Kojak, shouted triumphantly.

Lenrau was no linebacker for the L.A. Raiders either. He, too, was probably in his early thirties, compact, tense, square-jawed, a quarterback maybe who was not quite tall enough to make it in the pros. His intelligent blue eyes were dull with pain and, I thought even then, a hint of being recalled from somewhere else.

"Only the lord of death will triumph today," he murmured wearily.

I liked him at once.

Then another shift, this time to a field of battle in which men and women were fighting with spears and ray guns, killing and mutilating one another more bloodily than I had ever seen in a film, even worse than those news shots of war about which the anchor person cautions beforehand that they are unsuitable for children.

The gore on my screen was unsuitable for anyone.

2 The Other Side of Planck's Wall

Already I was hooked on the God Game.

I didn't know yet, however, that it was a God Game.

I did not bother to sort out the implications of what had happened. It was Nathan's game all right, but now working on a different dimension of reality than a couple of decision trees, a big parser, and some extensive but crude graphics.

Did I still control it?

I rushed to my terminal and typed in MAKE PEACE <cr>.

WHO? flashed on the screen like a subtitle.

I should have pushed a function key first.

I pounded the D&D key.

(In the rest of this story, I'll leave out the function keys most of the time and the carriage return signal always. The computer freak will read them in anyway and the noncomputer person doesn't need them.)

Cut to B'Mella: "Signal a truce," she said, looking as though she were about to become physically ill.

"But, Lady!" wailed one of the heavies around her. "We are winning! The evil Lord Lenrau will soon be dead."

The woman hesitated. An expression of terrible hatred crossed her lovely face.

OFFER TRUCE I told the program and held down the REPEAT button.

EXECUTING flashed on the screen.

B'Mella sagged against a young woman who seemed to be some sort of lady-in-waiting. She forced words out of her lips as though she was spending her life's blood.

"Offer a truce."

Cut to Lenrau's headquarters.

"It is a trick," screamed one of his advisers. "The witch seeks to avoid her fate. Do not be deceived."

The Duke glanced at him casually, as though he might be considering an interesting but unimportant insect. He looked back at the screen, hesitated, his face working with conflicting emotions. "She anticipated me, the foul whore. Very well. Let us see what she plans. Order a truce."

The next scene was the battlefield. The soldiers on both sides paused in their mayhem, receiving some orders that I had not heard. They glanced at each other warily, not sure that they should stop the killing. Then some of them backed off, torn between obedience and blood lust.

A warrior in red armor removed the oblong-shaped helmet which seemed to be required of Lenrau's warriors, shook out long black hair and began to push her colleagues away from combat positions. She had, I noted in passing, pale white skin and scorching blue eyes.

I figured I would give her a little help.

EXECUTE CLOUDBURST I typed in.

DO NOT KNOW CLOUDBURST it responded.

BIG THUNDERSTORM, REAL BIG.

EXECUTING.

The skies on my screen opened and the rain fell in torrents, making the downpour outside my house seem like a drizzle.

The opposing armies ran for cover, in the thick, twisted

forests which lined the battlefield. Nothing like a rainstorm to take the steam out of mass mayhem.

Back to the Duke. "She's proposing negotiations," Lenrau breathed. "Is there a mistake? Is the rain disturbing the signals?"

Proposing negotiations? I didn't tell her to do that. Did my instruction to make peace have a delayed impact? What were the rules of this crazy game? Were there any rules?

"It is a trick, my Lord," the Kojak type dithered. "A trick. Demand hostages before we send anyone to negotiations."

Lenrau nodded heavily. "Tell the whore," he snapped at his screen, "that unless she sends hostages, we will not enter into negotiations."

The poor man was confused. His world had suddenly come apart, so much so that his heart really wasn't in the word "whore" when he used it of his enemy. For good measure, I typed out a new instruction after the D&D keystroke. CONTINUE MAKING PEACE.

ALREADY EXECUTING, the machine flashed back at me impatiently. Then the screen cleared and I had a close-up of B'Mella's lovely face, calm, ravaged, beyond hope or despair, a Christian matron ready for the lions. Did they have Christians? Apparently they had a hell.

"The evil one demands hostages," a shrill voice said behind her.

She nodded, but didn't seem to hear.

"Shall we begin fighting again?" the shrill one asked hopefully, a woman's voice I thought.

"Tell them," her manner was cool, her face expressionless, "that I will offer myself as hostage."

I was not altogether pleased with the lovely lady, even if by now I had fallen in love with her. It was my story, not hers, and this little bit of melodrama was, I thought, going too far too soon.

With its now customary persistent tenacity, the program switched me back to Lenrau, also a closeup. He was angry, his lips pursed tightly, his eyes hooded, a man whose patience had been pushed too far.

"Accept her offer and kill her"—Kojak again—"slowly and painfully as she deserves to die."

The proposal appealed; a slow, cruel smile crossed Lenrau's face. Hey, what was happening to my nice-guy, half-mystical Duke?

NEGOTIATE IN GOOD FAITH, NO HOSTAGES, I ordered.

I DO NOT KNOW FAITH.

You wouldn't. SINCERELY.

NEGOTIATE SINCERELY?

EXECUTE, I pounded the keys.

The expression on Lenrau's face changed. His eyes softened. He seemed mildly curious. "No, let's begin the preliminary discussions on the battlefield without hostages. Maybe she is willing to end her crimes."

"Do you believe that?" The young, black-haired man who came into view behind his shoulder was genial and handsome. I thumbed through my manual to find out who he was. No luck.

"I'm not sure," Lenrau sighed. "That offer took courage. If I had accepted it and she came here, they would have killed her no matter what I said."

"You want to meet her?" The young man, a friend, I gathered, raised an eyebrow. Of all the people who had appeared so far, he was the most relaxed and self-possessed, a young James Bond completely in command, but with far more gentle eyes than either Roger Moore or Sean Connery (as Bond, for in other films Connery's gentle eyes are hard to match). He was, I would later find, not of the warrior caste that did the fighting, nor of the priestly caste that egged on the fighters, nor even of the political caste which sometimes advised peace and more often war, but of a class of courtiers and scholars, a handful of Renaissance men who wrote poems, played musical instruments, and did scholarly research.

Lenrau took off his helmet and ran his fingers through his tight curly hair.

"The ilel says I must."

The other nodded. "The ilel is hard to resist."

What was an ilel?

"Implacable." Lenrau gave a small weary smile of tolerant amusement, a father with a charming if undisciplined child. "Maybe it's time. How long, Kaila, has it been since our leaders have met each other face to face?"

"Three generations." The young man was now in my list of good guys. "You're right, 'Rau. Maybe it's time."

And it was time for me to remember that I had a SUSPEND GAME function key. The bloodshed had stopped, peacemaking had begun. Now I should figure out what kind of trick Nathan had pulled on me.

My battle with the Duke and the Duchess had lasted no more than a half hour, only long enough for the summer storm to sweep through our village and head for Notre Dame, where hopefully it would drench the Theology Department. Yet I was as spent as though I had sat through twelve films as scary as *Halloween*. My reactions had been purely instinctive. I was responsible for the people on the screen. I had to help them. It did not matter who they were or how I had been assigned responsibility for them. As the storm fled southwestward, I began to analyze what had happened. I didn't like it.

Let me deal with your obvious objections first. Why didn't I call Nathan?

Don't be absurd. I did that as soon as the screen returned to pink and green. No answer. Then I remembered that he was sailing the *Red Shift*, his Petersen, to Chicago to prepare for the annual lemming charge to Mackinac. No Nathan for a week.

How do I know that the lightning didn't strike me instead of the dish and that I was not temporarily round the bend, or more so than usual?

The answer is that during the next two days, while I was playing Nathan's God Game, I waterskied with Bob and Michele, talked to my office in Chicago, my sister, my agent, and my publisher on the phone, and carried on a normal life, as they will testify. They all agree that I seemed preoccupied, as I do when writing a novel, but, in Michele's finely honed phrase, "no more of an airhead than usual."

Finally, can I prove that I didn't make it all up?

I have tapes.

Yeah, videotapes. I thought to turn on the VCR towards the end of the game. They scared Nathan half to death as well they might; he found them so weird that he would have no part of using them even for marketing purposes. I'm not about to show them to you. In fact, they're locked up in another country where U.S. government bureaucrats can't get at them.

Why are they scary? Two reasons: the world on the tape is different enough from our to terrify you. It's one thing to imagine other worlds, like ours only a little different, and even to see these worlds in SF films. It's another to have one invade your parlor or lab or classroom. The other reason is that no film you've ever seen dares to be as honest about human passion, love and hatred, as these tapes. The fury and the affection between Lenrau and B'Mella are not toned down the way we tone down raw human emotion when we depict it artistically. This latter reason is why the biologists and social scientists who came to our seminars unanimously agreed that we couldn't show the tapes outside the controlled environment of a university.

And that was the reaction without a sound track. For some reason all the tape picked up was the visuals. It was worse when you heard them.

To a person, our colleagues found the love between the Duke and the Duchess more fearsome than their hatred.

I won't show you the tapes. But if you're sufficiently interested, I'll give you the names of two scientists who have seen them. They'll confirm this story for you, but most people don't want it confirmed.

So what happened?

As best as we can figure it out, the linkage between my PC, Nathan's game, the big screen TV, and the satellite dish, all messed up in the crazy system of connections that an electronic illiterate like me can put together without half trying, created or more likely invaded a "port" that was open to events happening elsewhere. I suppose that the world abounds with such "ports," but they are rarely activated because they are rarely struck by lightning precisely when all the links are in place. As I see it, the key factors were the lightning bolt and Nathan's game.

I'll admit that at first I suspected that Nathan had actually broken through to the other world and was as usual using me as his guinea pig. But he denied it, and I believe him. He is an honest man, and moreover his terror at the passion between B'Mella and Lenrau was unfeigned.

So was I for a few hours of electronic fluke in touch with another planet?

I doubt it.

More likely another cosmos, one existing "adjacent" to ours but on different dimensions of time and space. The theoretical physicists postulate such "adjacent" universes to explain some of the bizarre things that happen as they go back in time towards Planck's Wall (when the universe in which we live was only 10^{-42} seconds old). As one of those to whom we showed the tapes remarked, "My theory postulates such a realm. I don't want it to really exist, however. It raises too many other questions."

That's just about what a distinguished Protestant theologian said. "It's possible, but I don't want it to be true."

The Jesuit who watched the tapes, if you ask me, was wondering what B'Mella and Lenrau would do about the high-school education of any potential offspring.

That first evening, I turned the game back on after half an hour of dithering. The same amount of time had passed on the battlefield. In that part of my brain which was still thinking about Nathan, I congratulated him on that technical breakthrough.

The rained-soaked armies slowly backed off from one another and two men walked warily into the "no man's land" between them as the deep purple sun began to race through the thick black clouds towards the mountains on one side of my screen and a string of misshapen moons slipped over the snow-capped mountains on the other side and quickly hid behind the cloud banks.

One of the truce makers was Kaila, the handsome young man who had stood next to Lenrau and recommended the cease-fire. The other was a tall, silver-haired aristocrat named Malvau from B'Mella's court, a man whose every bone and muscle proclaimed that he was unbearably, intolerably distinguished.

They stared at one another in a long, tension-packed silence, as the rain streamed down both their faces. Some of the warriors began to finger their weapons nervously.

"I believe, most noble Lord Malvau," the younger man

bowed respectfully, "that our ancestors met on a field like this once before, though without the rain to mark the event."

"A hundred and forty years ago." Malvau sniffed haughtily. No bow from him.

"Actually a hundred and forty-two years ago." Kaila's second bow was a bit less than respectful.

"Our families have brought peace once before. Perhaps we can repeat the phenomenon." He still looked down his nose, but a trifle less arrogantly. "They are, after all, older than the families of the Duke and the Duchess."

"Yours, at least, appears to be continuing." Kaila permitted himself a smile. "A beautiful wife, two lovely daughters, a handsome son, healthy grandchildren."

"You continue your family's reputation for clever words." Malvau's lips moved slightly, perhaps a smile. "I for my part wish to protect the health of my children and grandchildren from an even more disastrous war."

"And perhaps to permit me enough life to sire children and even grandchildren of my own?"

"A most desirable possibility." Again the slight movement of his lips, a little more this time.

They exchanged elaborate and convoluted flattery for a time. Out of consideration for their sincerity I decided to improve the weather a bit.

DELETE RAINSTORM.

EXECUTING.

It stopped instantly. I knew that eventually I would have to cope with why I was able to do that sort of thing. But I was too interested in how Malvau and Kaila would work out the details of the truce.

It wasn't easy, despite their infinite—and as far as I could see sincere—courtesy. I suspected that both of them were conscious of the small delegations of warriors who were huddled within listening distance behind them and afraid to seem too accommodating.

The young woman with the long, black hair frowned angrily at each compliment. It was a shame, I thought, that her gloriously delicate features should be marred by anger. I wondered why someone who seemed to be a classic Celtic beauty would show up on this world.

As the compliments dragged on, the warrior delegations began to murmur uneasily. Malvau and Kaila hesitated. I started to wonder what I should do if the truce came apart. The woman warrior saved me the trouble. She turned on her colleagues and silenced them with a single furious glance. The warriors on the other side quieted down too.

The best that could be accomplished was an agreement that they would meet again tomorrow and that the armies would return to their quarters for the night. Both the negotiators seemed quite happy with this minute progress.

The warriors began to straggle away uncertainly from the battlefield, a soggy mass of partly disappointed and partly relieved fighters.

With rueful smiles the two lordly peacemakers bid each other farewell.

"We both live through another night, it would seem." Kaila bowed again. "You will present my respects to the excellent Lady N'Rasia."

"I will," the older man absolutely would not bow, "with gratitude that I'm sure she too will feel."

They both waited for several more moments, neither wanting to seem to be the first to leave. Finally Kaila bowed yet once more and walked off into the darkness, ignoring the stony-faced young woman in red armor who had lingered, intently watching his every move.

How come, you want to know, they spoke English pretty much like ours (though I'm the only one that can confirm it because of the absence of sound on the tapes), looked like us, and acted more or less the way we do? Why were their names the same as those of the Duke and Duchess (and all the other characters) in Nathan's "interactive fiction"?

That one I can't answer. I admit that its implications scare me. If they were for a few months of their existence part of a game I was playing, might we not be part of a game that someone in another adjacent cosmos is playing with us?

But maybe the question of the names is worded the wrong way. Maybe we should be asking how come Nathan's game was modeled after their universe and not vice versa.

Another possibility is that the port was also a translator. The whole crowd of them could have been scaly septupeds (though I will resist the possibility that Ranora is such a creature) with whirling antennae, speaking in beeps. Maybe the accidental concatenation of linkages and currents enabled me not only to enter their cosmos as a game player but to perceive it in images and language I more or less understood.

To complicate the issue, they were not quite like us, and their world was different from ours in the sort of tiny ways that an SF writer would not imagine. They wore clothes that were early medieval or late Roman but made out of some synthetic material that is beyond our capability. They fought with swords and spears and primitive zap guns, but they had techniques of visual and audio communication that none of us could figure out or even perceive as operating. Possibly, but only possibly, telepathic. Their religion was important to them. In addition to "The Lord Our God," whom both teams pictured as being on their side and with whom individuals seemed to relate on an "I/Thou" basis, they had a couple of castes of priests to whom I took an instant dislike, not because they were so different from us but because, alas, they had all our faults (I assigned some of the principal clerics names which matched those of some of the sociopaths who currently perform in the Roman Curia) and a lot less to do to justify their existence.

There seemed to be almost no formal worship ceremonies or ritual buildings, a simple religious system, it seemed, for such an elaborate priestly community.

The clergy, I theorize, represented an older religion most of whose doctrines (largely magical and superstitious) had been replaced by the more spiritual worship of the Lord Our God. The priests continued to provide the rituals for social and familial ceremonies but apparently had no teaching role. The Lord Our God on the other hand was worshipped privately with almost no formal ritual. He was addressed much like a passionately loving and indulgent parent, or even a sexual lover, in terms of endearing intimacy.

There were no statues or images involved in this prayer devotion. But neither was there any hesitancy in creating such images. Later I would see one of B'Mella's paintings in which the Lord Our God was presented as a sexually aroused young man in his late teens clad in a bulging athletic supporter (like some of the Renaissance paintings of the Risen Jesus analyzed by Leo Steinberg). It did not seem to have shocked anyone. Nor did G'Ranne's portrait of the Lord Our God as an elegantly dressed young matron in the advanced state of pregnancy. They had no problems, it would seem, with the androgyny of God. And no need for a theology to explain it.

Their world was "different" physically. It had trees and grass, mountains and rivers, forests and lakes, but the flora and fauna and the geology were not quite like ours. "That oak tree is a fooler," a botanist told us. "It is almost a perfect oak tree."

"How is it a fooler?"

"How? Oh, it's not an oak tree at all. The ribs on the leaves are different, the bark is wrong, the branches are at angles that none of our oak trunks could possibly sustain. A nice imitation, though."

"Or maybe ours are a nice imitation."

He looked hard at me. "That is always possible, of course."

Politically, they didn't seem much different from us. Two tiny principalities in adjoining broad valleys with a high plain uniting them and providing an arena for warfare. I would guess that neither duchy numbered more than fifty thousand citizens, of whom most were farmers or stolid burghers in the two towns. The warriors who so enthusiastically slaughtered each other were a kind of nobility who had larger farms in the countryside—farms which others worked because the nobles were too busy doing each other in.

Their principal occupation, agriculture, baffled the expert we brought in. "Damn impressive yields, but I don't know what the hell it is: I'm not even sure whether it's a vegetable or an animal." Some sophisticated manufacturing was done in buildings, or rather pavilions as I called them, all constructed with rainbow-colored, lightweight fabric, much like the glittering gowns they wore, but I never learned the exact nature of the manufacturing. I was too busy doing other things.

The politics were, one supposes, not unlike those of petty fiefdoms in early modern Italy. There would be only one exception to that generalization: at no time during my visit was there any reference to a world beyond the borders of the two duchies, no hint of an Empire of which they were a part or even of conflicts between great powers which would sometimes flow across their boundaries as did the wars of

France and Spain in Renaissance Italy. If there was a "rest of the world" it didn't seem to bother or interest them.

The two rivers which drained their circumscribed little environment must have emptied into something bigger, and they flowed in opposite directions, suggesting some kind of continental divide. Moreover, there had to be something beyond the massive mountain ranges, several of the snow-capped peaks at least twenty thousand feet high, which framed the two duchies. Yet I never heard a word about such other lands. It seemed that the produce in their valleys was sufficient to their needs (most families were at repro-duction-level size, two, sometimes three, children) and they had no reason to be concerned about the rest of their planet. If planet it was.

"A clever imitation," Nathan summed it up. "Hastily done, but not bad for a spur-of-the-moment job. When you stop to consider it, nothing is quite right, colors, shapes, angles, perspectives. But at first you are dazzled by the dramatic colors and hardly notice. The only problem is, why did whoever created that world permit it to be such an inaccurate reflection? If he could do it at all, he could have done it better."

"Maybe," I mused, filling up his glass of Baileys, "that's a problem of translation. Perhaps our receiving mechanism has to adjust to signals, electronic or spiritual, which it doesn't normally receive. Or perhaps only some of the signals get through. Or perhaps there is a mechanism, a cen-sor—make the "c" a capital if you wish—that filters out information that we don't need or shouldn't have."

"What kind of censor?" he demanded impatiently as though I was an undergrad retard or something.

"An author."

I think I won that point. Anyway, since it's my story and I'm God in it, I awarded the point to myself.

"It's still a weird little place." He shook his head in disapproval.

"Maybe that's what they would think about our cosmos."

Nathan didn't like that much. Most of our scholarly colleagues wanted to think it was an elaborate cosmic hoax. But they were dealing only with the replays, not the reality.

The reality that first night was an uneasy peace that could explode into a bloody war again at a flick of a finger.

3 A Cosmos Down the Street

I decided to follow the two negotiators home. It was not a reassuring experience.

Kaila walked wearily through the still-dripping trees to a small black-and-silver tent near the Duke's, hesitating briefly in front of an even smaller peppermint-candy-striped tent next to his. A girlfriend, I wondered, not dreaming of the complexity lurking in that tiny pavilion.

No one spoke to him as he slogged through the dark and the mud. Maybe I'd overdone the storm, but it was my first time, you see.

At the time, I thought the young man had incurred some kind of ritual impurity because he had spoken to the other side. Later I realized that it was much simpler: no one knew what to say to him, not even the Duke.

When he entered his tent, a number of the young warriors outside swarmed around the woman who had watched the negotiation up close. Armor tossed aside, arms folded across her breasts (magnificent by the way; the only authentically voluptuous woman I'd seen so far in that world), she stared grimly at Kaila's tent. Her colleagues began to babble, hinting that perhaps he ought to be killed.

"Have you no more respect for our leader than that? The Lord Kaila is not a brave man as we reckon bravery." She dismissed them with an imperious wave of her hand. "Still, he did what he was told."

If she didn't think that it was brave to walk out on that battlefield and begin to talk about peace, she didn't know what bravery was.

"Perhaps, G'Ranne," one of the men murmured, in the tone of a man thinking the unthinkable, "the leader is... not well."

"I will not listen to treason." She turned on her heel and walked away, the giant star on her cloak (the insignia of the Duke's army) trailing like a furious comet behind her.

The Duchess's symbol, by the way, was a string of four half moons, kind of reminding me of a four-of-a-kind poker hand.

An ice maiden, with a vaguely Celtic name and black-haired, pale-complexioned Irish beauty, constructed from honor and a warrior code of loyalty, a female samurai, a transplanted Gaelic warrior goddess. Not a thought of her own all her life, I wagered. She would have made a good novice in the pre–Vatican II Church.

I didn't like the warrior code in men. I liked it less in women. This young woman, I concluded, was the enemy. She'd fight treason until her code demanded that she turn traitor. Then she would kill quickly and heartlessly.

Dangerous.

Malvau's return home was equally unpromising. He kept up a brave front of Gregory Peck aristocratic dignity until he reached the darkened courtyard in front of his own purple pavilion. Then his pace slowed, his step faltered, his shoulders sagged. In the courtyard, worn, spent, exhausted, he sank into a chair—a flexible form-adjusting device which seemed to be made out of some sort of foam rubber.

I would have expected his wife, whose charm had been praised by the loquacious Kaila, to rush to his assistance. She rushed, all right, but to complain that he was late for a dinner party and that she was greatly embarrassed because the guests had gone home.

Not a word about the end of the war. She apparently could not have cared less about that subject.

Malvau paid no attention to her outburst. He was probably used to tuning her out.

She was dangerous too.

And, like the girl warrior, very similar to many inhabitants on this side of Planck's Wall.

At the secret Lakeside seminars after the game, we agonized over the "humans" if you want to call them that, and I do. Lenrau and B'Mella were, as I have said, attractive human beings, if not quite like anyone you've ever seen. Should you pass one of them on the street, you would hardly notice any difference. But later you would reflect that his flaxen hair was not quite curly the way you'd ever seen curly hair before, and the darkness of her skin was not like any hue you'd recognize. Lovely indeed, but just a tiny bit strange.

Our physiologists had a field day examining close-up shots of their bodies and heaven knows there were some scenes that left little to the imagination. They never did agree whether the cellular structure was identical with ours or not. Some of them thought that their whole muscle system, while an analog of ours, was fundamentally different.

"Hominid, all right," one of them murmured, "but products of an analogous evolutionary process."

The word "analogy" and its derivatives were used a lot at those seminars.

Not everyone agreed that they were full hominids. "I'm not sure they could reproduce with one of us," a young scholar observed with a tug at his beard.

"It might be fun to try." Nathan was the only one of the gang capable of humor during those sessions.

I had no doubts on the subject of their humanity. Their capacities for self-deception and self-destruction, love and hate, cowardice and bravery were indistinguishable from ours. What difference did muscle or cell structures make?

Of course, I was in love with them—with those inhabitants of an adjoining world.

Why am I convinced that it's an adjoining world, one existing in a different time-space continuum from ours but closely juxtaposed with us?

First of all, I can't imagine my "port" mechanism becoming a sending and receiving station powerful enough to reach other worlds in our cosmos. That would seem to be not merely improbable, as the whole experience was, but physically impossible without some kind of "subspace" communication link. The Star Ship *Enterprise* had one, but its electronics were never explained. If it was another world in our cosmos, it would almost certainly be at a minimum a few light-years away and more likely thousands of light-years from our planet. Yet my instructions through the Compaq 286 had virtually instantaneous effect. Hence I conclude that their world must be very close to us; perhaps, as I shall suggest later in this story, frighteningly close.

If it is in a different segment of the time-space spectrum, a different cosmos, more or less, why would my electromagnetic emissions have any effect on it at all? The theories concerning alternative universes about which the theoretical physicists are merrily chirping these days would suggest that very early on, substantially before the crossing of Planck's Wall at ten to the minus forty-two seconds (one over ten to the forty-second power), the alternative universes, necessarily according to some of the theorists, would develop force systems all their own.

My answer is that either their world has force systems relatively like ours (just as it seems to have produced an evolutionary process like ours) or that the influences crossing the barriers between the two cosmoi (Greek plural, note what even a bad classical education can do for you) are mental or "spiritual." If you, whoever you may be, juxtapose two cosmoi and permit/tolerate/direct/insist that mind develop in both of them, it is not impossible—it may be likely and even inevitable—that mind links build up occasionally or often. It may be, to fall back on Père Teilhard's vocabulary, that we begin to share the same noosphere.

Most speculative fiction, dating back to the time our ancestors acquired the capability of reflecting on the lights which hung above them by day and by night, has fantasized about rational, more or less, creatures like us, more or less, who lived on or near the heavenly bodies we can see. Hence Carl Sagan and his crowd (who leave me a little cold, to tell you the truth, mostly because they are not imaginative enough) send out probes and listen eagerly to static coming in from outer space. No one has bothered to snoop around looking for "ports" to alternative space.

But the theoretical physicists range from "possible" to "probable" to "certain" in their judgments on this subject. The last judgment even postulates an infinite number of actually existing alternative cosmoi, mostly to explain why ours seems so "anthropic" (apparently designed for humankind) or so demanding of "observership." (Wright of Texas points out that Planck's Laws don't apply unless there is an observer.) Either you have Someone engineering the whole business or you need a virtually infinite number of cosmoi to ensure that what seems like a plan in ours is pure chance.

Maybe both.

Over in the next neighborhood, if that is where it is, the pot was still simmering. Three young men had cornered the stony-faced young woman warrior in a dimly lit tent. Like her they were handsome, athletic, self-confident—true Academy graduates, if they had an Academy in that world, the kind of people who in our world won the wars in Korea and Viet Nam for the United States.

Unlike her, they had a wild gleam in their eyes. Not only dangerous, but mad.

"We do not need any of your inventions," she said somberly. "I will have no part of your insane schemes."

"How long will you tolerate this betrayal to our ancient enemies? Lenrau, Kaila, the witch child—they will permit us all to be killed in our sleep."

"I do not propose to die in my sleep," she shot back tartly.

"When will you resist?" another of them demanded.

"When my honor forces me to resist."

"You do not trust the Duke?"

She hesitated. "I will trust him until there is reason not to trust him."

"We think there is already reason not to trust him. The witch child..."

"I do not need to be told about her," she cut him off.

Who was this witch child?

"We will proceed with our plans," their leader warned. "We have our honor too."

"If you take actions against the Lord, your honor is that of mad fools."

They stomped out of the tent into the darkness, muttering under their breath to one another. As they faded away into the woods, the young woman stepped out of her quarters and stared after them, her lovely face blank and unreadable.

I told the 286 to scan the woods. All was quiet, though I thought I saw some clergy conniving in the darkness.

I wouldn't have wanted to bet on the chances of the truce lasting another twenty-four hours.

What does the existence of such a world mean, inhabited as it is by people who are disturbingly like us? To speculate about that, one must turn from theoretical physics to theology, two subjects which are clearly converging, or would converge if theologians would acknowledge that a degree in their discipline does not make them expert in international politics and economics and stick to their own last. I think you can make an excellent argument that God, being excessive in all She does (think of the poet's cliché about the flowers blossoming at the bottom of the sea), would be hard put not to spin forth cosmoi with the same prodigious and passionate recklessness with which He has produced stars and constellations and galaxies in our cosmos.

Why the hell not? If you're exuberant, you're exuberant, and by all signs and accounts Whoever is behind it all is nothing if not exuberant. Reread the parables of Jesus, stripped of their later allegorical interpretations; a father who forgives a spoiled brat of a son before the clever little fraud even has a chance to deliver his phony speech, a farmer who pays loafers a full day's wage for at most an hour of grumbling effort, a judge who dismisses a capital charge of adultery against a woman who is patently guilty without even bothering to ask her whether she has any regrets— there, my friends, you have exuberance with a vengeance. Indeed the last story was so exuberant as to be profoundly shocking to the early Christians and hence was cut from many texts of the Bible, not the first time Church leaders have tried to tone down Jesus's description of his experience of the Father.

A God like that limit Herself to just one old cosmos like ours? Don't be silly!

Does this admittedly odd kind of God permit creatures to move back and forth between or among various cosmoi? Only if He repeals Planck's Law or at least tears down Planck's Wall. God wouldn't do that, would She?

I tell myself "no way."

Yet there is Ranora.

Sometimes at night I even hear her pipe, not unlike an Irish tin whistle, blowing outside my window forty-seven stories above ground level.

Playing the theme which she had assigned to me.

I don't know; you figure it/her out.

My imagination?

SF writers, of course, men and women with much larger and more generous imaginations than I have, take such exchanges between alternative cosmoi for granted.

But this is not Speculative Fiction. This is an attempt at a sober report by a social scientist of what happened when he began to play an interactive fiction game of which he ought to have been more suspicious. I don't have the imagination to do Speculative Fiction.

Anyway, I suspended the game to watch the ten o'clock news.

When I returned it was the next morning for them. The sun rose above the snow-covered mountains which I think were in the west end of their land, though I'm not sure, and quickly dried up the remainder of my admittedly excessive rainstorm. Kaila and Malvau trudged wearily into the no-man's-land and sat on chairs which someone had arranged before their arrival. The young man carried a thick vellum book, his finger between two of the pages.

"A scholar's wisdom?" Malvau cocked a skeptical politician's eyebrow.

"A description of the arrangements for the peace conference a hundred and forty-two years ago."

"It was a short peace."

"Longer than any we have known.... Besides..."

"We can blame the format on our ancestors?" The movement of his lips was definitely a smile this time, though not
an uncynical one.

"Your words, my Lord."

Malvau leaned close to his opposite, so close that the
listening warriors could not hear him. "How long do you
think we have, my friend?"

"No longer than ten days."

"If that."

"Precisely."

"Does your Duke accept this format?"

"He awaits the approval of your Duchess." Kaila grim-
aced. "No doubt we will waste another day on this charade.
... You have more experience in this than I do, my Lord;
are we the only ones in the world who feel the urgency?"

"I think not." Malvau rose, the book under his arm.
"We are the only ones who are willing to admit openly how
near the fire is."

"The Lord Our God," Kaila murmured with more than
routine piety, "save and protect us."

"In times past," the older man replied, "He has not been
responsive to similar prayers."

I had yet to realize that in this other world, this cosmos
down the street, they meant me.

Anyway it took two days of huffing and puffing, of the
drawing of weapons, and the making of threats, of stony
glares from the ice maiden and manic whispering among
Larry, Curly, and Moe as I had dubbed her three buddies,

of secret conversations between the clergy of both sides (who seemed to have no trouble joining forces, thus it always is with the bad guys), of temper tantrums from B'Mella and long interludes of daydreaming from Lenrau, before the negotiations began.

Not a moment too soon. Kaila collapsed into his bed, too exhausted and sick to attend the opening session, marked by interminable clerical chanting and even longer washing of hands, and Malvau, his dignity offended by the Duchess's refusal to accept his recommendations quickly enough, had withdrawn to his courtyard to sulk and to ignore the not completely unattractive blond shrew to whom he was married.

The only men, in other words, with an admitted sense of urgency were absent from the negotiating table on the first day. The fire was even closer.

Kaila, gray and haggard, turned up the second morning, in time for the ilel's dramatic arrival. The next day, after what might be considered an apology ("I cannot deal with all this excrement myself") from the Duchess, Malvau, with singular ill grace it seemed to me, suspended his sulk.

I wondered whether they had any chance at all. It had not yet occurred to me that I was supposed to hurry the process along.

What process?

Let's leave it as a tentative system of hypotheses for further research:

1. There exist neighboring cosmoi.

2. The physical barriers between our cosmos and the neighbor are at the present state of our knowledge impenetrable.

3. They may be impenetrable physically forever because they were produced/emerged/were created so early in the big bang as to be operating with a different set of ele-

mentary forces from those which function in our world or even to be the product of a completely different big bang. (Who knows how many times She struck the cosmic matches?)

4. However, since love may be responsible for all the big bangs, and mind and spirit may be able to transcend physical barriers, it is possible that subtle and unpredictable influences, often erratic, may flit across these physically impenetrable boundaries.

5. Perhaps these influences are frequent *and for all their unpredictability growing more frequent.*

I submit the previous five hypotheses, verifiable or falsifiable by further research, though God, you should excuse the expression, knows who will fund such research. However, my own personal experience, acquired while I was playing Nathan's God Game, convinces me that they are all true and also convinces some of the scholars.

I include Nathan, of course; he'd like nothing more than to send some of my characters, most notably Ranora, who has some of the characteristics of his teenaged daughters/princesses, on a promotion tour for the revised version of the game.

And of course for the upgrade two years from now, when they bring on line the optical disks.

With fifty thousand story lines.

If anyone could pull that off, Nathan could. I'd like to see her dance around him blowing a wicked theme on her pipe.

The final hypothesis? I have a lot of hunches and one bit of physical evidence:

6. Some individuals on the other side, at any rate at certain times in their lives, can frolic across the boundaries between our cosmoi (and many other cosmoi too, for that matter) with considerable and mostly benign effect.

I use the term "frolic" advisedly, because I suspect/feel/ intuit that either you dance across them the way a little kid dances down a beach on a warm summer day when the lake is warm and calm or you don't do it at all.

I suspect further that those who can do it are virgin potential bearers of life. Not that there is anything less noble about a woman who has engaged in lovemaking or actually borne life. On the contrary, I think they have more dignity, and, all other things being equal, more inherent worth. But they represent a promise of life fulfilled. Creatures like Ranora symbolize a promise yet to be fulfilled and therefore have a certain, what to call it, freedom of movement which is appropriate for their phase of the life cycle, freedom of movement which makes Planck's Wall look liked a beaded curtain.

Women like Ranora and, maybe, like Mary the Mother of Jesus.

Well, having laid out that highly speculative possibility and acknowledging that (a) I can't prove it and (b) half the time I think it absurd and half the time I am utterly convinced that it is true, I must quickly add that even if it is true, it doesn't begin to explain Ranora or the role she seized for herself, unasked and not infrequently unwanted, in Nathan's God Game.

That however is not the issue at the moment. I did not think of myself as God for the people in the game, not in any real sense, until I was much further into it. When I paused for my reflection that night, I knew only that they needed me and I had to go back to them.

That brings us to the most important question of all, doesn't it? OK, you have a port to an analogous cosmos which may be very like yours or may be similar only because of a hastily constructed translation system. OK, you've broken into it by an accident which gives you both access and comprehension. So how come you're God? How come they have to do or want to do or usually but not always do what you tell them to do? How come the grace/free will game is being played out again with you (did I hear someone say "of all people"?) given the grace hand?

Beats me.

Maybe the situation in that place was so bad that they needed some special help and all the angels were busy elsewhere.

Wild?

Sure. But what can I tell you?

Author's Note _____

"The traveler," writes André Gide in The
Counterfeiters, "having reached the top of the hill, sits
down and looks about him before continuing his
journey, which henceforward lies all downhill. He
seeks to distinguish in the darkness, for night is
falling, where the winding path he has chosen is
leading him. So the undiscerning author stops a while
to regain his breath, and wonders with some anxiety
where his tale will take him."

Gide then goes on to complain about his part-time
narrator Edouard, who "has irritated me more than
once... enraged me even."

It is a natural reaction in the uneasy relationship
between author and narrator, inevitable given the
propensity of narrators to take stories away from the
author. "Marcel" drove Proust out of his story, even
converting Proust's homosexual lover Agostino into
the young woman Albertine. In later life, Joyce
ruefully confessed that he had given Stephen a hard
time; in fact, as is obvious, the exact opposite is the

case. Joseph Conrad, we know, was driven up the wall by the loquacious Marlowe.

Hence readers of this story will not be surprised that I am already irritated with the narrator's sly hints that he is me and with his clever schemes to take the story away from me.

As Michele observed when she read the story (the real Michele, four years older, four inches taller, and talking English as she always did instead of teen talk), "I totally like the leading character."

"The Duke?"

In full seriousness, "No, the narrator."

"He's not me."

"I know that."

I warn all readers against his pretensions. Consider how long it takes him to realize that I have cast him in the God role. Does that sound like me? Could anyone with a Ph.D. be that dumb?

In terms something like that does every author complain about the narrator with whom he is stuck, does every Other Person complain about the narrator with whom He is forced to work in order to manifest His wisdom and goodness.

Or Hers.

4 An Ilel Plays Her Pipe

Ranora's arrival on the second day of negotiations is branded into my imagination for as long as that dimension of my personality may survive. She added a Wonderland dimension to the story. I was Alice and she was the Mad Hatter, the March Hare, and the Red Queen all rolled into one cute little package.

I think if she could testify (maybe I should say when she decides to testify) she'd claim I was Humpty-Dumpty too.

I couldn't figure out why the game needed her. Or the worlds, ours and theirs. On the other hand, maybe both cosmoi need as many ilels as they can find.

I had the impression as I played the God Game that need, unspecific perhaps but powerful, was driving the game. Their world needed ours for a few months (a week or two of our time, but the time was all fouled up—sometimes the game was in real time, occasionally it was slower than real time and often much faster; I have no explanation for that). And they, especially the Duke and the Duchess, needed me.

Arguably it was the other way around. Maybe our world, in the persons of a score or so of befuddled scholars, needed exposure to their world. Maybe I needed B'Mella and Lenrau.

To be perfectly fair I should tell you about the parapsychologist. It was my idea to call him in. Our University, of course, does not permit parapsychology on the campus, so he had to fly in from Elsewhere. He puffed mysteriously on his pipe for several minutes after we'd run the last tape.

"Possible," he finally murmured.

"What's possible?"

"That these tapes are the result of a strongly psychic imagination sending out electronic energies which create visual images. We have been able to do it in a minor way in the lab. Nothing like these, of course, but still..."

I am, for the record, utterly devoid of psychic powers.

But, as the man said, still...

Finally, to end the speculation and get back to the story, I can't believe that coming to know Ranora was an accident. I still hear her pipe late at night. Or I think I do.

By that second day of negotiations, they had rigged up tents at either side of a clearing in one of their oak-that-wasn't-oak forests. Maybe I should call them pavilions because they were luxurious portable palaces. These people did not live poorly. They sat on plush lounges, which adapted to their body shapes, in glistening pastel gowns on either side of the clearing and went through the rituals that they considered negotiation—mostly shouting invective at one another and suggesting how they would carve one another up when the battle began again. They had rather unkind words for one another's leaders too, of which "foul-smelling whore" and "cowardly degenerate" were the mildest. It was hard to figure out what the issues in the conflict were. Some small tracts of land, fishing rights on a lake, and memories of unsettled vendettas from long ago. The exchange was curiously artificial. It seemed as stylized as black teenagers doing the "dozens" with each other. But then someone would rise to his feet and rush across the meadow, waving his (or her, because this was strictly an equal-opportunity war) sword or spear in the air.

One leader or the other would raise a hand and the charge would stop. I couldn't tell when these alarums and excursions were serious and when they were not. I had the feeling that the rituals had been played out before. But the young man had said earlier that Lenrau had never seen B'Mella. He wasn't seeing much of her now either. Her face was partially veiled by the collar of her magnificent glowing blue-green robe and he didn't look at her anyway.

I began to wonder what I was supposed to do next. I had imposed a truce on this world and forced the warring factions to negotiate; was I supposed to resolve the conflict too? How?

I felt like a benign British monarch who had forced the Prots and the Teagues in Belfast or Derry to sit down to talk with each other and now was baffled that mere negotiation didn't lead to peace.

How odd of them.

There was, however, Ranora to provide entertainment. How can I describe her? A luscious little middle-adolescent blonde in a short red-and-white peppermint-candy gown with a matching hood, pert nose, dancing blue eyes, an acrobat's responsive body, and a face which seemed to be made of rubber putty, but which, in its rare repose, was delicately lovely.

She emerged from the woods and marched straight across the middle of the meadow, blowing a dissonant melody on a small pipe, not unlike an Irish tin whistle in appearance but with a much greater range of sounds, also red-and-white striped.

The exchange of insults stopped and everyone listened

silently as she reversed direction and paraded right back across the meadow to the edge of the woods whence she had come. Instead of disappearing into the woods she flounced up towards B'Mella's throne, sat imperiously in the shade of one of those almost oak trees, tucked her legs under her, modestly arranged her gown, and, occasionally experimenting with a theme melody, stared boldly and I thought affectionately at the Duchess.

B'Mella turned crimson and tried to avert her eyes from the outrageous child. More notes on the pipe, demanding attention. B'Mella motioned the girl to come closer. She mimed a giggle, shook her head elaborately, and continued to stare and experiment with her pipe. The Duchess acted like a woman who had been captured on *Candid Camera*.

Like most warriors, this crowd was not strong on wit, but they knew they were being ridiculed. The debate continued with a little less vigor. The girl with the pipe refused to permit it to become serious. Whenever a warrior would start shouting, she would accompany him on her pipe with a mocking melody. Some of the victims had the good grace to laugh, others looked like they wanted to strangle her.

Malvau rose with considerable solemnity towards the end of the cloudless afternoon to deliver his daily summary, which normally was enough to put everyone, even his Lady, to sleep.

"We have a rare opportunity," he began, "for peace. You all know that either we will have peace now or the war will overflow from the warrior class and spread to all our peoples. The fields will be burned, the cities destroyed, women raped, men tortured to death, children mutilated and killed, as it was written that it happened in the time of the evil Duke Franon. Perhaps those of us who are warriors are not tired of combat. What else can we do? Our people are amused by the conflict much as though it were an athletic match, but they too know how dangerous it will shortly become. Can we not find the will for peace that will end forever this conflict which has no sense, no point, no reason, other than its own continuation?"

The girl leaped to her feet and began to do approving somersaults and cartwheels, like an Olympic gymnastics champion.

Kaila rose from the other side, handsome, casual, self-possessed.

"My distinguished colleague, the noble Lord Malvau speaks only the truth. Why must we fight? Cannot we become friends, fellow citizens, even perhaps some of us lovers? We are the same people, we worship the same God..."

"Blasphemy," shouted a tall, white-haired, handsome chief priest (dressed in crimson and ermine) on B'Mella's side. "Your God is the prince of darkness."

"And you are an effeminate coward," yelled a one-armed woman warrior.

"Your Duchess is a foul-smelling whore."

"Your Duke is a degenerate pervert."

G'Ranne the ice maiden said nothing. Her silence at insult time was rather un-Irish behavior.

The peppermint-candy girl did not elect to be quiet, however. On the contrary, she exploded with fury. She bounded across the meadow blowing vulgar insults on the contestants.

B'Mella lost her temper. "Lord Lenrau, are you so weak and ineffectual that you cannot control this obstreperous child?"

The obstreperous child wheeled on the Duchess and favored her with a rude and insulting melody, then removed the pipe from her mouth and made a rude face.

The Duchess, to my astonishment, did not reach for her own sword or order someone to remove the offending young woman. Instead she smiled graciously. "Small one, we must have our arguments first, before we can make peace. Come here."

The small one, pipe in one hand, rested her hands on her hips and considered the Duchess gravely. Then she shook her head and giggled. Instead of responding to the Duchess's invitation, she lifted the pipe back to her lips and played a sweet little melody, so lovely that it reduced everyone to reverent silence; she paused, considered what she had played, and played it over, making a few adjustments the second time.

Then she bowed elaborately to the Duchess, who in turned bowed elaborately back. "Is that me?"

The girl threw up her hands in a "sometimes" mime.

"When I'm good?"

She nodded enthusiastically.

"Which isn't very often?"

The kid shook her finger in a "shame, shame" gesture.

"I like the tune very much. Thank you. I'll try to be good."

The kid clapped her hands, did a couple of handstands, and began to march across the meadow, switching her cute little rear end defiantly as she played "B'Mella's tune."

The pipe, as I have said, was little more than an Irish tin whistle, but the child could make the most wondrous sounds come from it, almost as though it were an instrument from the fairie glen.

I began to wonder whether she was some sort of elf from some tiny, upcountry meadow of this country, a survivor of their fairie past.

"Ranora!" the Lord Kaila said firmly.

She took the pipe out of her mouth, stared at him impatiently, hands on hips, little foot beating the turf rhythmically, obviously displeased.

"Come here," he ordered.

She shook her head negatively, now a stubborn teen-aged brat.

"Don't embarrass me and the Lord Lenrau."

She sighed elaborately and with a great show of resigned displeasure stalked over to Kaila's chair and sat stiffly at his feet, telling the whole world by the cold tilt of her shoulder that she was greatly displeased with this handsome young courtier.

Five minutes later she was holding his hand.

He was too young to be her father, didn't look at all enough like her to be her brother, and didn't act, not then at any rate, like her lover. No one, I suspected even then, would dare to be her master.

So what was he?

I would learn later on that when ilels rose up in that world and attached themselves to someone who "needed" an ilel, they also elected someone else to be their "protector" or "keeper" or "minder." Or maybe the right word is "babysitter."

Poor Kaila had been given the nod. The courtly, scholarly humanist was stuck with a waif who was half child, half imp, half angel.

How would you like to have had someone like that dropped on your doorstep when you were maybe twenty-two or twenty-three?

Kaila seemed then to accept his mission with resigned good humor. As the story continued, however, his manner towards her changed subtly. More about that later.

I began to think she was a kind of slave and adolescent mistress to the Duke. She brought him his breakfast on his couch in the morning, laid out the gown he was to wear, bathed him in his pool, massaged the back of his neck, made him eat his food, provided a late night hot toddy, turned out his portable hand lamp, and tucked him into bed when it was time for him to sleep.

It soon became evident that she was neither a slave nor a concubine. Whatever the rules which regulated relationships with an ilel, she could hold his hand, kiss his forehead, caress his arm when she wished, but he dared not lay a finger on her. She was a mixture of Tinker Bell and Ariel, a sprite, an imp, a pixie (with small piquant features for the role), a female leprechaun, a trickster, a wise woman, a conscience, a sister, a daughter, a mother, and a haughty archangel.

She was also pure hell when she was displeased; fortunately that didn't seem to happen very often. In fact, her temper reminded me of Michele's. Very much so. In the back of my head I began to wonder if there was some sort of connection.

That's a tough one. I haven't figured it out yet.

God help me if they're in cahoots with each other, even unconsciously, across cosmos boundaries.

The next day the ilel was back, still fascinated by the Duchess. While the warriors were shouting at one another, she would prance around the edge of the meadow and sit twenty yards away from B'Mella, arranging her red-and-white gown around herself carefully, like a properly trained parochial school graduate. She would then rest her tough little chin on her hand and stare admiringly at the Duchess.

Again B'Mella blushed and looked away, somehow embarrassed by the sprite child's attention. Then she stole a cautious peek. Ranora giggled happily. The Duchess turned away, suppressing with difficulty her own smile.

The ritual became a daily affair, always disconcerting but pleasing the Duchess, who acted like a novice model under consideration by a trained professional. At least once a day Ranora would play her B'Mella theme. Unfailingly, the Duchess would turn her head away so that no one would see her tears.

Ranora was clinically blunt with her Duke. "Master, you must win her to your marriage bed, penetrate her most vigorously but with proper respect, and make her pregnant. That will end all this foolish fighting."

"Is she not a foul-smelling whore?" Lenrau asked with the faint smile that his ilel always seemed to excite.

"You like her." Ranora jabbed a finger at him. "You can't take your eyes off her. She likes you, too. I can tell."

"End the war on the couch?" Kaila asked tentatively— no other form of expression seemed to be permitted him when he was speaking to his lissome charge.

"Where else?" She jumped up, drew her tiny pipe from her gown, and begin to play it and dance to a lascivious tune. "I think she'd be fun in bed." The others laughed, it seemed to me, a trifle uneasily.

"You wouldn't have to sleep with her." The Duke smiled wryly.

"Don't be vulgar," the ilel fired back at him and stamped angrily out of the tent.

"If you can endure her," Kaila closed the book he was reading (he always had his head buried in his book), "you would have no trouble with B'Mella."

"I heard *that*!" Ranora bounced back in, blew a few cacophonous notes, and then stamped out again.

"You are right." Lenrau laughed. "B'Mella at her worst would not be that haughty," his eyes glazed a bit, as though he were drifting to a faraway world, "and probably not that loving."

"That we do not know." Kaila was ever the man of reason. "She has perhaps never been given a chance."

"Hmmn..."

If I were in the Duke's position I would have been meditating on that possibility. I'm sure he was preoccupied by something ineffable and distant.

"She is attracted to the ilel..."

"Can they attach themselves to two people at the same time?" The Duke struggled to return to his world.

"It is written," Kaila flipped open his huge folio book, "that five hundred years ago it may have happened."

"B'Mella was very courteous to her, was she not?"

"Indeed."

"That," the Duke sighed disconsolately, "would be all I need."

Neither of the two principals paid all that much attention to the negotiations, save when they had to intervene to maintain order. Rarely did they say anything, and, except for B'Mella's rebuke to Lenrau when Ranora was misbehaving, never a word to each other.

The Duchess would twist and turn nervously on her form-fitting chair, impatient, restless, bored. You thought she'd rather run through the forest or swim in one of the lakes or dance and sing with the ilel or fight another war—anything but endure any more tiresome talk.

Her counterpart often seemed asleep or so abstracted in thought that he might as well be asleep. Kaila, or one of the other young courtiers who hung around him, would often have to nudge him to pay attention if something important was being said.

Or Ranora would blow a soft little tune, a variation usually on her B'Mella theme.

She also had a Lenrau theme which sounded as if it might have been lifted from Elgar's "Pomp and Circumstance" or Handel's "See the Conquering Hero Comes."

It embarrassed the Duke enormously because he certainly didn't see himself that way.

"Well, I do," she said flatly when he tried to register a mild protest. "And I play the tunes, you don't."

So there, too.

After what seemed a particularly acrimonious negotiating session ended abruptly, as though someone had blown a whistle, everyone withdrew to their fabric palaces. I decided that I was after all the author of the story and I had let the plot get out of hand and turn dull, save for the appearance of the delightful but contentious ilel. It was time to reassert my authorship.

That was the second turning point in my active intrusion into the God business.

I suspended the game for a few moments and tried to think rationally about it. In the heat of the moment there wasn't much time to think and, anyway, when Ranora was dancing around, thought was impossible.

I was betting that the real issues between them were minimal and that like the Prots and the Teagues in Northern Ireland they were prisoners of a history over which they had little control. Maybe, I reasoned, if I focused a little more intently on the personalities of the principal figures I would be able to reverse the trend of history. Lenrau and B'Mella were the Duke and the Duchess, the hero and the heroine, the ones who really mattered. I had allowed myself to fixate on the process instead of attending to the principal characters—a major fault in a storyteller.

I informed the 286 I wanted to observe Lenrau.

He and Kaila and Ranora, the three of them in the most minimal of swimsuits (hers red-and-white striped and displaying a perfectly delightful little figure) were floating in a pool which seemed to keep them effortlessly on the surface—Dead Sea density. She leaped out of the pool as I joined them, did a number of quite impossible acrobatics, dove back in, and promptly shoved the heads of both the men underwater. Neither of them was in any mood to play. But Ranora wanted to play, so they both tried to dunk her and for their troubles were rewarded with vast lungfuls of water as she dove under them, surfaced behind them, and dunked them before they could lay a hand on her. Finally Kaila wrestled her if not into submission at least into powerlessness.

"Game's over, I win," she announced brightly.

Kaila released her, I noticed with a hint of reluctance. There was a glint of something in his eye which I thought not appropriate in a keeper of a vestal virgin. Did she catch it?

Don't they all. She showed no sign that she was pleased or displeased. She merely kept her distance from him for the rest of the pool session.

Were you an ilel for life, I wondered?

She began to devote her ministrations to the Duke.

"You are so tired, Master." She caressed the Duke's weary brow.

I thought that I wanted an ilel of my own.

"We must not despair." Kaila took her hand playfully. She let him hold it for a while and then slipped it away, but not without a hint of a promise that he might have it back later. "The master has kept us together in negotiations already longer than we have talked for three generations."

"Good master." She patted the Duke's forehead with her free hand. "I think the woman is as tired as you are and wants peace as much as you do and doesn't know how to do it either and is very pretty and not at all a foul-smelling whore. I want to talk to her. I'll tell her that you can hardly wait to get inside her thighs."

"You forget yourself." The Duke pushed her hand away.

"Ranora..." Kaila protested in vain.

"And you forget yourself too," she shouted, pulling his kinky hair kindly but firmly and dunking him briefly.

He came up sputtering, but no longer angry.

"I'm sorry, good Ranora," he sighed and sank deeper into the pool. "Strangely I want peace, so badly that I cannot drive the desire away from me. I want peace more than I want a woman...."

The young one laughed at that. He frowned but continued. "It is true. And I want a woman again, too. It has been so long. I don't know why the lust for peace is so powerful. They say I'm a coward. But perhaps the Lord Our God has put this desire for peace in me."

"And in her?" Kaila asked.

"Who knows? She is but an animal."

"A sleek and desirable animal." Ranora jabbed his ribs.

"In truth," he agreed.

They lapsed into silence. I cut to the Duchess and found her at prayer.

And felt my eyes pop out of my sockets.

As I learned later, the people in this world removed their outer garments when they prayed, a sign of humility and dependence which caused no scandal (they are prudes most of the time) because prayer was a private, very private activity.

However, my first view of herself in the undergarments of her culture (they would be a hot item at the exotic lingerie stores and would greatly delight your SF illustrators) took my breath away. I agreed with Ranora—she was no foul-scented whore.

Not one of Boris's more voluptuous dark women, but slender, almost thin, sleek, boyish at first glance, before you noted the slightly curving hips, the long elegant legs, the slightly convex belly, and the small, delicately shaped girl-ish breasts. At prayer all her arrogance vanished; she seemed a fragile little girl in the presence of a father whom she knew doted on her but whose ways were hard to comprehend.

"What do you wish of me, Lord Our God?" She seemed to be speaking to me. "I wish to do your will in all things. All my life I have been taught that it is your will that I kill them and seek especially the death of the evil Lord Lenrau who is the agent in our world of your enemy, the Lord of Darkness. Now I see that he is a human like me and on his poor face the same anguish that I feel. He seems to have suffered even more. I should feel guilty, but I don't: I want to make the pain leave him. I wanted to cuddle his poor weary head against my breasts. Is that wrong?"

Not wrong, but remarkably honest.

"In my heart I hear you demanding that I make peace with him. You tell me that I have always wanted the killing to end. How can this be? Are they not evil and your enemies?"

MAKE PEACE, I told her.

She heard me. "It is your will. I will try to turn my heart in your way. It is so strange." She stood up and reached for a thin robe. "Yet, Lord Our God, I like the way this new rule of yours makes me feel."

She paused as she was belting her robe. "But, how does one make peace? I do not know. I have never done it before. You made me end the conflict, you force me to control those who want to fight again, but you will not show me what I am to do next."

WHO, ME? I typed in.

WHAT? said the machine.

"Yes, you." She didn't wait for the machine to translate. "Please!" Tears in her soft brown eyes. "What good are you if you don't help me now?"

What the hell?

Thus far I had played peacemaker on instinct. I had kept them from killing off any more of one another. Now I had a choice: I could continue to be a spectator or I could begin to force my own solution on the Duke and the Duchess, a decision whose romantic implications should be clear to anyone who has ever read or written stories, even if it wasn't to the two idiots themselves.

It was, I told myself, only a story, a game, Nathan's game. Besides, clever little Ranora saw the same ending.

I didn't ask then what would happen if we were both wrong.

5 The Malvau/ N'Rasia Subplot

I was being seduced rapidly by the God Game. And subtly. By the time I realized what was happening I was hooked. Eventually I had to go cold turkey to end my addiction, but that comes later.

Let me illustrate what was happening to me at this stage of the story with a subplot, the sort of thing my publisher Tom Doherty and my editor Harriet McDougal and my agent Nat Sobel would insist, with every reason, ought to be in this story. The subplot concerns B'Mella's aristocratic councilor Malvau, whom I realized was a key to shoving the negotiations off dead center, and his wife N'Rasia.

I was already hooked on the game, enjoying my power (I mean, how many of you have put an end to a bloody war and forced the contesting parties to attend a peace conference?) and enjoying the game of manipulating people's lives—for their own good, of course. I was also beginning to discover that, just like characters in one of my stories, the people who were cavorting through my Compaq 286 and on my big-screen Zenith would do what I wanted them to do sometimes not at all, other times with grave reluctance, and yet other times without my lifting a finger.

I had yet to conceptualize my role in this game as a God figure and, I'll admit it, it had not yet fully penetrated my consciousness that these were very probably real people.

But even if it was much later in the game and I had a pretty good idea what I was doing, I would have leaned on Malvau and N'Rasia pretty much the way I did. The difference between me and the Other Person, I think (but who knows for sure), is that I knew what I wanted those two idjits to do but I didn't know whether they would do it or, more important, whether it was good for them to do it. At the time I intruded myself into their crumbling relationship, I didn't bother to ask such questions. They were characters in a story who would live more or less happily ever after if they did what I wanted them to do.

Later when I realized that the God Game, for me at any rate, was more problematic, I went ahead with my pushing them around because... well, because not to act when you have the power to act is in fact a form of action.

If you get to be God, no matter what you do, it matters.

OK. Malvau (I can't help it that his name sounds like a character from Shakespeare) was something like a cross between a Commissioner of Public Works and a States Attorney in B'Mella's government. He was on the right side, i.e. the peace side, but he was also a pompous bastard if there ever was one. 'Ella listened to him respectfully, but with obvious impatience. I had a hunch he might have been a kind of tutor for her at an earlier age.

One time when he had delivered himself of an oracular, ponderous, and obscure observation about the deteriorating peace negotiations, she barked at him, "The difference between communications from you, 'Vau, and those from the Lord Our God is that He would speak more clearly."

The remark didn't seem to displease him at all. Apparently he thought he was worthy of comparison with the

Lord Our God. (Their God and probably our God too, God knows, but I'll use their form throughout this story.)

Whenever he paraded solemnly by the spot Ranora had picked to listen to the negotiations, she blew a nasty, slightly off-key, pompous tune on her tin whistle. That sailed over his head too.

His insensitive arrogance wouldn't have bothered me, except that if these poor people were going to work out some kind of peace they needed his intelligence and political skills—characteristics which he occasionally displayed when he wasn't busy parading his massive dignity. I had no intention to become involved in his personal life. I didn't want to know about it. I followed him home because I wanted to jolt him into a constructive peace process. What happened after that was my doing, but not part of my original intention.

(To give the poor man his due, it seemed that his family were the oldest nobility in either kingdom and that he had been raised to believe in his own inherent superiority.)

B'Mella screamed at him the day I decided to follow him home. "Stop acting and start thinking, the Lord Our God condemn you!" (the strongest curse of which they seemed capable). "I'm a warrior not a thinker; how can I end this terrible bloodletting if you don't do some thinking for me?"

"I am always ready for my lady's command." He bowed superciliously.

"My command," she reached for the dagger she carried at her belt, a symbolic gesture rather than a real threat, I had come to realize (well, most of the time not a real threat), "is that you tell me how to end this foolish and boastful chatter."

"I will give it very serious thought." He bowed again.

I couldn't figure out whether the handsome, silver-haired bastard didn't have a clue or whether he was waiting for the negotiations to break down completely before he rushed in to save the day and become a hero, as his family image demanded he be. I suspected that he was angry that the Duchess had called a truce without consulting him. This may have been an enormous affront to his dignity.

"I do not know how N'Rasia puts up with your pomposity, 'Vau." The Duchess pounded on her table, a portable wood frame covered with the blue-green cloth which was her color. "Do you require that she kneel and adore you every morning? Does she pray to you at night and not to the Lord Our God?"

Pretty rough stuff by the standards of their world. You could call poor Lenrau an impotent pervert and no one thought anything of it. But with your own people you were supposed to be courteous and respectful. When B'Mella was upset, however, she could insult anyone.

"N'Rasia understands her position fully," he bowed again, "and embraces it willingly."

"She is a fool. I would not tolerate your pretensions to superiority for a minute."

"How fortunate it is, then, that we are not mated. Perhaps, the Duke Lenrau will be respectful of you."

Very dirty pool, I thought.

"The Duke Lenrau is an upstart, a pervert, and a pig," she said automatically, much the way kids used to mumble the act of contrition in the old days when we processed them through the confessional on the Thursdays before First Fridays. "From him I expect nothing, from a man with your heritage I would expect humility rather than arrogance."

There was something regal about her all right; alas, if it were only matched by stability of character, she would be an effective ruler. Nonetheless not bad for a woman whose first husband was killed when she was sixteen, as I had learned, and whose second died, just when he had appar-

ently recovered, after a long convalescence from wounds. It
was hard to tell whether she had loved either of them, but
such traumas were enough to explain some instability and
win her some sympathy.

Apparently the latter was not part of their rules: the
death of young spouses was a common occurrence, a matter
of course in their society.

She picked up no sympathy from that miserable so-and-
so Malvau.

"I will advise you, my lady, on affairs of government."
He bowed yet again. "I will not seek your advice on my
personal relationships or demeanor."

"So much the worse for you," she fired back hotly. "Now
leave me and go home to your poor adoring wife."

To give 'Vau full credit, however, he had quickly and
vigorously supported her decision to call the truce. Therefore he was not a complete fool. I needed to know more about
him before I could figure out what I should require him to
do.

It was obvious around B'Mella's pavilion that the man
was a bit of a lecher, though sufficiently charming and restrained about it as to not quite make it into the dirty-old-
man category. Many of the young women deftly avoided his
pinches and caresses; others seemed to enjoy them. A few
were undoubtedly "intimate" with him, though at times and
places I couldn't figure out and didn't want to anyway.

The Duchess clearly disapproved; her thin lips became
thinner and her flashing brown eyes flashed more vigorously when Malvau made one of his passes. She said nothing, however, apparently respecting everyone's freedom.

One point for B'Mella: a hot-tempered, fierce warrior
aristocrat, she was nonetheless gentle, almost maternal with
her staff and servants. In response, men and women both
seemed to like her, enjoy her company, and occasionally risk

a joke at her expense. She had, I decided, distinct possibilities.

So I instructed my machine, FOLLOW MALVAU HOME.

It complied without protest. I hope it's clear, by the way, that, as much as I respected his political acumen and as important for the peace process as I knew him to be, I had a strong distaste for the man. I'm experienced enough in dealing with characters like him to know that behind the arrogance there lurks a terrible feeling of worthlessness and self-rejection. They are pathetic, not proud; they play lord of the mountain who doesn't need to be loved because they're afraid that if they let down the barriers, no one will love them. Such understanding, however, is not much help if you're trying to help them salvage their marriage or their life. They continue to be unattractive boors encased in armorplate which will resist anything short of a direct hit with a sixteen-inch shell.

So you feel sorry for them and wish that they could escape from the armor of hate with which their mother (usually) had messed up their characters and pray that God will jolt them out of their stupid defense mechanisms, but you don't have much hope that you can do anything to help them.

Because you're not God, right?

But what if you apparently have picked up some Godlike powers in a story you're coauthoring with a sixteen-bit computer?

Anyway we (the Intel 80286 microprocessor and I) followed him home.

These people had the interesting custom of moving their homes when they moved, even for something short term like a peace conference. They stacked their room-divider screens, let the air out of their furniture, dismantled their colorful pavilions, folded their garments in neat piles, closed their ingenious sanitary and bathing facilities, carefully packed their portable lamps and loaded the whole business on flat-bottomed red wagons with thick, cushioned tires and compartments for each of their packages, hitched four white horselike creatures to each wagon and bounced casually and comfortably away. I watched one of these operations and calculated that it took a family of four—mom, pop, teenager, and brat—two hours and forty-five minutes to complete the whole process and even less time to unpack and set up camp at the other end of the line.

Travel light they certainly did. It sure solved the second-home problem. It was made possible of course by the incredibly light but durable multi-use fabrics that their mills ground out, apparently from the flaxlike material which was left over when they had extracted the food from their crops.

A word about the horselike creatures. They were shorter, faster, and sturdier than our counterparts. It's hard to estimate speeds from the perspective of a TV screen, even a large one, but the animals seemed capable of sustained speeds with full loads of perhaps forty miles an hour. So who needed automobiles?

Oh yes, they reproduced by laying eggs. I'm serious. So did most of the other animals which lived in the forests and on the mountains. I'm not kidding.

The humans? If we can use that word? I don't think so, though I wasn't around for any childbirth scenes. The pregnant women that I did observe seemed to be "normally" pregnant, though the biologists who watched our tapes up at Lakeside were not absolutely certain.

Anyway we soon arrived at Malvau's pavilion, a rich purple one, matching his garment of course, located in the woods behind the peace meadow where the upper echelons of B'Mella's staff were gathered, on the shore of one of the many attractive, silver-smooth lakes which dotted the forests.

He began complaining upon arrival. The food was not ready, and when it was, it was not cooked properly. The garden in front of the pavilion was not adequately tended, the house itself was fit only for pigs (their pigs laid eggs too, honest), the wine had begun to sour, the servants and his teenaged daughter were not prompt enough in responding to his requests, and his wife was, as usual, an incompetent housekeeper, mother, administrator, and moreover was unworthy to bear the distinguished name of his family, certainly in no way comparable with his own mother.

Know him?

Sure. They're a dime a dozen. You'd like to punch the bastard. It was this sort of grown-up little boy that my poor B'Mella had to lean on for advice. Note that, like all characters in a story, she belongs already to the author. Not that I owned her. The Lord Our God forbid that I or anyone try to own that one. She was mine in the sense that I had begun to love her and to feel responsible and protective about her. Soon like John Fowles's Mantissa, she would haunt my dreams, day as well as night.

She would not, however, give me a hard time in my dreams as some of the others would. But that anticipates.

Well, if Proust can do it, so can I!

While my B'Mella was moderately attractive, she didn't compare with the gorgeous Irish Catholic heroines of my other stories who cavort, haremlike, through my dreams.

Does God have fantasies about His creatures with whom She falls in love—and again if we are to believe the indications available to us, S/He falls in love with everyone? My guess is that, if you're God, you don't need to fantasize because your reality is good enough as is.

Presumably the Other Person had some affection for

Malvau. If She did, She was the only one. His family and servants ignored his self-pitying monologue, the way a mother learns to ignore a child's crying which is for the record and not a real protest. They tuned him out with routine and untroubled disgust.

His wife was blond, younger than him by maybe ten years, a bit overweight perhaps, round bland face, expressionless eyes, an unimpressive woman whom you could easily ignore at first sight. Only if you looked a second time would you notice that she was the kind of woman that most men would be perfectly delighted to have next to them in bed at night. Then you'd wonder why you hadn't noticed that before, and would probably conclude that her external boredom had become a protective armor with which she walked through life.

Nonetheless, when an insensitive dummy of the Malvau type washes up on the rectory beach with a wife like that, the professional celibate, having been forced to take a second look, thinks to himself that if he was involved with a woman that attractive, he'd certainly learn to be reasonably thoughtful and considerate with her, if only to assure himself some pleasant times in bed. The husband of course has never thought of it that way because he is too frightened of women to be thoughtful and considerate to one of them.

The professional celibate is wrong if he thinks there's any guarantee he would be different from the dummy if the circumstances were reversed or if, with or without permission of the Vatican, he takes unto himself a wife. He is on the other hand dead right to think that the species is organized in such a way that women require some relatively modest displays of thoughtfulness and consideration and that, failing all else, the sexual urge is designed to facilitate such attentions.

I didn't like N'Rasia any more than I liked her husband.

I would dread being burdened with such a superficial flake for the rest of my life. But from the security of my position I thought to myself that she was attractive enough that, flake or no flake, I would certainly work at being nice to her if only to keep the passion going.

That is, mind you, a minimalist approach. Obviously love demands much more. On the other hand, there are times in any relationship when you are thankful (presumably to the Other Person) for providing you with the minimum on which, you should excuse the expression, to fall back.

Presentable physical charms notwithstanding, 'Rasia would have been hard to put up with outside of the bedroom. Like her husband, she was a complainer, a nagger, an unhappy, frustrated, and dissatisfied woman. Her beef was that the prolonged peace negotiations were interfering with the social season back in the city and the plans for her daughter's first official dance (that's what they called it). She was uninterested in and did not care about the deadly serious issues of war and peace with which her husband was preoccupied.

"Will this foolish nonsense never end?" she complained. "There have always been wars. There will always be wars. That's what we have warriors for. What will they do if there is peace? That foolish girl will get herself killed eventually just like her mother and father and husbands. We should be thankful that our children are not of the warrior class. But why should their foolishness interfere with our children's lives? There is so little time for a girl to find a proper husband."

And on and on and on.

You know that type too?

Right.

He complains and she whines. He moans and she bitches.

And they haven't listened to a word the other has said for a long time, years perhaps. The Lord made them, as the Irish put it, and the divil matched them.

But once they had been in love with one another or at least thought they were. A storyteller, unless he's writing for university professors and book reviewers, would perhaps want to bring them to some self-understanding if not renewed love. You can get just so much fun out of Elizabeth Taylor and Richard Burton (God be good to him) shouting at each other just so long before it becomes a drag. God who is a romantic, on the basis of the evidence, and indeed a passionate one, almost certainly will settle for nothing less than romantic passion between the two once and future lovers.

(A pig of a priest once patronized something my sister wrote on the ground that it seemed quite strange for a married woman, mother of seven children, to believe in romantic love. My sister in reply wisely observed that if you are married and the mother of seven that's the only kind of love that matters.)

Your parish priest does his best to prevent spouses like Malvau and N'Rasia from killing each other and perhaps even to keep the marriage together, though often it is not altogether clear why. If you're playing storyteller/God, you figure why not go for broke.

OK, so 'Vau gets his jollies with the young women around the Duchess, those that are interested anyway. And, as it happens, 'Rasia has an occasional stud on the line too. An adjustment, not a perfect adjustment, mind you, but it functions more or less, the best, if you will, of a bad situation. The Other Person in Her wisdom may choose to leave it that way, knowing, Grand Improviser that He is, that any alternative strategy will make a bad situation worse.

A novice at the God Game will rush in where angels fear to tread and muck things up considerably.

As I have reported before, the people in this neighbor world have interesting late-night customs: they remove their outer garment, folding it with the care that sister sacristans (in the old days when we had them) used to fold Mass vestments. Then in their undergarments they kneel to pray to the Lord Our God, either silently or aloud, and if they are married, either together or separately.

Their undergarments, as I noted before, are limited in scope but highly effective in function. I cannot testify for the fantasies of women, but the "unmentionables" of the womenfolk in this cosmos next door would delight the fantasy of the adolescent male that lurks in all of us. Moreover, N'Rasia is the kind of woman who improves as clothes are shed. It is possible to kneel next to a womanly body like that, communicate intensely with your Maker, and not feel the slightest twinge of desire. Possible, but you'd really have to work at it. Alas, as we all know, a lot of men manage to put in the work as their marriages deteriorate.

The next step in their bedtime practices is to bathe naked and together in the elegant and spacious portable bath which is next to every bed, and almost as big as the bed. These people are into bathing rituals with almost the same fanaticism as the ancient Irish or the folks who assembled around the Wadi Kumran near the Dead Sea. There's ritual significance in the custom, a bath is always associated with some sort of prayer to the Lord Our God. Moreover, you could make the case that the culture displays considerable wisdom to put the naked bodies of lovers together in warm water before they go to bed. Like the ancient Irish, they have a fetish about personal cleanliness and domestic cleanliness too, a trait which the ancient Irish and, according to some, the modern Irish and Irish Americans lack. Their pavilions are neat enough and clean enough to win approval of the most rigorous Eastern European homemakers on the Southwest side of Chicago.

OK, then they get out of the tub, wrap themselves in a vast towel to dry off (all the gestures seemed to be determined by a ritual as timeless and as unconscious as were the motions by which a priest used to remove vestments after Mass), discard the towel, replace it with a kiltlike garment at the waist and slip rapidly under the covers (the women have taken care of their hair before the process begins).

Within the room created for Malvau and his mate by the portable screens, all the fabric, including his wife's lingerie and his jockstrap, was his color of rich purple that was his official badge. This was something of an affectation on his part, since even the Duchess didn't seem troubled by the need for consistency of her blue-green color scheme.

The two of them hardly said a word to one another as they went through the ritual.

I told myself that the nighttime ablutions of a middle-aged couple that I didn't particularly like were none of my business and that their lack of sexual attraction to one another was hardly worth even a voyeur's attention.

Yet something fascinated me. As I look back on the night it was the strange, tormented face of Malvau. The mask of self-satisfied complacency had slipped away, to be replaced by sadness and infinite weariness. How come, I wondered. Had the verbal beating from the Duchess hit him harder than I had thought? She might be an upstart from an unimportant family, but she was still the Boss, an almost sacred person whose displeasure could hurt even such a distinguished aristocrat. Especially if, like most of those around her, he treasured a secret worship for the lovely, tragic Duchess.

Like I've said, I was already in the ranks of the worshippers, so why not even our vain Malvau. Vanity does not protect you from pain, rather it makes it worse.

His wife lifted herself out of the tub first and promptly enshrouded herself in the vast towel. I thought he looked at her with the faintest hint of admiration and regret.

She lifted the patch of fabric that shielded their window. The light of their moons poured in. She extinguished the hand lanterns.

"I didn't tell you that you might turn off the light," he complained.

"I didn't ask." She tossed aside the towel and, briefly glowing in the silver light, wrapped the kilt around her loins, climbed into bed (a large, inflated cushion lying on the floor), and pulled the purple coverlet up to her neck.

For a moment, however, as she belted her kilt, her heavy, conical breasts glowed in the light. Unseen by her, his face contorted in swift movement of desire and affection. Maybe not quite as high and firm as when she was a virgin brought to his bath and bed for the first time, but still unbearably attractive.

Grace in other words. Elementary, temporary, ordinary grace. But still grace.

Without any reflection, I jumped into the scene. I keyed his shift/function and typed, APOLOGIZE TO HER, YOU STUPID IDJIT.

He stiffened in the tub, harsh and firm resistance.

IT'S TIME TO STOP THE NONSENSE. YOU STILL LOVE HER. I SAID APOLOGIZE.

I pressed the REPEAT key.

Sheer agony for your noble lord. Had he ever apologized to anyone in his life? Yet, part of him wanted to humiliate himself to his wife. Otherwise he would have simply tuned me out.

SHE'S A LOT MORE WOMAN THAN THOSE LITTLE WITCHES AT THE DUCHESS'S PAVILION. IT'S TIME TO WIN HER BACK. APOLOGIZE AND NOW.

Slowly he climbed out of the tub, went through the ritual of drying himself, walked over to the window and lifted the patch higher so that the room was illumined by silver light, discarded the towel, and stood over his bed and his wife, hesitant and yet eager.

DO IT, CLOWN!

DO NOT KNOW CLOWN.

IDJIT, DAMN FOOL.

EXECUTING.

With the elegant movement of a courtier he knelt next to his bed.

"What foolishness is this?" She was scared stiff, so of course she turned nasty.

"I...I am sorry, 'Rasia," he stammered, pulling back the coverlet to seek encouragement from her torso.

"Sorry?" she sneered. "For what?"

REPEAT. EXECUTE.

"For having been such an arrogant, insensitive husband all our life together."

Hey, I didn't mean the whole life, I just meant today.

"No woman at the palace would give herself to you today?" She turned away from him in disgust.

KICK HER IN THE REAR END, I told the machine.

EXECUTING.

She jumped on the bed, as though someone had really kicked her. My damn machine was too literal.

"I don't deserve to be forgiven." Once launched he could not stop. How many years must it have been pent up inside him?

And how clever of the author to force it out whether 'Vau wanted it out or not.

"You certainly don't."

RESPOND TO HIM. I had to create a shift/function for her. In the meantime, the Compaq more or less on its own kicked her again.

She listened silently as in a clear firm voice her husband described his faults and failures.

THAT'S NO RESPONSE, I typed in. FORGIVE HIM, LOVE HIM. IT'S NOW OR NEVER, YOU BITCHY LITTLE FOOL.

I held down the REPEAT button.

"Torment yourself no more, my dearest one." She cut off his sentence of self-accusation and drew his head against her belly. She didn't want to do it, she resisted the words and the movement every inch of the way, but she was dealing with powers stronger than her own shallow, selfish flakiness. "I will love you always."

My power or power within her? Or both?

Grace or desire or both? Or are they different?

REWARD HIM.

She glanced up at me, wondering how she should reward him.

She knew the author was around. Or did she think it was the Lord Our God invading her boudoir? Or did she care?

OVERWHELM HIM WITH PASSION.

She nodded, smiled, and set to work.

I keyed myself out of their privacy. An author may have to involve himself in the foreplay of his creatures, but under most circumstances he should leave their coupling carefully veiled. Anyway, I wanted out of their relationship, which my instincts said would get much worse before it got better.

I was pleased with myself. I had given these two unappealing people a new chance in life. I had forced a new chance on them whether they wanted a new chance or not.

That's what authors do, they are supposed, *pace* Berney Geis, to ignite hope in their characters.

Even if they don't want hope or don't know what to do with it.

6 The Feast of the Two Moons

The night wasn't finished. Caught up in the fever of the God Game, I intended to continue going around doing good.

The most subtle of all temptations.

I decided that I would look in on the high priest I called the Cardinal because of his red robes and ermine cape. He looked like a Cardinal from central casting, with a sharply cut, aristocratic face, long thin nose, thick wavy white hair—very much unlike the squat, ugly types who actually preside over the curial dicasteries. To my surprise, he was locked in a tête-à-tête with his counterpart from Lenrau's priestly caste. There were others, two of them ancient, witchlike priestesses (the Other Person forgive me for it, but I coded them MOTHER SUPERIOR), huddled around a table in a dimly lit cave deep in the forest. There was a brazier burning incense, I guessed (remember, there was no smell in the story) in the corner, and a couple of sinister-looking snakes crawling around.

No spiders or black cats.

"There will be no peace," the Cardinal said flatly.

"The ilel may force it," croaked one of the priestesses.

"The ilel should be eliminated," screeched the other.

"We must restrain her," the Cardinal said prudently (Cardinals are always prudent), "not eliminate her. Firstly, she may be dangerous, secondly, there might be a terrible reaction to her death. Counterproductive. Thirdly, it may not be necessary."

No remark that it would be evil. I said Cardinals were prudent, not necessarily virtuous.

"Kill her!" The Mothers Superior, sounding like the witches in *Macbeth*, cackled in unison. "Kill her!"

A couple of the snakes did a nifty little dance.

"They are right." One of the men leaned forward on the table. "Noble Lord, she could frustrate all our plans. Peace will only be restored when the warrior class destroys itself and we resume our ancient rule of the land. She must die as they must die, for the good of all, even for their own good."

"Kill her for her own good," another cleric chimed in.

All this time, I was pushing my ABORT PLANS button and holding down the REPEAT key.

No impact. None whatever. I could force Malvau and N'Rasia into each other's arms and bodies, but I couldn't force these clowns to think twice about their plans to dispose of my Ranora. Conclusion: you can as an author shake those who are open to lust of one kind or another, but not those who are into power.

No wonder the Other Person has so much trouble with the Curia Romana.

So I told the Compaq, EXTINGUISH LIGHTS.

Bamm! Total darkness.

Cries, screeches, alarms.

KILL SNAKES.

The damn thing knew what a snake was. Of course, the

parser knew about snakes from *Adventure*. There were three or four rapid explosive retorts and then a much louder blast.

Then frightened silence.

The light came back on.

"What happened?" The Cardinal was pale and shaking.

"The Lord Our God has struck us for planning to desecrate his ilel!" wailed one of the priests.

"Nonsense." The Cardinal began to regain his cool. I doubt that he worried much about the Lord Our God.

"The snakes are gone, He's taken our snakes."

"Demons!" screeched the Mothers Superior.

"I said the ilel might be dangerous." The Cardinal smoothed his robe. "Killing her would serve no useful purpose at this time. She cannot impose peace. Our true enemies, as always, are the warriors. If anyone is to be killed, it must be the Duke and Duchess. Together they could stand in the way of our return to power."

"Kill them! Kill them!" yelled the witches.

"In due time, if necessary to restrain them," the Cardinal said softly, "for their own good and for the good of the land, of course."

Not if I can help it, you bastards.

The night, theirs as well as mine, wasn't over yet.

I looked in briefly at Malvau and N'Rasia. They were huddled close together, hands affectionately resting on each other, peacefully and complacently sleeping. Well, score one anyway.

Then I reached for the SUSPEND GAME key, hesitated, and decided to have one last look around.

SCAN FOR TROUBLEMAKERS, I told the program.

EXECUTING.

It began to move rapidly across the countryside, over the forests and the lakes, down the rivers, up the sides of the mountains. Near the top of one mountain it focused in on a large hut in a snow-covered meadow.

What kind of troublemakers were messing around way up here?

The interior of the hut looked like a low-budget set for a film based on *The Guns of Navarone*. A group of very young warriors, under the command of the Three Stooges, were working on what I can only describe as a piece of heavy artillery—a big cannon, surrounded by computerlike consoles and several large cranes. The warriors wore the star of Lenrau's army.

A number of fur-clad peasants were stumbling around carrying boxes and bags under the watchful eye of a warrior with a zap gun. Two men, apparently the leaders, were huddled over the largest console.

"It is aimed at her pavilion, is it not?"

"See how the lines intersect? Right at the whore's bedroom."

"Send the peasants into the snow," the first one barked, rubbing his gloved hands together. "If our, ah, experiment is successful, we may dispose of them later."

The poor people were herded out into the snow.

"We will destroy her, and then the Lord Lenrau will sweep into their city, and we will take power away from the effete Kaila and his weakling friends. You may have the honor of pressing the button, my friend."

"First, let us make a final adjustment. It would not do to miss." Someone spun a few wheels and the canon shifted ever so slightly.

I wasn't going to try to reason with these clowns.

DESTROY CANON.

DO NOT KNOW CANON.

A spelling purist. CANNON. EXECUTE.

EXECUTING.

Did it ever.

The roof of the shed vanished in a cloud of dust, the cannon collapsed on the floor, crashing through its supports, a ball of fire exploded high in the sky, a noise like thunder trailed after it, and then the walls of the shed fell in on the wreckage of the mechanism.

FREE PEASANTS, I demanded.

One of the peasants complied with my instruction by bashing the guard over the head with a tree branch. He grabbed the zap gun and the whole crowd of peasants took off for the woods.

Inside the wreckage of the hut, the leaders were extricating themselves from the rubble.

"We will have to build it again," one of them said, his breath turning to mist on the cold night air.

"Then we will rebuild it," another replied calmly.

You just do that, fellas. I'll be back.

A hundred yards down the mountain, I saw a white-clad figure on a white "horse." Another plotter?

I told the machine to IDENTIFY RIDER.

G'RANNE. REPEAT G'RANNE.

I heard you the first time.

The ice maiden, in her element now, flipped the white scarf away from her face, rose-red now in the cold night air and pondered the rubble that Larry, Curly, and Moe had produced.

She turned and rode back down the mountain. What sort of devious game was that one playing?

Enough trouble for one night. I suspended the game.

Ranora danced in my dreams that night. Not B'Mella nor the somewhat outsize but nonetheless attractive N'Rasia, but the teenaged imp with the peppermint-candy clothes and her witty little pipe.

I think she said something like, "I'll please my Master and darling Kaila—isn't he *totally* cute?—and you too!"

She played her triumphal Lenrau theme and her gentle Kaila theme and then something, well, amused and tolerant, which she seemed to be assigning to me.

It was, of course, only a dream. And very different from my later dreams.

I think it was different, anyway. My altered states were already becoming confused.

The next morning I told myself that it was only a game, a storytelling game with a few extra fillips that writing an ordinary story didn't have. Not quite so complete control of the material. Made it more interesting.

But nothing real.

So I picked up the adolescents, was reprimanded (by Michele) for being "grossly" late (five minutes), and headed for the lake. While Bobby and Lance skied double with the banana peels, Heidi watched them for the inevitable noisy collision. She was troubled because someone had asked her the day before "when the lifeguard would come" despite the fact that she was wearing her official whistle. Apparently he had never seen her daily confrontation with the hapless Joseph, a well-meaning and genial but maladroit young man who is *always* banished at the end of the confrontation. Michele sat across from me, looking reflective (a rare event) and humming a hauntingly familiar little tune.

The melody which had been played for me on the pipes in my dreams the night before.

"What's that song, Michele?"

"Hmmn . . . oh, I don't know." She hummed it again like she was listening to it for the first time. "That one?"

"Yes."

"Something I must have heard on the radio."

"It doesn't sound like rock."

"*Well*, I'm not totally into rock."

I told myself then that it was all in my imagination, that Nathan's God Game was taking possession of me as a story does when I'm deeply involved in it.

After all, I had heard the tune in a dream, had I not? Not in the game.

And Michele was not really like Ranora. As positive and as outspoken indeed, but a bit older, less exuberant than an early teen, brown hair instead of blond. She didn't play any musical instrument, much less a tin whistle. Equally bossy and definitive, seldom in error, never in doubt. Same stubborn jaw, but very different face (equally pretty, I add to protect my life).

Cognates, not identities, to use words I came up with later.

After skiing, I made a few phone calls and sat back to reflect on the game. I told myself that I was still in control, I could stop anytime I wanted to, I was not hooked on the plot or the characters. I could turn on the machine, press the TERMINATE GAME function key and that would be that.

However, I had to find out about that tune.

So on went the game.

FIND ILEL, I ordered the program.

It searched around in her usual haunts and finally found her strolling through the forest, where the birds seemed to be delighted by her imitations of their love calls, and occasionally singing in a language I did not understand.

Did the ilels come from elsewhere? No one had mentioned her family. Did they come over the mountains occasionally and intrude in the lives of these peoples and then perhaps disappear again? What kind of thoughts raced through her pretty little head?

At any rate she wasn't playing the tune I had heard in my dream and on the ski boat.

She came to a little lake, apparently her destination, felt it with her fingers, nodded approvingly, glanced around to see if anyone was watching, threw off her clothes with a couple of quick movements, and dove into the water.

Her swimming stroke, a slightly off-key (like everything else in this world) variant of the Australian crawl, was strong and determined. This was not ministering to her master in the pool, this was serious exercise.

I let her swim and went to the kitchen to prepare a ham and cheese sandwich on rye bread and a chocolate ice cream with chocolate sauce. I don't know what would have happened if someone had come into my house and seen a naked girl swimming across a weird-looking lake in the middle of an odd forest on my big screen. I guess I had come to expect that there were rules written elsewhere that said I was not to be disturbed and that I was not to consider calling anyone else to play the game/write the story while I was working on it.

By the time I was finished with lunch she was out of the lake, lying on a slab of rock, her blond hair plastered against her head, greedily absorbing the warmth of the sun, looking quite chaste and virginal despite her nudity.

She picked up her pipe, blew a few notes, and then played the theme I had heard in my dreams.

"*Well*," she looked directly at me. "What now?"

I didn't say anything.

"You made me an ilel and sent me to that poor silly man," a few more notes of the theme, "and told me to be obedient to Kaila..."

I never did. It was someone else. Don't blame me. The Other Person...

"...*and* he won't court that poor lovely lady *and* Kaila has begun to like me *and* I think I like him *and* they talk all the time *and* I can sing and dance and make faces and be good to him *and* that doesn't bring peace at all *and* I don't know what to do next *and* anyway what about Kaila?"

Gee, kid, don't ask me.

She played the Kaila and Lenrau themes, mixing them up in an ill-fitting combination.

She sat up and made a face at me, disgusted.

Then she played the Lenrau and B'Mella themes and they didn't fit either. She pounded the rock with her little fist.

"It's *all* your fault. I'm only an ilel, not a princess or a politician or even a scholar like poor dear Kaila." She grinned and played his theme. By itself it was wonderful. "Isn't he cute? What am I supposed to do about *him*? I mean, I'm not afraid of him...or anything like that..."

She frowned, turned deadly serious, and knelt reverently on the slab. "I can't deceive you. I'm terrified of him. He's not going to hurt me or anything gross like that..." She paused as though that were an absurd notion. "I mean, he totally respects me. But..."

She grinned.

"I don't like it when he looks at me like I'm a silly little girl, but I'm scared when he looks at me like I'm a woman. I'm not a woman yet, am I? I'm only a poor little ilel. I'm not old enough to drag him into my bed, am I?"

She was trying to manipulate me now.

"So what should I do? Like I know you want me to shove those two silly people together, but it isn't working very well, is it? And what's wrong with the Master anyway? Where does he go when his eyes glaze that way? I don't know."

She struggled to her feet and donned her red-and-white-striped bikini-type undergarments, as though more modesty was required for further conversation with God.

"Well?" she persisted when she was comfortably stretched out on the rock again.

DO WHAT YOU'RE SUPPOSED TO DO. I was playing the role of the Great Improviser or Master Model Fitter with a vengeance.

She sighed, "I know *that*. And I'll do it, really I will, except that it's hard being an ilel with such silly people. Anyway, you don't mind if I complain occasionally, do you?" She smiled a wheedlingly attractive smile. "Just a little bit? I know you don't!" She played my theme again and giggled when she was finished. "I knew you wouldn't."

What can I tell you?

SING AND DANCE AND MAKE PEOPLE SMILE AND LAUGH AND BE HAPPY, I typed in. THAT'S WHAT PEOPLE LIKE YOU ARE FOR.

She considered me shrewdly, or rather she looked at the sky above her where the port between our worlds seemed to be located. "Are *you* always that way?"

AN IMPERTINENT QUESTION, YOUNG WOMAN.

"I know, but *are* you?"

AS LONG AS THERE ARE ILELS TO AMUSE ME.

She rolled over on her stomach and pounded the rock as she laughed.

I'd said the right words, I guess.

She put her gown back on, frolicked through the forest, playing with the birds and picking flowers, and ran the last hundred yards to the Duke's pavilion.

Inside he was staring glumly at the sky. She kissed him and threw the garland she had made on the run around his neck.

"Happy today, noble Lord and Master?"

"As long as there are ilels to amuse me," he replied with a brave smile.

That freaked her out completely.

In a way the conversation I didn't have with Ranora was as decisive a turning point as my meddling in the marriage of 'Vau and 'Rasia the night before. I knew that this was not just a game and not just a story and that I was not merely a game player and a storyteller. Something totally weird was happening. People, most notably Ranora, were confusing me with Someone Else.

And I seemed, temporarily, to be playing that Someone Else's game; and it wasn't Nathan's either.

And I was beginning to love it.

Next stop was Malvau's.

He was fully dressed for his walk to the central pavilion. His wife, looking disheveled and abandoned, was still asleep. He paused above her, glanced down proudly, kissed her lips, and fondled her lightly. She opened her eyes, smiled warmly, and embraced him. Only after he had left did she shake her head in confusion, as though she were trying to drive away sleep and figure out what the hell had happened.

The clergy's secret meeting cave was empty save for the conference table and the brazier.

ELIMINATE FURNITURE, I ordered.

A couple of rocks fell out of the wall and smashed the table and the brazier. Nice going.

Up in the mountains the renegade warriors were shivering despite the sunlight and lifting rocks off the wreckage of their cannon. I thought I'd have some more fun with them.

BREAK CANON.

I DO NOT...

I cut it off. CANNON.

The round tube cracked neatly in half. One half of it rolled off the braces on which it still rested and smashed into several more pieces. Larry, Curly, and Moe sat around the wreckage of their toy and wept as they shook in the cold. I actually felt kind of sorry for them. Nonetheless it served them right.

I was handing out justice with a fair and even hand, wasn't I?

Then to B'Mella's chamber where the dark Duchess was poring over several stacks of paper, marking them with a strange scrawl which was, I presume, her signature.

(Kenny, a political scientist like Nathan and a good friend of ours, was somewhat upset that I didn't learn more at the seminar about the operation and function of the administrative elites in this world. "What's the point," he said with his usual Calvinist intensity, "in breaking through a cosmic barrier if you don't find out how they run things in your neighboring cosmos?"

(That's Kenny for you. No problem at all with the existence of another cosmos. The only problem for him is why I didn't do something useful during the time I was more or less in charge. By useful he means, as befits the President of the SSRC, something that would add to the store of human social science knowledge. "Kenny," I told him airily, "God is too busy to pay any attention to those things.")

"Good morning, my lady." Malvau smiled complacently and bowed. "I see you are at work early."

"I must deal with this excrement before we have the excrement of the negotiations." She glanced up at him. "You look very satisfied with yourself this morning, 'Vau. Bed another woman?"

"A very familiar woman, since you ask, my lady." He looked so damn proud of himself that you would have thought that it was his idea instead of mine.

She leaned back in her chair, and put aside her trapezoidal-shaped writing implement. "N'Rasia?"

He bowed again and smiled quite happily. "Old loves are the best are they not? Especially when rediscovered?"

"Does she look as self-satisfied as you do?"

"I cannot answer for how I appear, my lady, but, since you ask, I must report that my mate seemed quite content when I left her this morning."

A smile played at the corner of the Duchess's lips, making her very lovely. "I must congratulate you both." She half rose from her chair and kissed her blushing councilor on the cheek. "I hope your happiness continues."

"We pray to the most high that it does...now, if I may make a suggestion about the negotiations?"

His suggestion was that since it was the Feast of the Two Moons the next night, she would invite Lenrau and a few of his aides to eat the sunset meal in her pavilion. He would be there along with a few of her advisers, Linco, and one or two others. They might over the fruit and wine arrive at some "principles."

"With some good fortune, we could even establish groups which would sort out the more complicated issues that separate us."

"If we can remember what they are." She grinned wryly. "Cancel the other negotiations?"

"Oh, by no means. The heat can be radiated in public, the light shed in private."

She nodded. "How very wise. The Lady N'Rasia will accompany you. We owe her a debt."

"My wife is not concerned about such things..." he stammered.

"I want her here at the meal," she waved away his objection. "If I say she is to be concerned, she will be concerned...but will they accept our invitation?"

"Would you, if it were reversed?"

"After some hesitation."

He nodded wisely. "So will they."

It was a near thing, however.

Ranora, naturally, clapped her hands, executed a joyous somersault. Kaila smiled pleasantly, as much enthusiasm as he ever displayed. But the warriors were against it and voted unanimously at a meeting (in which one of the men from Navarone on the mountain inveighed against the foul-smelling whore in language I will not repeat). G'Ranne, who seemed to have lost her power of speech, contented herself with watching Kaila intently.

The priests, horrified to learn of the invitation, whispered that it was sacrilege to eat the Meal of the Two Moons with blaspheming infidels; a delegation of prosperous overweight burghers from Lenrau's city appeared towards the end of the day to register their fears and anxieties.

"She'll kill you," screeched a Mother Superior of the previous night. "She'll kill all of you."

"I hardly think so," Kaila murmured gently.

Ranora stuck out her tongue behind the woman's back.

"We could ask for hostages." Lenrau cocked an eyebrow. "I'm sure she'll offer herself again. No, the Lady may and doubtless does have her faults, but treachery is not one of them. The question is not safety. It's whether any good can be accomplished." He glanced at the stony face of the ilel who, arms akimbo, stood at the door of his chamber, building up to one of her towering temper tantrums. "Or perhaps whether it will do any harm." She climbed down from the tantrum and smiled approvingly at him. "Kaila, will you convey to the Lady B'Mella our grateful acceptance of her most charming invitation? G'Ranne, will you accompany us to the dinner?"

The ice maiden was startled. "I have nothing to wear!"

"I'm sure that can be corrected."

"As you wish, my lord."

Smart move, coopt her.

"It will be the first time in four hundred and thirty-nine years that our leaders will eat the Meal of the Two Moons together." The courtier could on occasion turn pedantic. "I shall tell her that too."

"Doubtless she will be pleased to learn that," the Duke smiled ruefully. "Also the first time in either of our lives."

"Which is more important," crowed Ranora.

So Kaila crossed the meadow, Ranora piping his way with a dramatic variation on his theme. She called forth the Duchess with a burst of sound that could have come from a trumpet, bowed very low when the Duchess emerged, then scampered away from the pavilion like an eighth grader who has broken a window in the public school.

"I cannot recall that the ilel is included in the invitation." B'Mella found Kaila's smile as hard to resist as anyone else and treated him with the same deferential reverence he accorded her.

"As you know, my lady, I am responsible for the spirited little wench. If I give an absolute order she will obey me."

"I will not put that burden upon you, my lord. Indeed, I would be disappointed if the magic imp did not appear."

"I think we will both agree that she would be intolerable if I told her that.... She is very fond of you, my lady."

"I cannot imagine why."

The courtier had the last word. "If you will permit me to say so, my lady, I can."

It did not work out so easily for Malvau. His edgy wife, trying to pretend that nothing had happened the night before, greeted his return at the end of the day with perfunctory neglect. He in turn proclaimed pompously that the Lady B'Mella required her presence the next night at the Meal of the Two Moons.

Both of them were trying to return to their old ways. I began to wonder whether I'd made a mistake.

I also found, to my dismay, that they were no longer

pawns to be manipulated in my story, but people I cared for. I was now emotionally involved in their evolving love/hate connection. Dear God, or Dear Other Person, how the hell did I get into this?

"I despise that woman. At her age, no husband or children and no concern about either. I will not eat with her." She was working herself up into an enormous rage, the kind I bet she'd used often in the past to control and dominate her husband. "Nor with that evil blasphemous pervert from the other side. It is a sacrilege the Lord Our God will abominate."

'Vau had been, I think, of mixed mind about the invitation. On the one hand, proud that his wife had been invited, on the other fearing the negative reaction he thought he would encounter. I could see in his face, hesitant and weak, that he was about to agree with her and phony up an excuse through which the Duchess would instantly see.

DON'T LET HER DO IT, I advised.

He nodded, took her arm firmly, and said, "It is necessary for us to have a private talk, my dear."

While the servants and their daughter watched wide-eyed, he virtually dragged her away from the tents and into the forest.

She was terrified, fearing I think that she would be beaten. Their society, like ours, has deadly violence lurking beneath the surface. I can't judge whether there is more or less husband/wife violence on their side of the barrier. The wives over there, however, are generally in excellent physical condition and give as much as they get. Battered wives they have, and lots of battered husbands too. Perhaps these two had never physically punished each other—they had more effective ways of inflicting pain and humiliation. N'Rasia looked sure she would be hurt.

DON'T HIT HER, I warned him.

If he heard me, he didn't show it. I guess he really had no intention of hitting her.

"Now listen to me, woman," he said quietly, one hand digging into each of her arms, "and listen carefully. We have three children and five grandchildren, have we not? Good. And a virgin daughter we both love very much? Do you want her raped by warriors before the Feast of Four Moons? Do you want the heads of your grandchildren to be smashed against the rocks? Do you want you and your other daughter and your daughter-in-law to be stripped and sold on the auction block? You don't? I thought not. You think those things can't happen now, because they have not happened in fifty years? You think that only the warriors fight wars in our modern days? I tell you that we are on the edge of a return to barbarism. There are many who wish it, some who will stop at nothing to accomplish it. If this attempt at peace fails, the night will return again."

"Why me?" She struggled to break free of his hold.

"Because the Lady requests it, because she realizes that she needs another woman at the dinner, because the woman should be the wife of one of her councilors, because you are attractive and, as I learned again to my delight last night, capable of great charm. If those are not enough reasons, then the final one is that I want you there."

You'd better accept, I warned her.

"Very well," she said ungraciously. "I will obey."

What came next was entirely his idea, not mine.

"No," she exclaimed as he began, "not here, not now."

He didn't force her, though he wouldn't let her out of his grasp either. But he knew all the skills of seduction and applied them to her with ruthless cunning. Probably, I reflected, as I bowed out of the picture, for the first time in their lives.

I ventured into their city and discovered that sentiment

there had turned in favor of the meal with the other side. The people were dancing and singing and guzzling large amounts of wine. It was part of the festival, but also hope was in the air.

And hope between 'Vau and 'Rasia. When I checked in with them later, they were ambling back to their tent hand in hand, 'Rasia unabashedly wanton. The servants pretended not to notice. Their daughter rolled her eyes in astonishment.

"You must explain to me what I ought to know about tomorrow night," she said respectfully to her husband as they ate their dinner. "You know so much more about these matters than I do."

I glanced at my watch. Six o'clock. I had spent almost seven hours with the game and it had seemed no longer than seven minutes. I was completely hooked.

Didn't I have something to do tonight? I glanced at the calendar. The Goggins were picking me up for supper in a half hour. I was barely ready when they arrived.

Now here's where things get strange, real strange.

7 A Midnight Visitor

Gail and Terry took me to a classy new restaurant on the Red Arrow Highway. The food easily beat McDonald's, which in that part of the world meant that it was a place where on any night of the week you could meet at least five or six and maybe a dozen or more couples from Grand Beach.

"Would you look at those two," my hostess said in astonishment. "They look like something good has happened to them."

Joan and Tom Hagan were in one of the community's more perennially troubled marriages. He was an important political person and she an active social climber. They should never have married, it was generally agreed up and down the beach. This summer rumors of divorce had become statements of fact. Yet here they were, holding hands and smiling dreamily at one another like young lovers.

He seemed as self-satisfied as Malvau, she as contentedly wanton as N'Rasia.

"Anyone," I said cynically, "can have an occasional happy summer romp."

"Not those two, not after what they've said and done.

There's something much more powerful going on. I wouldn't have believed it."

"Will it last?" her husband wondered.

She smiled as only Irish women can when they're not certain but intend to sound as if they are. "Of course."

Well, maybe, says I.

They stopped over at our table on their way out, blissfully content and somehow grateful, though we had done nothing to help them and, like a lot of other folks on the beach, had written off their chances a couple of years ago.

"What could have happened?" Terry Goggin wondered.

"They've fallen in love again," Gail said promptly.

"It won't work." I helped myself to another spoonful of chocolate ice cream. "Unless they deal with the underlying problems."

"Maybe," she replied, "they'll be able to deal with them now."

I began to worry about it on our way home. Did the rebirth of passion to N'Rasia and Malvau, a second if very thin chance for their love, influence our neighbors? Or vice versa? Or were the two merely utterly unrelated coincidences? Or was there some complex interrelationship which could not be described by any pattern available to us? Note, by the way, that the last explanation is an academic copout.

However, if there is a port between our cosmos and theirs and if that port happens to be, on our side, in the vicinity of Grand Beach, and if there are spiritual links through that port, ought not the relationships on one side to be possibly graceful for the relationships on the other?

Or also possibly harmful?

It was true that on our side the woman was blond and the man silver-haired, though he was not as tall as 'Vau and she not as attractive as 'Rasia. He was a political influential, though not the most important one of Grand Beach and certainly not of the high status of Malvau. Cognates, when you looked at the hope and the contentment in their eyes, rather closely linked cognates, but not the same. Not quite the same. And, as the next phases in both their lives would indicate, the processes were not the same.

Strange, however, scary strange. I didn't even share this part of it with Nathan, nor the encounter I would have that night.

Anyway, how did Michele know Ranora's song? Or was that vice versa too?

In short, why do the ways of grace have to be so mysterious especially when you are, for the moment, in the grace-dispensing role?

Maybe.

After an Irish Cream at the Goggins' I wandered by the Brennans' to talk to Michele's parents. Bobby and some of the young apes with whom he associates were in the other room listening to rock and talking about beer and broads, presumably. Michele was out with her latest date who, thank heavens, is not the courtier/scholar/poet type.

But the news was that she was to sing her medley of Irish folk songs at a formal dinner dance at Long Beach the next night.

I didn't like that at all.

Not so badly, however, as to refuse my third Baileys of the evening. Or a fourth.

My head was whirling with possibilities and speculations, all jumbled up together with the two worlds rushing one upon another in exotic confusion. I was, however, now so deeply involved that I was determined I would work it all out myself.

The confusion was not unpleasant. I was in fact having the time of my life. And in love with everyone.

Just like God.

I had a hard time falling asleep. I think I did, anyway, because now it gets really weird.

Unable to sleep, I got up, climbed down the stairs, and sat on the deck by the beach, watching the stars on a moonless night and wondering how many other cosmoi there might be linked with each of them.

I was now and would be for the rest of the game in an altered state of consciousness, or, as my friend Erika would say when I consulted her after the Lakeside seminar (she was unable to attend because she was lecturing in Zurich), I was in a number of different altered states: "an unusual but not unknown phenomenon."

I heard footsteps on the tiny beach. Someone had been walking along the sandbar a few yards out and was now coming ashore.

"May I sit with you for a while?" A woman's voice, familiar but yet not familiar.

"What is it you want?" I demanded nervously. I mean, who knows what can happen to you on the beach at night?

"I would like to talk to you." She climbed up the steps and sat on the chair next to me. "At least I have the right to do that, after what you've done to me."

"What have I done to you?"

"Come now. You know what you've done. I'm a grandmother, well into the middle years of life, at an age when passion cools. You have addicted me once again to my husband. It is a disgrace. I can think of nothing else. I want to be with him all the time, to make love with him every minute. I cannot stand to be separated from him."

Her low voice was intense with anger and embarrassment.

"It was your fault, woman. Flaunting your breasts at him that way was bound to get to him eventually."

"Do you like my breasts?" She sounded bold and proud.

"That is not the issue."

"But it is. Do I have good breasts?"

"As I've already said..."

"Heavy and conical, not as firm as they once were but still appealing. But that's what you make my husband think."

"No, that's what he makes me think. Anyway, you're a vain woman if you want us both to praise your body."

"You both have." She laughed. "I am vain and I do enjoy it."

I could now see her clearly enough in the starlight. N'Rasia, all right. Wearing the white swimsuit Joan Hagan sometimes struts down the beach in, but filling it out much more nicely.

"What do you want? You're on the wrong side of the wall, you shouldn't be here."

"I'm part of your dream about me. I'm on the other side, but you've seen me, so I can come over here in your dreams. Simple, isn't it?"

"How do I know I'm not part of your dream?" I demanded. The conversation, you will note, is utterly impossible—but nonetheless, given its impossibility, by no means irrational.

"That's possible, but then we both might be part of her dream, might we not?"

"Whose dream?"

"My counterpart, the woman I borrowed this swimsuit from so as not to shock you by appearing naked on your deck, though since it's a dream you wouldn't be shocked, would you?"

"You don't sound the way you do in the game." I was trying to change the subject.

"You think I'm a bit of a bitch in the game."

"You act like one."

"A woman acts like a bitch because she's frightened."

"So frightened that she flaunts herself for a few seconds at her husband every night even though she's treated him with indifference and contempt for the rest of the day."

"All right, I'm a real bitch," she said disconsolately.

"You still haven't told me what you want."

"My husband," she said firmly.

"I gathered. Well, I gave him to you, didn't I?"

"And I'm very grateful." She touched my hand. "Poor man took such a risk because you made him."

"Helped him."

She giggled. "We did it together."

"So?"

"Do you know what I'm going to do tomorrow?"

"Prepare for the Feast of the Two Moons dinner, I devoutly hope."

"Exactly. How?"

"You tell me."

"All right. And then when it happens tomorrow you'll know this isn't merely a dream. I'm going to make him have an orgy with me. Hours and hours of love."

"He'll need hormones."

"I won't?"

"Not if what you tell me is true."

"All right, you're God, provide him with hormones. You see, a wonderful afternoon will make him self-confident and brilliant and it will make me glow with beauty and those degenerates we have to learn to love will love us. What else can I do? I can't understand all the political issues he talked to me about after you left."

"Let's get one thing straight," I insisted. "I'm not God."

"Sure you are," she said confidently. "Who else could have done what you did for us? And," she turned somber, "if it doesn't work, it's all your fault. You probably shouldn't have messed in our lives anyway."

"Would you like a drink?" I deliberately changed the subject again.

"I would love some of that Baileys you have with you. We haven't developed it on the other side yet. Too many oviparous creatures you know." She laughed at me.

How did she know the name?

I didn't bring any Baileys down to the deck. But this was an altered state so there was a full bottle, and Powerscourt tumblers to drink it from too.

"Do you mind if I take off this horrible swimsuit?" she asked. "Your fabrics are not nearly as comfortable as ours."

"It's your dream." I handed her the glass of Baileys, filled to the rim. Ice cubes had appeared in it too. Another advantage of an altered state. "Do what you want."

She placed the glass on the rail of the deck, went through some awkward twisting movements, sighed with relief, and sat back on the chaise, Baileys in hand. "That's better and uhmm . . . this is good."

"Glad you like it."

"Your health," she said gravely and I saw the outline of an arm raised in the night. "If that's appropriate for God."

"I'm not God."

"Sure you are. Do you love me?"

"I thought I said that once."

"I know, but I'm not very lovable."

"You weren't at first. Neither was his nibs. Then I became involved and got hung up on you."

"Would you believe I fell in love with him when I was ten and have loved him every day since?"

"If you say so."

"I tried. He tried. You made us and the divil matched us."

"That's my line."

"It's your dream. May I have another drink?"

"You can't drink it that way."

"Maybe my metabolism is different. Maybe I have scales and seven feet."

"For all I know."

"I'm terribly grateful for the last chance with my man." She was weeping now.

"Not last. Only most recent. Anyway the Other Person made you."

"I don't know what you're talking about. You love that bitch B'Mella more than me."

"She's the leading character, I've got to love her more."

"And that teenaged demon. Of course, you have a thing for teenagers, don't you?"

"Regardless. She's a leading character. You're only a subplot."

"The story of my life." Her tears were bitter now. "Always a subplot."

"In this story. That doesn't mean there won't be other stories."

"You'd destroy me and 'Vau," her voice turned musical at the sound of his name, "if it fit your plot, wouldn't you? In fact, you may still do that, just to prove that even God shouldn't meddle in people's lives. Isn't that true? You'll do all you can to make Lenrau and the bitch happy and you'll let us go down the drain, just so there'll be some contrast."

"You aren't even important enough to be in my dream," I responded cruelly.

"I know, but I'm here because, damn you, I want to be important and not because I have 'presentable' breasts and a nice ass."

"I never wrote anything about your ass."

"I know, and that makes me mad. I think it's nice. As nice as the little demon's and you mentioned her ass."

"Yours is delightful too, 'Rasia." I was lying because I hadn't noticed but I'm sure it was. "The point about you, however, is not your physical aspects, though you do all right there, but your redemptive capacity."

"Oh," she said in a tiny voice. "Really?"

"I stole the idea of a wife's familiar breast as a sign of grace from David Lodge's *Small World*."

"I haven't read that."

"No matter. I'm trying to argue that you're grace in a special way. And be nice to the ilel, she's going to do something very special for you tomorrow."

"What?" she demanded like a little kid promised a present.

"You'll have to wait and see."

And I'll have to figure it out.

"Will it be nice?"

"Very nice. And I don't want you being harsh with the Lady B'Mella either. She has enormous respect for you. Why else did she invite you to the Meal of the Two Moons?"

"Only because I made that damn councilor of hers human again," she snapped.

"Isn't that enough?"

"So I'm a good screw for him? What does that matter?"

"You know better than that."

"All right," she sighed. "There's no point in arguing with you, anyway. You will promise not to destroy what... what's happened between my man and me?"

"I have my story to tell."

"So we don't have any chance at all."

"You haven't been listening. A storyteller can't make a character do what he or she doesn't want to do. You have free will."

"You sound like a Jesuit."

"I'm not."

A long silence.

"May I have another glass of Baileys? I don't know when I'll be back."

"Do you have to swim over to your side?"

"Of course not. The beach idea is your part of the dream. Your stories are filled with beach trysts. We don't have lakes this size on our side. Or if we do I've never seen one."

I filled her glass, draining the Baileys bottle. I had had only one glass. She must be more than a little tuned by now. "I think you'll be back," I said. "You've intruded pretty deeply into my unconscious, more than I realized."

"You do have a weakness for handsome middle-aged women, don't you?" she giggled tipsily.

"I sure fell for you," I agreed.

"Are you sure you love me?" Now it was tipsy tears.

"Yes, N'Rasia," I said it straight out because she needed to hear it and it was true. "I do love you."

No questions about comparisons.

"Do you enjoy it when my husband fucks me?"

"You are picking up our bad language."

"I'm sorry. I shouldn't talk that way with God ... I know you're not God, but I don't believe that. You didn't answer my question."

"Of course I do."

"More than he does."

"Differently."

"Do you want to make love with me now?" A shy, girlish offer.

"I would love to, 'Rasia, but it wouldn't be right."

"I'm only a dream figment."

"It still wouldn't be right."

"I know. I thought I ought to offer. Maybe in another

world. Anyway, I want to go back to our side and wake up my husband and persuade him to love me again."

"I'm sure he'll be delighted."

"I can hug you?"

"Why not?"

So she hugged me, modestly enough, and was gone. Then she faded back in. "Don't forget the hormones. It's important."

I had. "Haven't I taken good care of you so far?"

"Oh yes. Please don't stop."

This time she was gone for good.

And I woke up. In my bed, of course.

Still, the next morning I went down to the beach deck. There was a white swimming suit on the railing. I threw it in the trash can.

I was deeply enough into the story by now that I had stopped trying to figure out what was happening. It was like being halfway through a novel. All that mattered was finishing it. This one was even more compelling because I couldn't be sure how it would end.

I went skiing in the morning and was accused by Michele of not paying any attention when I was driving the boat. "You want to drive?" I asked her.

"No way. Other people drive me."

"Then be quiet."

"All *right*!"

Which means that it's neither all nor right.

We saw the Hagans strolling down the beach hand in hand. She was wearing a red swimsuit.

"Isn't it really excellent, how happy they are?" Michele enthused as she put on her ski jacket.

"Hormones," I said.

"Huh?" she and Bobby exclaimed together.

"Never mind, just trying to remind myself."

While she was spinning across the wake, I remembered that I should check my supply of Baileys when I returned to the house.

"You remember Rick?" Bobby asked with a wink.

"Herself's boyfriend, the fierce linebacker with the gentle soul?" I grinned. How could you forget Rick?

"'Chele may go off to Ohio for a few days to see him," Bobby offered as his sister wiped out for the third time.

"So?"

"And Heidi will be working mornings as lifeguard."

"So?"

"So maybe I can bring one of my own chicks."

"What chicks?"

"I don't know. I can always find some. They really dig me."

"Funny, that's not what I hear."

As far as I know there's no cognate for Bobby on the other side, unless it be one of the sword wavers—a good-guy sword waver of course.

I mention this conversation because it is necessary to plant some information here which will be pertinent later on. The difference with planting it in this story is that I didn't know when I heard it that it would be pertinent. You see what I mean by this story being different from the others?

As if someone else was planting things as part of my story.

I checked the Baileys supply when I returned to the house. Sure enough, there was one bottle missing. I found it, quite empty, in the kitchen trash can.

Also I discovered two of my Powerscourt tumblers in the dishwasher—strictly a "no-no." Bitch, I thought, she's smart enough to swim into my dreams, she should be smart enough to protect my glassware.

Do I expect you to believe that any of this happened?

I don't care much, because I was so enmeshed in it all by then that I don't know what happened myself. The basic facts of the game have been documented. If you've played the game, you know that N'Rasia, as sumptuously drawn by Boris (he knocked a few years and a few pounds off her, but he got her right), has been upgraded to a major optional character. And of course her husband was part of the original story.

Boris did not see the tapes of N'Rasia—before or after he did the painting. So she's as real as the story, however real you may finally judge that to be.

My shifting states of consciousness? That's up to you. Draw your own conclusions. All I want to contend is that such shiftings back and forth are not inherently impossible once you admit that a port existed or had been called into existence at Grand Beach. If you breach Planck's Wall with spiritual energies, almost anything can happen.

You want to know what I think? I think that 'Rasia and I linked up somehow in dreams or maybe her silent prayers and my dreams, as a parallel to the link in the Compaq 286 port. I don't think she really leapt over Planck's Wall.

Ranora, on the other hand ... but that's getting ahead of our story.

I cleaned my Powerscourt with cautious care, phoned my office, called Nat Sobel to tell him to negotiate for more money with Tor Books and also to call Larry Kirshbaum at Warner's with the same ultimatum, and then, the decks cleared for action, unsuspended the game.

First stop was the small black-and-silver tent of Kaila. He was poring over an old vellumlike manuscript, taking notes, and writing what I thought was a poem on a sheet of modern paper. (These folks do not have word processors or TV and are not, in fact, a terribly literate society, though most of them can read if they have to. Communication, as

I have said, rapid though its means were, was obscure to me and to the Lakeside team. Entertainment is mostly verbal: plays, storytelling, songs. Hence the importance of an occasional ilel or ilellike creature.)

"Do you like me, Lord Kaila?" Ranora burst into his tent, swirling. Her red-and-white promlike gown had thin straps, considerable cleavage, and a long flowing skirt.

"I always like you, Ranora," he replied with his usual civility. "I think you look especially attractive in that gown. It is perhaps a bit revealing, on the other hand..."

"Oh, pooh!" She sat on the edge of one of his chairs. "You're too young to be a prude."

"I was thinking of the Lady B'Mella." He closed his inkwell, knowing that his peace was to be disturbed as long as the ilel chose to disturb it.

"I'm not competing with her." His fears were dismissed with an airy wave of a hand. "*Anyway*," she jumped up and spun off the skirt, "this is for dancing. Is it *too* revealing?"

The question, asked of the skintight leotard which she was wearing under her skirt, permitted an affirmative answer only at risk of one's life. Kaila, courteous, respectful, well-balanced, ducked the question.

"I am not certain, wise and gentle Ranora, that you are even properly invited to the dinner. However, I know there was no mention of you entertaining."

"Ilels go where they want and do what they want," she grinned impishly, "wear what they want and entertain where they want. Read it all in your book. Anyway, my Master will insist that they let me play my pipe."

"Then it shall be as you say. Though in truth, gifted Ranora, I can't recall ever reading that an ilel performed uninvited on the Feast of the Two Moons."

"*Well*, you haven't read your old books carefully enough." She flounced over to his bookcase, pulled down a volume almost as big as she was, flipped through the pages, and pushed the book under his nose. "See!"

He read it carefully, made a note on his pad, and agreed. "You continue to astonish me, 'Nora, absolutely astonish me."

"Pooh," she said haughtily, but still flattered.

"The Meal of the Two Moons is very important," he said, a little sententiously.

"I know *that*." Then came the quick change of mood so characteristic of her age and sex. She bounded into a chair, curled up in a knot, rested her jaw (truly a Michele-like jaw) on her fist, and looked admiringly at her "minder." "Explain it all to me again."

He closed his volume with a sigh, but he was not at all displeased by his attractive audience. "Well, I suppose the best summary" (a fellow academic, I knew one when I saw one) "is that peace is like love. Both are highly desirable states which look easy and require great skill and discipline and practice to exercise properly."

"Uh-huh." Eyes open wide in respect. Betty Coed. I know her well too.

"Our warriors have been fighting so long and so furiously that they don't know how to be peaceful. We pay respect to the idea that we have noble warriors only for self-defense. If it wasn't for the wicked, evil, blasphemous, infidels on the other side..."

"Our cousins."

"Of course. We need our warriors to defend us against them. And vice versa, of course. A purely defensive arrangement. But we train them from their earliest years to fight. They are not much good at anything else. They are convinced that their work is peace, but they are ready to fight at the slightest pretext. So they create wars, sincerely enough, in which they fight with extraordinary bravery and skill against equally brave and skillful people from the other side."

"If there is no war?"

"We'd have to retrain them. Their courage and dedication could presumably be put to peaceful uses." He gestured towards his bookcase. "It's been done before. My ancestors were warriors and look at me."

"An effete, effeminate coward." She winked at him.

"When you wink at me that way, good ilel, you unman me utterly."

"Pooh." She giggled happily. "Go on with my lesson."

"Sometimes the balance of conflict swings towards barbarism and war that involves everyone—farmers, workers, burghers, scholars. Then there is terrible violence and slaughter. One side or the other determines that it is not enough to stay even with the other but decides that total victory is possible and the land will be reunited under their rule. We are at a time when there are strong parties in both armies that believe in the obligation to total victory. So many noble leaders have been slain and must be avenged. Moreover, the priests are pushing for an all-out war because they say it is necessary for the good of the land. In their hearts they believe that the warriors will kill one other off..."

"And most everyone else too."

"And then they can restore peace permanently and rule as the clergy once ruled long ago."

"No more ilels." She waved her arms in a grand, dismissive gesture. "No more scholars either."

"The people don't take this talk seriously and are not worried about being raped and enslaved and slaughtered. Some of us scholars are, and some of the politicians—Linco and Malvau on the other side for example."

"And the Duke and Duchess..."

"Ah." He smiled. "That's where the ilel comes in, isn't it? And appropriately. For they are different, aren't they? Neither of them quite fits the pattern. The Lord Our God knows they are brave enough, but 'Rau is both too sensible and too much of a dreamer to like the endless violence. 'Ella? She's harder to describe. As hot-tempered a woman warrior as you could imagine, yet..."

"Yet sweet and kind and good..." The stubborn little jaw went up sharply. "And beautiful and loyal and wonderful."

"You see those qualities better than the rest of us, except for the beauty, which is obvious. She has lost two husbands. She is sick of the killing. She has...what I would call a certain sensitivity which warriors rarely possess, since we breed and train it out of them. They are not greatly different from the pattern, but sufficiently different so that they offer us some little hope."

"You agree with me that they should marry?" In tones which meant heaven help him if he didn't.

"It would perhaps help." He shrugged his well-shaped shoulders. "Yet both of them, in truth, are ill equipped by the past for either love or peace. They would have to learn slowly and painfully and are quite capable of killing each other in the process..."

"The Lord Our God wouldn't let that happen."

"He's let some bad things happen before. Moreover, neither of them has children—which is fine so long as they are able to produce a child. If they should mate and there is no heir, well, then the priests would make terrible trouble in the Lord Our God's name."

"Everyone wants peace..." she began.

"Certainly. The warriors by victory, the clergy by power, the politicians by subtle compromises, the scholars like me by wisdom, and an occasional ilel," he smiled fondly at her, "by love."

"*Well*, we need wisdom and compromise and love *anyway*."

"That's what tonight is all about, 'Nora."

"And you," she bounded to her feet and wrapped herself in her formal skirt, "aren't very hopeful."

"The only thing which makes me hopeful is that the Lord Our God sent us as He did long ago an ilel."

"The greatest ilel ever?" She swirled her skirt.

"At least."

She scampered across the room, kissed his hand quickly, and then bounced out of the tent.

Kaila flipped up his window patch and watched her as she dashed madly across the meadow.

"I hope," he glanced up at me, "you know what you're doing."

So did I.

8 The Port Opens Up

We were all winging it.

I didn't send Ranora, and I had not the foggiest notion of what an ilel was supposed to do.

I want to emphasize that point. It's one thing to be the Great Improviser when you're playing with a full deck and know what all the cards are and who has them. It's quite another to be improvising and model fitting with an undetermined part of the deck. It's also one thing to be a storyteller when you have reasonable control of your characters, it's quite another when most of them are out of control and have to be knocked into line by such gimmicks as kicks in the rear end, rocks falling into caves, and experimental cannons exploding.

As both improviser and storyteller, Nathan's God Game put you at a disadvantage.

The theological issue, which I will raise but not try to answer, is whether that's what it's like to be God. In the grace/free will game, is grace always at a disadvantage till the last of the ninth anyway?

Think about it.

I had almost forgotten about the cannon so I instructed the machine, ACCESS CANNON.

Spelled it right that time, you so-and-so.

Sure enough, there they were back up in the mountains, in the melting snow, painfully putting the pieces back together again.

ZAP CANNON.

HOW?

OH, I DON'T KNOW. HOW ABOUT A SNOWSLIDE?

EXECUTING.

A cloud of snow appeared on the mountain above the reconstructed hut and slid towards it, accelerating as it came. The warriors ducked behind walls, like characters in a slapstick comedy. The snowslide swept over them, obliterating most of the hut.

Doggedly, Larry, Curly, and Moe climbed out of the snow and began to shovel it away. Nothing if not persistent.

ACCESS CARDINAL.

The Cardinal, the two witches, and the high priest from Lenrau's crowd were hiding behind a great rock, bent over what looked like a large kettle.

Eating a missionary?

"This sauce," the Cardinal said in his sweetest, most pious voice, "should restrain them. Poured over their fruit, it will taste sweet but turn their dispositions sour. The meeting will serve no useful purpose."

"Maybe they will kill the ilel," cackled the Mothers Superior.

"Possibly. If that happens, we will of course deny involvement."

"Excellent," said the other priest, the man whom I had dubbed "the Admiral," because he seemed always to be making statements for the TV camera.

"Kill her! Kill her!"

Not my 'Nora, no way.

ZAP POT.

ERROR. ERROR #39. NO MARIJUANA PERMITTED IN THIS WORLD. DEA ORDER. ERROR ERROR.

KETTLE, YOU IDJIT.

PREFERRED MODE ZAP KETTLE?

DEFAULT.

EXECUTING.

The Admiral, as clumsy as he was mouthy, leaned over to peer into the kettle, which was bubbling away enthusiastically. "I'll stir the pot up a bit," he announced.

Before anyone could stop him, he pushed a large ladle abruptly into the kettle and swept it around in a vigorous, military movement.

The kettle tipped dangerously in one direction. A Mother Superior tried to tilt it back. The Admiral swept the ladle around again.

The kettle then tipped the other way, hesitated on the brink, and began to sway back.

I pushed my REPEAT key.

The kettle resumed its sway, tilted beyond the point of no return, crashed with an earth-shaking rumble, and shattered into hundreds of pieces. The liquid darted in all directions, turning the ground around the broken pot brown.

The Cardinal sat down alongside the rock. "Too many witches," he sobbed, "spoil the brew."

Now it was time to deliver on my promise of the night before to N'Rasia, a promise about which I was very dubious.

The yard in front of Malvau's pavilion was bedlam. As the one in charge of the physical preparations for the feast, he apparently felt that he had to organize and instruct all responsible parties, even though their culture seemed to be notably ahead of ours on organizational skills. He was in a vile mood, snapping at servants and family and staff members, and even at a remarkably calm B'Mella who stopped by to chat happily with her councilor and his wife.

"It will go well." She smiled. "The Lord Our God wills it."

"With my help," 'Vau said irritably.

Both women laughed at him. He flushed angrily, and then, realizing without my help that their amusement was based on love, laughed with them.

After the Duchess had left, N'Rasia said timidly, "Noble Lord, I need more instructions about my role."

"Look beautiful and be silent," he snapped.

"I believe you mean that," she snapped back.

"I do..."

CUT THAT OUT, I demanded.

"...not mean it." He patted her rear end, to the shock and dismay of 'Rasia and all who were watching.

It *was*, as she had claimed, more than presentable.

"Malvau!" she exclaimed in horror.

"Excuse me, noble lady." He was not at all sorry. "I am so preoccupied with my responsibilities, I tend to forget myself."

She took a deep breath. "Perhaps we could walk briefly to the lake and you could explain to me again."

He glanced at the sundial in the middle of the courtyard. "A few minutes, surely."

I'm sure love was the farthest thing from his mind. So it always seems. When men want it women don't, and when women want it men don't.

I say this on the basis of others' testimony, not personal experience.

So they walked towards the nearest lake, hand in hand once they slipped out of sight of the pavilion. It was really nothing more than an oversized pond, but private enough on a day when most people were already in their own homes getting roaring drunk.

"Actually," he began, "we may be the only sober men and women in the land this evening. It has been agreed that we will drink lightly. That means that wit, wisdom, good conversation, and a few crucial agreements, contained in an exchange of nods and silences between our leaders, will be enough. The Lord Kaila and I have agreed in principle to the conclusions. He's a splendid young man, by the way, even if a bit bookish and over-formal. We only need the right chemistry between Lenrau and B'Mella to accomplish our initial goals. That's why your wit and charm are so important."

He swatted her again; this time she chuckled complacently. A time and a place for everything.

"He is not a degenerate?"

"Lenrau? No, of course not. You will be sitting on one side of him and the Lady on the other. I doubt that there is a man in the land who can resist your judicious mixture of charms."

"The Lady wishes this?"

"It was her suggestion, as I have tried to tell you."

"Are they planning just as carefully?" She snuggled close to him.

"At least as carefully." His hand took permanent possession of her rear. "This is a critical time in our history. Fortunately both our leaders want peace, even if they don't know how to achieve it."

"What about the demon child?"

"Ranora? Don't listen to the stupid priests. They envy her because she is clearly from the Lord Our God. She will be outrageous, of course. What else? When our leaders become deadly serious and reach for their weapons, she will blow her silly little pipe and they will make peace. I want you to be nice to her, 'Rasia."

"As you wish. I really did not believe she is a demon. She's like our daughters were at that age ... only ... only ..."

"More so?"

"Much more so." She put her arm tenderly around his waist. "Will they mate, 'Vau? Our leaders, I mean."

He pondered that. "It is likely. Risky of course—Kaila and I agreed about that—but probably necessary. They are not well matched."

"That can be overcome."

He turned her around, so he could face her directly. "That is difficult but not unpleasant work. Pray the Lord Our God that they have time."

IT'S YOUR IDEA, DUMMY, I told her. WHAT ARE YOU WAIT-ING FOR?

"We will not have time for an orgy tonight, will we?" she said bluntly.

"I fear the Feast of the Two Moons will be over before we can return to our pavilion." He touched her face affec-tionately. "But when did we celebrate it with an orgy?"

What a dolt! He wasn't receiving any of the signals. We'd have to provide a lot of hormones.

"Indeed never. But now it is different between us."

"Thank the Lord Our God," he agreed piously.

"So," she pulled her gown over her head with a quick, graceful movement, "let's have an orgy now!"

"N'Rasia," he protested in dismay, "we can't; there's no time."

ORGY, I told the Compaq.

It hesitated as it scanned its parser.

ONLY TWO CHARACTERS PRESENT.

Hmmn ... Nathan's hobbits had interesting minds.

EXECUTE.

DEFAULT. EXECUTING.

A default orgy? Only in the digital world of computers.

She was smothering him with passionate affection. Wisely he stopped resisting.

I opted out, remembered my promise, and returned to see the poor councilor on the flat of his back as the afternoon of orgy was beginning.

"Sorry," I said aloud.

HORMONES, LOTS OF THEM, I typed in.

EXECUTING, it responded instantly, as though it were a word it heard all the time.

Very interesting hobbits.

I got out of there in a hurry.

The Two Moon Meal was a complete success, a mellow, pleasant mixture of solemn ritual and delightful conversation, with some deeply moving incidents.

N'Rasia and G'Ranne, as unlikely a team as one can imagine, made the meal work.

There were seven men and three women inside the brilliantly lighted chamber, surrounded by screens with rich abstract paintings. The men wore long robes with short cloaks in contrasting colors like those of nineteenth-century cavalry officers and large jeweled medallions around their necks. The women were clad in what might be tolerable as nightgowns in our world—pastel gowns with thin straps, deep necklines and long slits in the side.

It was a fertility festival, after all.

B'Mella was tense, jumpy; G'Ranne icy cold, the most skeptical as well as the most physically attractive person at the table. (She had found something shimmeringly beautiful to wear despite her protests that she had nothing appropriate for the festival.) You didn't even want to look at her too long lest she distract you from the purposes of the evening.

Lenrau did not notice her, however; he was tongue-tied at the sight of his enemy in a nearly transparent blue-green gown which made her about as desirable as any woman could possibly be. Kaila and Malvau made awkward small talk.

No Ranora. Where the hell was she?

ACCESS ILEL.

INPUT/OUTPUT ERROR ATTEMPT TO GO BE-YOND EOF.

HUH?

It repeated the message, which I took to mean that in this game, the ilel finally did what she damn well pleased.

So N'Rasia, looking gloriously wanton after her orgy with her gold and silver hair falling on splendidly naked shoulders, took charge. She became the woman I had spoken with on the beach the night before— Was it the night before? I couldn't remember.

Lightly, graciously, with a joke here and a smile there, she assumed the role of hostess and gradually cracked the ice. It was a marvelous performance, as unlike the shallow bitch I had first encountered as I could imagine. The bitch, I told myself, was still there—a frightened, self-hating child, temporarily replaced by the magnificent woman who was presiding over the making of history at this meal. The bitch had dominated for most of her life. At least for these happy moments the other N'Rasia was free.

Even G'Ranne melted and chatted pleasantly about her interest in painting. How the hell N'Rasia had learned that this lovely ice cube painted I didn't know.

Unless Kaila and 'Vau had briefed one another pretty thoroughly.

Then very tentatively N'Rasia guided the Duchess and G'Ranne into a discussion of their artistic efforts.

"Do you find painting preferable to combat?" the Duchess asked bluntly.

The girl blushed. "Certainly, my lady. One has something at the end to show for one's efforts."

For the first time I became aware that there was intelligence lurking behind those scorching blue eyes.

"I quite agree, child." B'Mella smiled her approval. "The Lord Our God approving, we will soon be able to view each other's work."

"May it please His Holy Will."

I didn't even know that they were into painting.

'Vau beamed at his wife's performance, and B'Mella, liberated from her obligation to be the hostess, turned from the warrior maiden to a very close study of the Duke, as though she were studying a battlefield before a campaign began.

He, poor man, was swiveling his head back and forth, like a Ping-Pong watcher, between the dazzling women on either side of him.

"Do I smell particularly foul tonight, Lord Lenrau?" she asked lightly, her jaw tilted upwards, that wonderful little smile playing at either end of her mouth.

"If I were a poet like Kaila, I would think of a better image, my lady. At the moment all I can say is that you smell as sweet as this fruit tastes."

She laughed and blushed a little. "That will do very nicely as a compliment, my Lord. I wasn't searching for one, however. I was looking for something to say and, being what I am, started contentiously."

He was now fascinated by something more than the nearly visible charms under her dress.

"The issue, my lady...may I call you B'Mella..."

"Even 'Ella...'Rau."

"The issue, 'Ella, is not your physical loveliness, which

not even the most foul-minded can deny in their sane moments, nor the wisdom of your rule, nor your courage, but whether you can endure for a little while someone who is so much less endowed with these qualities than you are."

She put down the broad spoon with which they slurped up their fruit, lifted her wine goblet to him, and offered him a sip from it. "If we are to be friends at all, 'Rau, you must permit me to deny your last statement without any responding argument."

He sipped the wine and offered her his goblet. "Can I at least say that you have a quicker tongue than I do?"

"You can say it, but it isn't true."

"Noble Lord Kaila." N'Rasia beamed like a proud mother. "It would seem that the day of contesting courtiers is returning."

Everyone laughed, and two quick political deals were made. Fishing and lumbering problems were solved deftly, with nods from the rulers, who were much more interested in each other than in the casual but deeply serious political conversations that were taking place around them. It was agreed that a commission would be set up to supervise disarmament.

G'Ranne was watching the peace process with eyes that were now searchlights, taking in every nuance, evaluating it, filing it for future reference. How had I missed her intelligence before?

ACCESS G'RANNE, I instructed the 286.

EXECUTING.

She sat up straight as though she were listening for my instructions.

FACILITATE PEACE.

She nodded slightly, quick and responsive agreement.

"If my lady permits," the ice maiden spoke reverently, "I would serve with you on such a commission."

"No one I would prefer more," B'Mella turned on all her personal charm, "if your own Lord does not fear that we two women will connive against him."

"I do much fear that," he said. "But I cannot think of more appropriate or effective connivers. Be it done."

A lot of progress, then a loss of nerve. Even the recklessly engaging N'Rasia couldn't keep the conversation alive. Enemies of the decades and the centuries could not possibly be this pleasant. The room filled up with the poison gas of second thoughts. The Duke and Duchess turned away from one another, suspicion replacing interest.

CUT IT OUT, I demanded. CONTINUE FRIENDSHIP.

They paid no attention. I held the REPEAT button down. Still nothing.

Bastards. Resisting grace, that's what they were doing. Poor N'Rasia was close to tears.

The main course was brought in to dead silence—a dish which I can describe only as a monumental soufflé.

And with it arrived one ilel, right on time.

Her time, that is.

She piped her way in, playing a nonsense tune; then she looked up at me, blew a few notes on my theme just to keep me on my toes, and flounced up to the Duke. She bowed to him with elaborate respect and then held her pipe behind her back as though she didn't want anyone to know she had it.

"My lady," you could hear Lenrau's sigh of relief all over the room, "I believe you have on more than one occasion encountered this maiden, but now permit me to formally present her to you. This is Ranora."

"Good evening, Ranora," the Duchess said gravely. "It is a very pretty dress you are wearing."

The ilel sniggered, blushed, and hid her face.

"She regrets," 'Rau was talking easily and smoothly

again, "that we did not accept your offer to become a hostage when these conversations began."

Ranora nodded vigorously.

"Oh? Why is that? I would have been a very difficult hostage, I fear."

"She is not mute, you know, 'Ella. It is a game she plays."

Ranora made a face of displeasure.

"She can be shy if she wishes, 'Rau." The Duchess was just as smooth. "When she wants to talk to me she will."

The ilel sniffed saucily at her master. So there, big guy.

"But why," the Duchess went on, "did she want me as a hostage?"

"Her argument, gracious Lady, is that we could keep you forever and she and you would become great friends."

More vigorous nods.

Brilliantly executed, my friends. You don't need me.

"Why should she want to be my friend?"

"*Well*," 'Rau grinned broadly, "she thinks you're beautiful and sweet and good and wonderful."

Ranora clapped her hands in agreement. Everyone else in the room was leaning forward to see what would happen.

"Gentle ilel," the Duchess said sadly, "some think I am beautiful and others do not. But I am neither wonderful nor good, nor sweet."

Poor woman, she meant every word of it.

Ranora threw her arms around the Duchess and held her tightly. "Don't ever say that again," she said fiercely. "It's not true."

Quite overcome, B'Mella clung to the ilel as fiercely as she herself was held. "You make me weep, imp child."

"Now I'll make you laugh." She broke away from the Duchess, discarded her skirt, which she draped ceremoniously over the head of poor Kaila, and began her dancing, piping, and singing.

The songs were in a language I did not understand—and neither did the other guests, though they were constrained to join in the choruses. I guessed they were mild spring fertility songs—what one would expect and accept from a spritely young virgin.

She made them hold hands as they sang. The Duke and the Duchess hesitated, sensing that they were being shamelessly manipulated. Ranora forced their hands together. She didn't have to force G'Ranne to take Kaila's hands. I had beat her to it with my instructions. The ice maiden was certainly obedient.

Kaila didn't seem to mind a bit.

Then when they were worn out with singing and the wineglasses were refilled, she performed a solo "concerto" in which she blended in pipe music and wordless sound her "Lenrau" and "B'Mella" themes. The piece was just light enough so that she could get away with it and not offend the mildly embarrassed leaders.

"I fear you have rather definite plans for me." B'Mella shifted awkwardly in her chair when the music and applause stopped.

The ilel held out her hands innocently. Who, me?

"She has rather definite plans for everyone." Lenrau had not drifted away to his distant world once that evening—just as the Duchess had not lost her temper once. "Welcome to the group."

"One must listen carefully to the advice of such a wise old woman." B'Mella held out her hand to the ilel, who kissed it reverently. "Especially since she will give you no choice but to listen."

More laughter. Then while an ice-cream-like dessert

was produced, a couple more commissions were set up. Everything was on track.

Then I remembered my other promise. What the hell should I do? Ah.

I keyed Ranora. DO MELODY FOR N'RASIA.

She spun in my direction with an expression of unabashed astonishment. What the hell are you talking about?

EXECUTE.

EXECUTING.

I doubt that the algorithm could make that one do anything she didn't want to do. Still, she strolled over to the councilor's wife and began to peer at her intently, as though probing into the older woman's soul.

Embarrassed, 'Rasia tried to turn away. The ilel boldly took the other's face in her hand and turned it back so she could continue to probe. 'Rasia flushed and squirmed, but she was not displeased with the gentle examination.

Ranora nodded wisely, turned in my direction with a "So all right, you were right" expression and lifted the pipe to her lips. She fluted a few high notes, examined N'Rasia's crimson face again, nodded brightly, and began to play "N'Rasia's theme."

I am sad that my musical skills are so inadequate that I can't play it for you, not even pick it out on the piano in the house at Grand Beach. All I can tell you is that its pure delicacy reminds me of the post horn passages from Mahler's Third.

Occasionally I imagine even now that I hear it outside my 47th-story window in Chicago.

N'Rasia folded her arms across her breast and bowed her head as the ilel celebrated depths that only the two of them knew. Her husband knelt at her side, his arm around her shoulders. The Duchess, tears streaming down her face,

knelt on the other side. Even the ice maiden buried her
head in her hands.

Why? It's hard to say. A human person was portrayed
for us in that music, a woman with faults and weaknesses
we all knew and with strengths and beauty of which we
were more or less aware. But the music cast those superficial traits aside like discarded garments and plunged deeply
into the colorful, luxurious, sacred garden of the woman's
soul, exposed for us her deepest and richest beauty as a
person, and bade us to celebrate her wonders as we heard
them sung. We were introduced into the secret N'Rasia, the
one she hardly knew herself, and invited to share in worship
of the goodness that was reflected in her most hidden and
splendid self.

Sexual love with her would have been, by comparison,
only a minor and transient possession of some shallow secrets. All of us, for a few moments, possessed her as fully
as we could ever hope to possess anyone in our lives.

Then, just when it all became too unbearably painful,
Ranora broke the spell with a nutty, comic ending. Thank
God. We were able to end with laughter instead of hysterics.

COMPLIMENT ILEL, I told G'Ranne, mostly to see whether
she was unfailingly docile.

She nodded imperceptibly and ruffled Ranora's hair, big
sister to little sister. "When I am older and have as much
character as the Lady N'Rasia, small imp, perhaps you will
do that for me too."

For once the ilel was surprised. She threw her hands
in front of her face as though blinded by the light of such
a possibility. Then she responded by hugging G'Ranne.

Fooled you, kid. You didn't expect support from that
quarter for another hundred years, did you?

She didn't even seem to mind when G'Ranne and Kaila

left the party together, not exactly hand in hand but close to it.

It was a good way to end the Two Moons Meal. The ice of the ages had been broken, everyone set out for home happy. Politics, wisdom, and love had triumphed. The author/player had very little to contribute, besides a whisper into the ear of the ilel. The plot was coming together. The way towards the denouement was open.

And my promise to N'Rasia had been kept. She'd had her orgy, her triumph, her celebration. How could she doubt any more that she was loved or that I—in my role as author/God to her—loved her?

I was as exhausted as though I had written twenty thousand words in a day—try it for two days in a row and you'll end up in the hospital. I suspended the game with relief and collapsed into bed.

You may have guessed that I was overinvolved. Later I would scratch a note for Nathan: "Provide author/player warning about overinvolvement."

There is a note, which I'm sure you've seen, on the box of the game which says, "Psychologists recommend that no one play this game for more than two hours a day. Studies have revealed that it exhausts most players after that period of time."

Actually the research says you can keep at it for four hours without freaking out. But do more than that for a couple of days and you become a blithering basket case.

Like me.

And there was worse to come. Even that night—their time—as I was to find when I returned to the game the next morning.

The next day was Saturday so we left for waterskiing absurdly early, 7:30 A.M., to beat the weekend crowds who create wakes and put your life in jeopardy by mixing boat driving and boat drinking.

The adolescents were in a giggly mood. It had been, I gathered, a wild night among the natives. "Like really excellent, but kind of *crazy*."

Fine. You guys should know what kind of party I went to. No ilels in your bash on the beach.

Michele, of course, was humming N'Rasia's theme.

I didn't ask her about it.

But I did ask whether she ever blew on any kind of a horn when she was a little girl.

"No way," she insisted vigorously. "You mean a trumpet or a French horn or a sax or something like that?"

"Well, or a penny whistle?"

"Certainly not... what's a penny whistle, anyway?"

"Oh, a kind of Irish thing."

"Is it," giggle, "made out of pennies?"

"No, they call it that because it's so inexpensive. The Chieftains and groups like that use it."

The Chieftains not being a rock group, I'm sure she had no idea who they were.

"*Well*, if they're still *real* cheap, would you get me one the next time you go to Ireland? I'd, you know, kind of like to play something like that."

I don't even want to think about that, especially with what happened later. Of course, 'Chele being 'Chele I'll be in a lot of trouble if I don't return from poor old Erin with a penny whistle next year.

I dropped them off at their various stations after the skiing was finished: Heidi with her whistle at the beach (the secret of the whistle, I was told, to use it as little as possible), John Larkin at the clubhouse "Pav" where he served up the best hamburgers in Grand Beach, Lance and Bobby at their respective homes so they could "cash out" (go back to bed), Michele at the local Nautilus installation because "once you're awake it's totally silly to go back to bed."

I then drove into New Buffalo to buy some salami and to pick up *The New York Times* (so as to learn what had officially happened in the world yesterday) at the Buffalo drugstore. Coming out, I encountered the States Attorney of the County of Cook and his near-teenaged daughter. (Her name is Nora but I don't think she fits in the story. If she does, I don't want to know about it.)

"Strange night in Grand Beach." Rich Daley withdrew his unlighted cigar and smiled the most dazzling smile in American political life.

"Restless adolescent natives?"

"Restless everyone."

"A lot of the drink taken?"

"Funny thing," the cigar back in his mouth. "Less than usual. People were sort of laid back and relaxed, like they should be at a resort, instead of uptight. It should always be that way, shouldn't it?"

"Sounds almost like a religious festival."

"Just what I thought, peaceful, and," big grin, "really sensual."

"Heaven help us all when the Grand Beach Irish turn sensual."

"Less work for my people if everyone was that way all the time."

"My mommy," Nora piped up with that mixture of affection and disrespect which only a kid that age can blend for a paternal parent, "says my daddy has turned psychic."

"Really!" Only if several generations of acute political instincts made you psychic. Instinctively he could sniff a restless precinct.

"I don't know...there was something funny last night ...did you hear about the poor Hagans?"

"Only that there was a reconciliation."

"No." He shook his head. "They were mugged last night in Michigan City coming out of Maxime and Hymie's. She's in St. Joseph's with a brain concussion. Still unconscious. Wrong time for them, just when things were beginning to straighten out."

"I'll stop by and see her."

"I think they'd appreciate that very much."

Was the port between our cosmoi opening wide? And if I suggested that to Rich, would he call the men in the white suits?

Probably not. He'd want to find out more about how the port worked.

But it was my game and my secret and up to me to control the influences which might be flowing back and forth. As you can see, I was now acting as if I thought I was God. However, I wasn't quite ready to admit that to myself yet.

I drove well above the speed limit back to Grand Beach, so worried was I about what might have happened to Malvau and N'Rasia on the other side of Max Planck's Wall.

On Lake View I discovered the remnants of Diamond (the village's rock group) acting out for an imaginary video camera another chapter in the John Larkin disappearance. After one of their concerts at the clubhouse, Diamond had staged an imaginary TV interview with John in the midst of which someone set off firecrackers. Paul and Mike had immediately turned it into an assassination attempt and a long-running joke. Millions of dollars of reward were posted to find out who was behind the attempt and then to discover whether John was still alive. Rumors were spread that he had fled to Brazil. Other rumors insisted that his body had been found buried in a beach near São Paulo. John himself visited New Buffalo merchants and raspberry farmers, displaying pictures of himself, asking whether such a young man had been seen. (Almost always he had been seen, but the interviewee could not remember quite when.)

Great if slightly weird fun. But today they seemed to have become quite mad. Paul shoved an imaginary mike in my face. "Do you care to comment on the rumor that John Larkin is returning tonight from Brazil for a triumphant farewell concert?"

"Or," Mike demanded, notebook in hand, "do you believe that he really is buried in that beach?"

"Not without Heidi's permission."

"Does she hold the secret to the John Larkin case?" John himself demanded of me.

"Dux femina facti," I replied.

"Huh?"

"Cherchez la femme."

"Heidi!"

"She's the lifeguard."

"One last question." John, it occurred to me, bore a remarkable physical resemblance to Kaila. "Before we *cherchez* for her. Did you really visit John Larkin in Rio last year?"

"Salvador. He was living at the home of Calisans Neto, the famous artist."

"Is that on the record?"

"He was alive and well and living in Bahia. That was a year ago of course."

The camera crew raced off for the beach.

"Beware the whistle," I yelled after them.

Diamond was a mad crew. They had never, however, been quite this mad. The port was wide open.

Back on the other side, however, the carefully orches-

trated peace scenario had mostly fallen apart. I activated
the game just as the Two Moon Meal was breaking up and
followed 'Rasia and 'Vau through the soft night as they
dreamily walked home, hand in hand, quietly proud of their
achievement.

No one, I swore, was going to mess up the game plan
I and my allies in this land had put together. I'd protect my
two friends—friends and lovers they had surely become—
from any random muggers.

I failed them completely, despite the fact that I was
ready for trouble. It happened too quickly for my reactions
to be any help. It was a random event, not even intended
by anyone to be a disaster, a bit of the drink taken, an
accident, and almost another war. For the first time I understood that random events—built into the algorithm by random numbers, of course—could undo the best laid plans of
mice, men, and storytellers.

And possibly of God too.

You've probably figured out that their society was rather
rigidly ritualistic. They had tried to confine violence to the
warrior castes and sex to the elaborate and carefully pre-
scribed day-end ritual. Remember everyone's shock when
Malvau mildly patted his wife's rear end? Sex is too powerful
a human phenomenon to be so completely contained, but
retreats into the abundant privacy of the forests and lakes
of the sort in which 'Vau and 'Rasia had engaged twice were
rare events. Even they were ritual echoes of wedding night
and honeymoon behavior, as I was soon to learn.

Under ordinary circumstances, then, the people in the
land (I never learned whether it had any other name but
"land") were sober, self-controlled, responsible, even prud-
ish people. Dull bourgeoisie, you might want to call them.
On the various festival days they let off steam, eating and

drinking and making love as though all three behaviors were going out of fashion.

Not everyone blew their lid. As we saw at the ducal meal, the style was light and festive, made so first by the radiance of N'Rasia (how that was acquired earlier in the day was another matter) and then by the divine zaniness of Ranora. But if you were wandering around the meadows and the woods late in the evening it was not unreasonable to assume that you were interested in the more extreme variety of festival behavior.

So 'Rasia and 'Vau encountered three very drunken warriors on the path from the Duchess's pavilion to their own. Probably the men did not want rape; rather only some kissing and feeling. But 'Rasia was from the class that did not wander about on festival nights and surely had never been pawed without her consent by anyone but her husband. The men came suddenly out of the dark. One of them laughed cheerfully, grabbed the woman, and tossed her playfully to another. The third immobilized with broad arms the gamely struggling 'Vau.

I reacted as quickly as I could. STOP ASSAULT!

It didn't have much effect. The big guy with 'Vau tossed him to the ground, the way Richard Dent of the Bears sacks quarterbacks, leaving them dazed and motionless. The three of them then "played" with 'Rasia, as I suppose they had "played" with other, quite willing, women earlier in the evening. They kissed her and caressed her and tore at her gown and passed her back and forth with drunken laughter, all, as far as they were concerned, in the festive spirit of the late night.

She fought back like a tiger, kicking, clawing, biting, screaming. They were too drunk to notice that she wasn't enjoying the game.

I continued to press the REPEAT key. Nothing happened. I changed the strategy. ZAP ASSAILANTS.

ERROR. ERROR. CANNOT ZAP ASSAILANTS WITHOUT INJURING MAJOR CHARACTER. ERROR ERROR.

Well, she had become a major character anyway, as she had wanted.

'Vau shook off his daze and charged back into the fray. The big man swept him out of the scene with a single blow of his tree-trunk arm. 'Rasia dug her teeth into his shoulder, biting hard.

He screamed like the proverbially stuck pig and tried to shake her loose. She clung to him like a Gila monster, scratching at his face while she continued to bite his shoulder. The other two, confused and tipsy, tore at her already ripped garments, not quite sure what was happening, but doing what seemed to them to be the natural thing on a festival night.

Finally, the big man, bleeding profusely, succeeded in throwing his counterattacker off him. He swung his uninjured arm, really intending nothing more than shoving her away. The furious, and, looking back on it, incredibly brave N'Rasia charged him and collided with that huge swinging tree trunk. She flew back, stumbled over her husband, fell violently to the ground, and lay still, unnaturally still. The three drunks took off as if the hounds of hell were in pursuit.

Which they soon would be.

ACCESS COPS, DUCHESS, I demanded.

The local cops, not much more efficient than the teenager harassers in Grand Beach and Long Beach, showed up quickly and dithered ineffectually. 'Vau regained consciousness sufficiently to mutter "warriors" and then freak out over the body of his prone and barely breathing wife.

Then the Duchess arrived and all hell broke loose.

"Take them both to the medical tent. Tell the doctors I insist on their complete recovery." Then to one of her sleepy-eyed woman staffers, "Assemble the warriors, we march for vengeance at once."

Clever, you stupid little bitch, real clever.

By sunrise the two armies were assembled in the *quondam* peace meadow, ready to resume the war. Lenrau had heard at once that the Duchess was assembling her sleepy hungover warriors and he promptly did the same, not sure why the fight was to be resumed but not waiting to find out.

Cooler heads tried to prevail. Kaila and G'Ranne, the latter still instantly responsive to my commands, tried to talk to the Duchess and were summarily dismissed as "rapists," hardly a fair charge against either of them. Poor old Linco dithered like the cops and tried to argue the perfectly reasonable position that there was no reason to believe that the warriors were on the other side. He was banished as a "senile old man."

When my B'Mella loses her temper, she really loses it, a fact which would cause even greater trouble later on.

ACCESS ILEL, I cautiously recommended to my Compaq.

Without any difficulty it located Ranora in her tent, draped in a long black gown, pale and angry, kneeling on the floor, praying intensely.

STOP WAR, I told her, unwisely.

She looked up at me, made a terrible face of anger and disgust, and turned away.

HEY, IT'S NOT MY FAULT.

She resolutely refused to listen.

I tried B'Mella. STOP WAR, YOU LITTLE FOOL.

Her look of stony contempt was as bad as the ilel's. As an author/God I was not having one of my better days.

The two armies were stomping restlessly, eager to be

back at what they knew best. If you took a closer look, you would observe that many of them were not all that enthusiastic about resuming the war. They had, perhaps, learned to enjoy the little bit of peace they had.

G'Ranne, again at my suggestion, pleaded with the Duke to restrain his own anger. Larry, Curly, and Moe were dressed up in their fancy red armor plate, but restlessly watched the snow-covered mountains in the distance. They had discovered that it was more fun to play manic games than to actually fight.

I tried the medical pavilion. Malvau, his silver hair still stained with blood, one of his eyes terribly black, was hovering with a doctor over his unconscious wife. Her breathing seemed normal, maybe a little shallow; but the doctor types looked worried.

All we need is a long and lingering coma.

GET OUT THERE AND STOP THE DAMN FOOL WAR, I told him.

He shook his head, not so much declining the command as trying to think.

DO YOU WANT TO BLOW IT ALL? I demanded.

He sighed, straightened up, put his hand reassuringly on the shoulder of one of the doctor types, found a chariot outside the pavilion, and galloped rapidly to the battlefield.

The armies were approaching one another warily when he rode up to B'Mella's position on the hill.

STOP THIS DAMN FOOL WAR, I told all and sundry.

The Duchess did not want to listen. I was too far away to hear what they were saying. 'Vau grabbed the Duchess and shook her like an unruly and irresponsible little girl, which of course she was.

Her eyes opened in furious surprise, she reached for her sword, and then dropped it back in its sheath.

STOP WAR! I demanded, pushing her function key.

She patted 'Vau's arm, turned to an aide and whispered, "Signal truce."

Lenrau was by this time distinctly unamused by the events of the day. "The Lord Our God condemn her truce," he fumed. "It was her warriors, not ours, who assaulted the councilor and his wife. Continue the attack."

Kaila and G'Ranne had to shake him back to sense. From the warm and gentle glances with which they favored each other, incidentally, and the occasional lingering touch, I concluded that they were having a love affair. The ice maiden was not, after all, made of ice, but perhaps of fire. And as for her perhaps not being a maiden any longer, that was their business and I proposed to leave them alone. I had more than enough problems as it was. I couldn't help but notice, however, how radiantly lovely G'Ranne was.

So peace returned. No thanks to the ilel who had opted out of this one.

I was wiped out. Despite my morning exercise with the kids, I could not long survive this kind of tension. It was already three o'clock in the afternoon, Saturday afternoon at that, and all I'd done for hours was play the damn game, with the only effect being to keep my characters from killing one another. It had to stop soon.

Meanwhile something must be done about poor N'Rasia. She would surely blame me for what had happened. In the hospital pavilion I ordered, REVIVE N'RASIA.

EXECUTING.

Nothing happened. I pushed the REPEAT key.

EXECUTING.

She did not stir. The medical types were fretting and stewing. Malvau and the Duchess entered the chamber and appeared profoundly worried.

I leaned on the REPEAT key.

I/O ERROR. ATTEMPT TO GO BEYOND EOF.

In other words, it couldn't revive her and was blaming me. But it gave me an idea.

ALL RIGHT, I told the truculent little imp in her red-and-white-striped tent, CURE N'RASIA.

"How?" she snarled, still very angry at me. And at that moment looking like Michele did when she was very angry. Boy, I was in real trouble.

PIPE HER BACK TO CONSCIOUSNESS.

She frowned, considering whether this absurdity was worth her notice. She pulled her pipe out from under her discarded prom dress (and I must report that unlike the rest of the people in this land, and very like the teenage women in our land, she maintained her quarters in a constant state of pure chaos) and blew a few notes on it tentatively, as if she were thinking about it.

Then she played the first few bars of the "N'Rasia theme," nodded her agreement, winked at me, and slipped out of the tent.

For reasons beyond me, she marched solemnly across the meadow and through the outer tents and pavilions in her black dress as though she were a banshee going to a funeral. It was, I suppose, a protest. We would see it again before the story was over.

Inside 'Rasia's chamber, the whole family, including grandchildren, was assembled. The Duchess, clinging to poor old Linco (no longer presumably a senile fool), stood next to sad-faced 'Vau, whose hair was still stained with blood. Most of the other family members were weeping.

How late in your life they all discovered you, including, sadly, you yourself.

Ranora entered so softly that no one noticed. She slipped through the group, hugging the youngest daughter briefly as she moved her aside, and sat, crosslegged, next to the dying woman's bed.

The others drew back, not quite sure what was happening, but wary of the supernatural influence which had entered the room.

Candidly, Ranora, grim-faced and clad in black, would be enough to scare the hell out of almost anyone.

She examined N'Rasia carefully, touched her face, lifted her eyelid, nodded, blew a few test notes on the pipe, and then started N'Rasia's theme, now somehow far more melancholy than it had been only a few hours before.

I decided that the least I could do was help. I pushed the N'Rasia shift/function (still a minor character in that respect anyway) and instructed her, WAKE UP, KID, THERE'S A LOT OF WORK FOR YOU STILL TO DO.

"Sing with me." The ilel lifted her lips from the pipe. "Wordless song."

They joined in.

WAKE UP, DAMN YOU, I ordered and pushed the REPEAT button down.

Her eyelids flickered. Ranora leaned even closer and played the pipe next to her ear.

'Rasia's eyelids flickered again, a little more vigorously.

I SAID WAKE UP. YOU'RE TOO IMPORTANT TO THE STORY NOW TO DIE.

Ranora changed the rhythm of her melody, jazzing it up, making it comic, demanding attention.

The injured woman opened her eyes, glanced around, lost her focus, then looked around again, smiling slightly.

Ranora jumped to her feet and turned the theme into a triumphal march as she sashayed around the bed. N'Rasia, still a classy broad, laughed.

And then so did everyone else.

What a twenty-four hours for the poor woman—orgy, triumph, celebration, fierce fight, knock on the head, and then a recall from the grave.

Well, she wanted to be something more than a minor subplot, didn't she?

It probably would take her a long time to recover completely. Too many vulnerabilities at one time. For the moment, however, that was her problem. I suspended the game. For a time, at any rate, they didn't need me.

By the way, and for the record, they never did find out which side the warrior assailants were from. Later B'Mella admitted as much, with what I thought was a notable lack of graciousness.

I drove into Michigan City to visit Joan Hagan. She too was conscious, but dazed and unsmiling. She looked hauntingly lovely, a Violetta in the final scenes of the final act.

Her husband, his usual noisy bluster gone, sat next to her, holding a totally unresponsive hand.

"It was a freak accident, Father. They only wanted her purse. She stumbled and fell as they yanked it away from her. If the police catch them, they will will probably call it attempted murder."

"I don't remember a thing," she said dully. "I don't think I had that many drinks."

"Only two. The blow on the head, the doctor told me, will make you forget what happened for a long time."

Forget consciously, but the terror of the mugging will remain in your unconscious, just as will the terror of the assault on your cognate will remain in her unconscious. Somehow the two of you will have to deal with what you cannot even remember.

Was it two attacks or only one?

I must emphasize that, except for Tom Hagan's silver hair and Joan's blond streaked with gray and the fact that they are both handsome people, there is little physical resemblance between them and my friends on the other side of Herr Planck's Wall. Tom is shorter, less dignified, but more of a lighthearted comic than Malvau. His wife is thinner, more ethereal, and much less earthy than N'Rasia. They have six children instead of three. The strain in their marriage is less created by a blend of pompousness and shallowness than that caused by a little boy who refuses to grow up and a stiff, somber woman who was never a little girl and refuses to become one even when she should, mostly, alas, because she doesn't know how.

"Things were going so well for us," she said, "except I can't remember how or why."

"It'll come back, no rush." He patted the hand tenderly and sympathetically. "We have lots of time."

"I'm not sure we do."

I wasn't sure either. But I insisted that God always gave as much time as we needed.

Does S/He now? As the Irish would say.

I was afraid that the blow on the head might have knocked the emergent little girl out permanently.

One blow on the head or two? Had my port, I wondered, made it possible for the attack on Joan Hagan to cause the attack on N'Rasia? Or vice versa? Did one marriage have to survive if the other was to survive? Or was it all merely coincidence?

At that point I was leaning pretty much to a mechanistic view of the relationship between the two worlds. Since then I have rejected that interpretation in favor of a more elaborate and complex one which sees spiritual influences bouncing back and forth in intricate and unpredictable patterns.

Consider that last sentence: it's a masterpiece of academic scholarship. What does it really say? Not a hell of a lot.

It says I don't know how the two cosmoi affect one

another; they do, but I haven't been able to figure out how or why. I don't know and probably I'll never know.

But no scholar will ever admit ignorance in quite so candid a fashion, not unless he's trying to tell an honest story like this one. So we make up sentences about elaborate and complex interpretations of intricate and unpredictable patterns of spiritual influences.

Practically, all I know is that Tom and Joan in our world and Malvau and N'Rasia in the other cosmos were unconsciously linked with each other. Their problems and their possibilities were cognates. Grace and ungrace flowed back and forth, sometimes helping, sometimes hurting. But neither couple, I now firmly believe, determined the outcome of the other couple's "subplot."

I was responsible, more or less, for the subplot across the wall; the Other Person, presumably, was responsible for the subplot on this side of the wall.

But that makes it too simple, doesn't it? Since I'm telling the whole story, I'm cooperating with the Other Person on both sides of the wall, in different ways because on this side Tom and Joan are not really part of Nathan's God Game—as computer program, anyway.

I said three paragraphs back that neither couple was conscious of the flow of grace and ungrace back and forth. But if I am to be precise I must modify that statement. There were certainly strange things happening in Grand Beach those weeks and especially that weekend.

The folks in the other cosmos, less reflective and self-conscious, didn't seem to be aware of a reverse flow of influence. But that may not be altogether true either, as I will have occasion to note shortly.

As I drove out of Michigan City on U.S. 12, I noticed for maybe the millionth time a sign that said, "Leaving LaPorte County."

That hit me kind of hard. LaPorte, a town down by I-90, is very old. The Catholic church was built in 1852 and, alas, covered by stone a couple of decades ago. The town received its name because it was on a strip of prairie between the Great American Forest to the south and the Dune Forest to the north, through which the very early settlers came, and the Indians before them. It was the gate to the prairies and the world beyond.

Presumably it was merely an accidental juxtaposition of names. Two utterly different kinds of gates. If there was a juxtaposed cosmos in our neighborhood, it was there long before the forests came into being and before the name LaPorte was given to the town and the county. Anyway, Grand Beach is not in LaPorte County. Still...

We had Mass as always on Saturday in my parlor. I preached about two of my favorite characters, who appear in a novel about a novel, too, named Finnbar the Fair, Emperor of All the World and Everything Else Besides, and his girlfriend, Countess Deirdre the Dark, who works after school at McDonald's selling Big Macs. Deirdre was fed up with how dull the colors were in the Empire, so she made Finny—who is also the greatest wizard in all the world—take her on a trip to lands which were in different colors, a red world, a green world, and so forth. I was, of course, stealing from G. K. Chesterton's colored lands. Finally they come to a world where all the colors are perfect and Deirdre claps her hands for joy. Then they turn the corner and what do they see?

All the little Goggin kids watch with big blue eyes. No, what do they see?

Deirdre's McDonald's. The end of all our search is to return to where we started and know it for the first time.

I don't remember what the gospel was, to tell you the truth, but it's a good story and kids love it. I figure if you can tell a story the kids like, you've talked to everyone else in the congregation too. We prayed, since there were astronauts traveling in space at the time, for those who traveled between worlds. I had other intentions in mind, needless to say.

The point in repeating the homily is to record that, while I was under strain certainly and worried about my characters surely, I was not yet a blithering basket case. I was, rather, carrying on my normal summer-vacation routine with people who didn't notice any particular change in me or if they did, like Michele and her mother, they figured I was busy with one of my stories again.

Which of course was true, but it was a different kind of story. It was Nathan's God Game.

The Brennans were staging one of their Saturday night dinners, not only for invited guests, but streams of teenagers related in various ways to the four adolescent Brennans. Even for the usual standard of fun-filled evenings at the Brennans', it was a magically joyous evening.

The meal had hardly started when, no drink having been taken, I announced that I could create a better Archdiocese of Chicago than God had. In fact, I had already done so. In my fictional Archdiocese, Sean Cronin, a man of courage, honesty, and integrity, was Cardinal Archbishop, and Blackie Ryan, wise, gentle, insightful, was Rector of the Cathedral.

"God," I said firmly, "hasn't done nearly so well."

"Maybe he has more obstacles," Jeanine Brennan observed.

A point, I suppose, well taken.

9 Another Visitor

That night seemed a perfectly normal Saturday evening at Grand Beach in the summer, less harried than some, but if I had not been alerted by Rich's comment in the drugstore that morning I would not have speculated about energies rushing back and forth through the port.

Even then I was not ready for what happened next.

Why not close off the port and protect Grand Beach from possible harm?

A perfectly good question; that I didn't ask it indicates how deeply I was involved in the game/story despite my externally normal behavior. Besides, thus far there was no reason to think Grand Beach was in danger, was there?

Today I'm inclined to think that while both grace and ungrace can pass back and forth between neighboring cosmoi, the energies are normally either benign or sufficiently weak as to do no serious harm. Joan Hagan had not been badly hurt, not nearly as seriously as poor N'Rasia. Moreover, if we are truly juxtaposed in a close, tenement-house superuniverse with another cosmos, one temporarily wider port is not going to increase notably the flow of spiritual energies between cognates in the two cosmoi.

It is perhaps a self-serving view of things, but it does seem to fit the data. Were things a little different in Grand Beach that weekend? OK, if Rich Daley says they were, then they were not greatly different, not so much that anyone besides a gifted political leader could notice.

If Grand Beach were under assault, I could always pull the plug, couldn't I?

Besides, who knows how much energy may have leapt back and forth over Planck's Wall every weekend of every summer for ages in that spot on the shore of Lake Michigan? It is not unreasonable to assume that the port was always there, in some less-defined fashion than my electronic link-up had temporarily created.

Nothing happened to Grand Beach, did it, that would not have happened anyway?

Well, maybe with one exception. And that may prove the speculation in the next paragraph.

There is another possibility that I was not considering at the time and which may be very important. If there was any sense or plan in all of this strange affair of the leaks in Max Planck's Wall created by Nathan's God Game, the key theme might be that finally the critical energy was curvilinear, like a boomerang. Or, to change the metaphor, maybe Grand Beach was a transformer on the energy circuit. Or to try yet again, perhaps it was the prism that refracted lights back to the other cosmos.

Arguably, as you shall see, just in the nick of time.

Well, the Brennans walked me home after the dinner party, as they always do. I felt quite relaxed and unworried. Joan Hagan was fine. N'Rasia was recovering. The peace negotiations and the romance between B'Mella and Lenrau were back on track. I was in control again of my material, so in control that I could enjoy the usual summer Saturday evening in Grand Beach without any serious distractions.

I had not much of the Irish Cream taken, not nearly as much as 'Rasia had in her visit, not by a long shot.

Before I went to bed I prayed dutifully for those who traveled between worlds. I fell promptly to sleep, *dormitio justorum* as we used to say in the seminary.

Now, you're going to think that because I had N'Rasia on my mind before I went to bed, I met her again in my dreams. That would, after all, not be surprising. Maybe at some level in my consciousness, that was what I wanted, right?

Well, when I woke up and saw someone familiar sitting at the desk which is at the other side of my room, reading of all things Wendy Doniger O'Flaherty's *Dreams, Illusions, and Other Realities*, it was not, let me assure you, herself at all at all.

Who was it?

None of you will guess.

Kaila.

"This woman has a point, you know," he nodded politely, every inch the well-trained and respectful courtier. "It may be that dreams are real and that the real are dreams."

"That's not quite her point. She's merely investigating the Indian stories and legends about the reality of dreams."

"Hmm . . . well, I don't believe that she's persuaded that dreams are just energy discharges in the brain at the end of the day. Neither are you, or I wouldn't be in your dream."

"Or I in your dream."

"A possibility." He smiled. "I don't see how we can know for sure. This conversation, however, in some deep sense is certainly real, isn't it?"

"W. I. Thomas."

"I'm afraid I haven't heard of him. . . . Do you mind if I speak very candidly? You won't be offended?"

"Of course you may. You are the most courteous person in the story."

"So you made me," he said grimly. "I really don't have much choice."

"So you are," I insisted. "I couldn't make you what you're not even if I tried."

"The problem," he leaned back in my enormous desk chair, "is that I am a little too well bred to be angry at God."

"I'm not God; but why are you angry?"

"Surely you know?" He looked genuinely surprised. "The ilel, of course. You don't expect me to be pleased with you about her, do you?"

"I hadn't thought about it from that perspective. Anyway, I did not send her. She was there when I came. I don't know what she's supposed to do in the story either. I don't even know what the word 'ilel' means."

He ran his fingers through his curly black hair. "You can hardly expect me to believe that, can you?"

"She's not mine. I didn't send her. I don't know where she came from."

"You will certainly admit," his smile was sad, melancholy, forlorn, "that you made her what she is? She's part of your story. You make all the characters to be what you imagine them to be. You made that delightful little creature delightful because you wanted her to be that way. That's why I'm upset with you. Didn't you realize I'd fall in love with her? How could I not have fallen in love with her?"

"Perhaps," I said guardedly, "you have a point."

"It was not till you intervened that I began to find her sexually appealing." He drummed his long, artistic fingers on the side of my word processor. "You are well aware of that, are you not? With all respect and reverence, of course."

"You'd like to blow your stack at me, wouldn't you, Kaila? You're furious because you think I dealt you a bad

hand and you want to rant at me, but your good manners
and your charm get in the way."

He laughed and shifted in the chair. "What good would
it do me? Have I not told others that there is no sense in
being angry at the Lord Our God? If you choose to make
me a shadow in your picture, will protesting do me any
good? I think more might be accomplished by reasonable
conversation between..."

"Colleagues?"

"I would not dare use the word." His scholarly meth-
odology was not mine, but he'd make a good graduate student and more respectful than most.

"Let me set the record straight. I don't know where she
comes from any more than you do. I didn't send her. The
Other Person did that. She's a character in my story, so I
guess I'm responsible, partly anyway, for her outrageous
behavior. To be candid" (good academic phrase, that) "I doubt
very much that you were totally unaware of her sexual
appeal before I took over."

"I cannot debate theology with you." He smiled ingra-
tiatingly. "The distinction between you and the Other Person..."

"Maybe Other Persons..." I remembered the Trinity.

"...Escapes me completely. I am a monotheist."

"So am I. So are they—the Other Persons, I mean."

He shook his head. "You cannot escape your responsibility for that impudent little wench." He said the harsh
words fondly. "She's your creature now, whoever else may
have sent her."

"And it was only in the pool that day you noticed she
was not merely a little wench?"

"At first," he stood up and began to pace the floor, "she
was a mild nuisance, a hoyden for whom I was responsible
far too young in life to have a hoyden daughter. She attached

herself to me as soon as she appeared. Ilels have masters and keepers—odd, isn't it, to use those words? I certainly don't keep her, and 'Rau surely does not master her. I knew the historical literature better than anyone else; I was patient and kind; I was the natural choice, or so everyone thought."

"And a little flattered... if the wandering ilel had chosen anyone else you would have been offended."

"I can hardly deny that, can I? At any rate, at first she was amusing—an appealing, often impudent, but in her own way, docile child. I began to enjoy having a daughter who was only a few years younger than I was, especially a sacred child who had come to save our Lord Lenrau and our land, for such is the mission of ilels."

"Then you discovered she was more than a child and that without realizing what had happened, you'd fallen for her."

"You made me do that." Hands on hips, voice tense, he turned on me. "You needed my sexual frustration for part of the drama of your story."

"One of the rules of the game, Kaila." I got out of bed and sat in the reclining chair in my #3 work station (as the decorator calls it). "An author can never force a character to do something the character doesn't want to do. Your falling for the sexy little imp was as natural as the sun rising in the morning. Don't blame me for your own needs and desires."

"You made me with those needs and desires." He glowered darkly, and looked even more handsome.

"You don't want them? You want me to rewrite your healthy male reaction to a beautiful girl out of the story?"

He considered thoughtfully. "I'm afraid if I say yes," he laughed lightly, "you might do it. I don't want that to happen. And before we go on, may I have some of that wonderful wine you served to N'Rasia when she was here?"

"She told you about it?" I asked incredulously.

"Of course not." He seemed offended that I would even make such a suggestion. "They're your dreams, aren't they?"

So I put ice in the glass which was instantly available, brought it over to him with the bottle of Baileys which was also available, and filled the one with the other. He removed the bottle gently from my hand and placed it next to Wendy's book.

"An excellent wine," he murmured, as he guzzled a quarter of the tumbler.

"We call it a 'cream' or an 'Irish cream,'" I said, "and it's meant to be sipped, not chugalugged."

"Interesting..."

He sipped it more slowly but still with remarkable persistence. Given a chance they would notably improve the exports of the Republic of Ireland—and end up a land of drunks, perhaps peaceful drunks, but not necessarily.

"So you are tormented by the winsome imp but you don't necessarily want those torments to be removed?"

How God-like can you get?

His fingers tightened around the Powerscourt crystal. "My mind is filled with images, my body with needs, my fingers with imperative demands. I want to do the most terribly obscene things to her..."

"With her," I added the ideological caution.

"Yes, of course," he agreed automatically and then chuckled. "With Ranora it would necessarily be that way ...I think I will go mad with the terrible lusts I feel for her, for a holy one of God."

"You think we should have ordered the mechanics of procreation differently?"

He threw back his head and laughed enthusiastically.

"It is inconvenient and troublesome, isn't it? Yet...who would really want to change? Nonetheless, an ilel is sacred, she ought not to be the object of such desires."

"Only if her guardian is immune from the human condition, young man. Don't the ilels ever take mates?"

"The historical data are thin. Most ilels are killed; their goodness and charm and wit and kindness, of course, lead to their death. You have made that even more likely in this case by giving her magical powers."

"Me?" The so-and-sos were blaming me for things that I hadn't done at all. At all.

"Ilels historically have saved our land—when they have been successful, which as I have said is in a minority of cases—by ordinary human goodness directed in strange, appealing, and wonderful directions. But you have seen it with 'Nora. Even gloomy old Lenrau melts into honey when she blows her wicked pipe at him. They are essentially magical spirits, caring magical spirits to be more precise. They are not wizards or witches or wonder workers. Ilels don't trade in the miraculous. Now you've given us one that does."

"I'm sorry, but I don't understand."

He filled up his Powerscourt tumbler. "She brought that woman back from the dead."

"Oh, nonsense, Kaila; and rubbish and hogwash and a lot of other more scatological words. N'Rasia wasn't dead. She was in a coma. All our friend did was pipe her awake."

"It was your idea?"

"Sure it was my idea; I'm the author, am I not?"

"So it was a miracle?"

"It most certainly was not, young man, and get that into your thick skull. Ranora activated the deep-seated will to live in a woman in a coma and called her forth from the coma. It was a purely natural phenomenon."

"The doctors said she would not live." He rubbed his chin dubiously.

"What do doctors know? You're supposed to be a scholar; do you rush to a supernatural explanation anytime something new happens for which there are obvious natural explanations? You heard that melody. If it were about you, wouldn't you want to live?"

"She hasn't done a Kaila theme yet," he said sadly.

"Give her and me time. An author can't crowd everything on one page."

"The danger comes from the priests. They say she is a false ilel because she brought a woman back from the dead."

"As one of my mentors once put it, by their fruits you will know them."

"The little imp," he changed the subject rapidly, as a man in love would, "is terribly proud of herself. She blows the noisy pipe more than ever."

"How does she explain what happened to N'Rasia?"

"She gives your explanation, what else? She says she just woke her up with her little pipe."

"That's the truth; you should believe it."

"The priests fear her." He filled his glass again. "They are capable of sticking a knife in her back, you know; that's their way of disposing of their enemies."

"*Stylus curiae.*"

"What?"

"A bad pun from one of our archaic languages. Don't worry about them. While I'm around no one is going to hurt my Ranora."

"So you love her too?"

"We're not rivals, Kaila." I put my hand on his shoulder. "Authors fall in love with their characters." I filled up his glass with Baileys. "How could anyone not love her?"

"My frustration," he sighed, "is part of your story, isn't

it? Good, loyal, steady, charming Kaila; in love with an untouchable virgin whom he must protect and occasionally restrain, but never violate. A willing sacrificial victim for his Duke and the cause of peace. Oh, it makes a great contrast in the story, doesn't it? 'Rau beds B'Mella, Malvau beds his fat wife, and I cannot bed the one I really love."

"You are unkind to N'Rasia, and the story need not end that way at all."

"Have you made up your mind?"

Make up my mind about the two of them when I was barely in control of the narrative? He had to be kidding.

"Even if I had, I can force neither marriage nor celibacy on you and that sexy little imp; authors can't make characters do what they don't want to do."

"She's not sexy, she's innocent."

"None of them are innocent, Kaila." I sipped my Baileys very slowly. Tomorrow was another day. "She uses her sexual appeal very shrewdly. She caught your changed attitude instantly and has gently kept you at a greater distance ever since. The young woman knows what she's about."

"Does she love me?" His eyes glistened momentarily.

"Ask her."

"I can't do that."

"Sometime you'll have to."

"You will try to force me? I would be too embarrassed."

"For the last time, young man," I heard my voice rising, "I can't deprive you of your free will. If you're dumb enough and cowardly enough not to confront her with your feelings eventually, I can't make you do it. I'll sure as hell lean on you, though."

"You can tell me if I have a chance," he pleaded like a lovesick child.

"I can tell you the obvious." Keep him on the defensive, that's the ticket. "At the present moment in the story, if

Ranora is going to fall in love with someone and mate with him, you are not only the leading candidate, you are the only candidate."

"Would that please you?" His spirits picked up.

"If it didn't, I would have created someone else who was better qualified. But consider this: are you sure you want her as a wife? She is a difficult, stubborn, unpredictable, fiercely independent, and, alas, domineering woman. You'd never have a moment's peace. Fun in bed, doubtless, but do you want that hoyden interfering with your scholarship and writing every day for the rest of your life?"

"Yes," he said with a broad grin. "She'd keep me from drying up and withering away."

"God knows."

"Will she go away?"

"Huh?"

"She speaks of leaving, vague hints which she will not or cannot explain. Nor will she tell me if she'll come back if she does leave. Some ilels disappear when their work is done."

I was the author, wasn't I? How could she leave without my knowledge or permission?

But not an author the way most authors are authors. I was playing Nathan's God Game.

"But some do mate?"

"It is not unknown. On one or two occasions, it may have happened. They continue to be ilels, of course, though with less intensity. I," he swelled his chest a little, "may even be a descendant of one."

"How appropriate!"

"But there is no record of an ilel ever mating with her protector." He emptied the Baileys. "Do not worry, I will not harm your precious goblets, like that sloppy woman."

"You really are in love with her, aren't you? Poor N'Rasia

has done nothing worse than stir up the priests' envy because Ranora piped her awake and you hate the woman."

He actually blushed. "God always knows too much."

"I'm not God. But let it ride. Moreover, it is not impossible that you and Ranora can make history: the first ilel ever to mate with her protector. Have you noticed, by the way, how she looks at you when you lecture her about the history of your land?"

"She finds my pretensions amusing." He turned over the empty Baileys bottle and seemed disappointed to discover that it was empty.

"She has a teenaged student's crush on a good-looking teacher."

He scowled blackly. "Don't speak that way of a sacred virgin."

"You wanted to know whether she loves you. You can't have it both ways."

His good humor returned quickly. "I suppose part of me wants her and part of me is afraid of what happens when and if I get her."

"Wise man."

She'd lead him a merry chase.

"I want her so much." Fists clenched again. "Do not be afraid, I will not spoil your story by raping her or seducing her. I am a man of honor and self-restraint, no matter what the cost. That is, after all, the way you made me."

"Rape you'd better not try or I'll delete you totally. Seduction? That's up to you and her."

"Seduce an ilel?"

"Why not?"

"I love her, I do not lust after her."

"Nonsense. We are designed so that the two cannot be completely separated and ought not to be."

"You too?"

"In a certain sense."

Finally, I was betting, she would have to do the seducing, once she made up her mind that her "vocation"—I could think of no better word—did not preclude marriage. If that were indeed true—and I didn't know the story well enough yet to be sure—Ranora was a wild card someone else had slipped into my deck.

What would it be like married to a vestal virgin emerita? Poor young man would never think of that in time. Perhaps I should really take steps to warn him. No, if 'Nora set her cap for him, I wouldn't stand a chance if I tried to intervene.

"There is of course G'Ranne," I said tentatively. "You seem to be relating rather well with her."

"She is an incredible woman." He shrugged his shoulders. "So much passion and dedication. Too much for me, perhaps."

"Obedient warrior type, is she not?"

His eyes widened. "You are jesting. God knows better than that."

"I'm not God."

"Of course not." He laughed, going along with the joke. "You don't have to be God to know that she is a very special woman, in her own way as fascinating as the ilel."

"So you wouldn't be bored?"

"Oh, no. But that's not the point, is it? I should be going." He rose politely, flipping his silver cloak over his shoulder. "I have occupied too much of your dream time. You must sail tomorrow."

"Another few minutes won't hurt. How do you evaluate" (more academic shop talk) "her plan to play matchmaker to the Duke and the Duchess?"

"It's your story, isn't it?" He picked up the empty bottle

and the two glasses. "Don't you know what will happen in such a mating?"

"An author is never sure what will happen until it happens."

"Even God?"

"In some theologies, about which we're not arguing."

"Well." Hands on hips, he considered thoughtfully. "It would be the most approved happy ending. Do you like happy endings, by the way?"

"Of course. That's a stupid question."

"Sometimes I wonder...In any event, it is not the Duchess who worries me. She is a choleric woman warrior with the gentleness of a mother with a newborn babe. Not uncomplicated, surely, but not a difficult challenge to a man with some sensitivity to women. I flatter myself," he looked at me sideways, "that I could keep her happy rather easily—not, you may be assured, that I intend to try. A little patience, a little firmness, a lot of affection, an occasional stern warning: 'Ella would become not perhaps the ideal wife, but certainly a good and loving and lovable wife. Again I emphasize," he grinned wickedly, "that my interests are not of that sort, as you well know, but she does seem to respond rather well to me."

"So if I want to change the plans..."

"*NO!*" he exploded. "That is not the way you made me. I am too loyal even to consider such an ending."

The hell he was, but he was probably too young to be forced to face his deep and secret desire for the Duchess.

"You do, however, worry about your Duke?"

"Where does he go when his eyes glaze? Do you know?"

"An impertinent question which I won't answer." Authors can make up the rules as they go along.

"You see the point, however: he's three quarters in love with the woman now. In most respects he is the calm, steadying influence she needs. Yet if a vain and not quite secure woman like B'Mella thinks her husband has lost interest in her because he is preoccupied with some mad vision..."

"Hell hath no fury like a woman scorned."

"Pardon?"

"Forget it."

"But you agree we have a problem?"

"We?"

"I had gathered from our conversation that storytelling is a joint venture; author, you seem to suggest that one can be a monotheist and still admit the possibility of several authors and characters working together."

"Grace and free will in cooperation?"

"Whatever that means. Now I must leave. I feel my dream, or is it your dream, ending."

"It was nice of you to stop by."

He faded out, then faded back in again, a haze of dots and lights dancing incandescently in my room. "Please, dear God, please let me have her. I will love her and protect her and cherish her life and laughter for as long as I shall live. Only don't take her away from me."

"I'll see what I can do. There's always G'Ranne."

"A man must be more God-like than I am to marry her. I want Ranora."

"I'll see."

Which you have to admit is a really poor answer to such a moving prayer.

What can I tell you?

The next morning, before I went off to the marina to sail with the elder Brennans, I dug out my battered copy of *At Swim Two Birds* and hunted up the section where the characters constitute themselves a jury to vote on the fate of the author. It made sobering reading.

"Do you think it would be safe to go to bed and leave him where he is in the morning?"

"I do not," said Orlick. "Safety first."

Shanahan took out his thumb from the armhole and straightened his body in the chair.

"A false step now," he said, "and it's a short jump for the lot of us. Do you know that? A false step now and we're all in the cart and that's a fact."

Lamont came forward from a couch where he had been resting and inclined his head as a signal that he was taking an intelligent interest in the conversation.

"Will the judges have a bad head tomorrow?" he asked.

"No," said Orlick.

"Well, I think the time has come for the black caps."

"You think the jury has heard enough evidence?"

"Certainly they have," said Shanahan. "The time for talk is past. Finish the job tonight like a good man so we can go to bed in peace. God, if we gave him a chance to catch us at this game..."

"The job should be done at once," said Lamont, "and the razor's the boy to do it."

"He can't complain that he didn't get fair play," said Furrisky. "He got a fair trial and a jury of his own manufacture. I think the time has come."

"It's time to take him out to the courtyard," said Shanahan.

"A half-minute with the razor and the trick is done," said Lamont.

"I only hope," Orlick said, "that nothing happens to us. I don't think the like of this has been done before you know."

My nighttime visitors—and for all Kaila's appealing good looks and good humor I would have rather more enjoyed N'Rasia as a dream guest than Kaila—hardly seemed to be of the sort of Orlick, Lamont, Furrisky, and Shanahan. They were still under my thumb, still reverential and respectful most of the time.

But a lovesick young man and a frustrated middle-aged woman—put them together and you have the kind of team which created the Reign of Terror during the French Revolution. They had learned, somehow, to intrude themselves into my dream life with ease. Once they found out I was not really the Other Person, I could be in serious trouble.

Then there was the quote from the other Irishman, a Prot this time, at the end of *Mantissa*. He is closing the scene in the hospital room in which he has committed fornication with a number of his woman creatures/characters:

> Merciful silence descends at last upon the gray room. Or it would have done so, were it not that the bird in the clock, as if feeling not fully requited, as if obliged one last time to reaffirm its extraneity, its distance from all that has happened in that room, and its undying regard for its first and aestho-autogamous (Keep the fun clean, said Shanahan) owner; or as if dream-babbling of green Irish fields and mountain meadows, and of sheer bliss of being able to shift all responsibility for one's own progeny (to say nothing of having the last word) stirs, extrudes and cries in an ultimate, soft and single, most strangely single, cuckoo.

Well, I hadn't even come close to fornication yet, and given my habits and experience probably wouldn't. Furthermore I was not crazy. Finally, while Shanahan was to

be found in both Flann O'Brien and John Fowles, he was
not in this story, not yet.

As I left for Snug Harbor, the clock on the ground floor
sounded its routine note—a cuckoo, of course.

Not once, but ten times.

Why talk over the game/story with two of the lesser
characters? All right, they may be interesting enough, but
the plot really doesn't revolve around them. Nathan's God
Game will not be won or lost because of what Kaila or
N'Rasia does. If the author/player/creator wants to get inside the head of some of his creatures in a dream world
conversation, why not Lenrau and B'Mella? After all, this
is a romance, maybe a divine romance, and are they not
the romantic leads? And surely Ranora is the most whim-
sically interesting person in the story; it is a fair bet even
now, that somehow it will be her task to pull all the pieces
together at the end, if they will be pulled together at all.
Perhaps she will be called upon to straighten out the mess
that the author/player/creator has created. So why not en-
gage in a dream conversation with her?

What goes on inside the head of an ilel, anyway?

Is that not more interesting than the agonies of a middle-aged matron (slightly overweight) in a midlife identity
crisis, or of a lovesick young man? Our lives are filled with
such people; how many ilels have we ever met?

In my defense (and creators always must be prepared
to defend themselves—take for example the scene in Yah-
weh's court when Satan, still a good angel at that late date,
demands that the Creator defend his work), I must say first
of all that you can't pick the people who come to your dreams.
You can see a rather ordinary-looking someone briefly on
the bus or the train at night after you have seen *Witness*;
while you'd much rather dream about the luminous Kelly

McGillis, you dream instead about the ordinary someone. You take your dreams where you find them.

Moreover, 'Rau and 'Ella are the larger-than-life romantic leads. We must learn something about them, especially about their tragic flaws and their saving strengths, but if they stretch themselves out on a psychiatrist's couch and bare their souls to us, it's pretty hard for them to be romantic heroes.

I have no idea what goes on in the mind of an ilel, and I'm not sure I want to know. Mostly, I think, on the basis of a sample of one, they operate on instinct and intuition. Probably they are like totally geeky when it comes to self-analysis.

Besides, I don't want that one intruding in my dreams. No way.

So, OK, I have some resistance to letting them into my dreams, which is probably why they didn't come or maybe why I suppressed the conversations I had with them. I had no particular resistance to Kaila and N'Rasia, both of whom had powerful motivation for demanding that the story/game/world be modified to take into account their desires, the former for a woman he wanted, the latter for a more important life.

Already, I'm sure, N'Rasia was having second thoughts. And if it should work out that Kaila really does bed the ilel, he'll have second, third, fourth, and fifth thoughts. But they both wanted to push their way into my story and change it. So they pushed their way into my dreams, with what outcome remains to be seen.

Sunday is supposed to be a day of rest and relaxation. Definitely not a day for working on stories or playing exhausting games. So I sailed, swam, skied, slept, and made a supper of "uncle burgers" for a horde of my nieces and nephews who had descended upon Grand Beach for the wondrous blue-skied, white-foamed perfection of a summer Sunday, the kind of day which heaven had better be like or I'll organize a petition of protest.

Michele and Bobby joined us for supper, the former to have her favorite repast of French fries and Tab. She was going off to Ohio next weekend to see her boyfriend, the gentle-souled linebacker, and she took a lot of teasing about it. The crowd departed my house quite late, the cars sped through the tree-covered dusk for the expressways and the rush home. Unresolved and unresolvable question: do you return to the city very late Sunday night or very early Monday morning, and the routine Sunday melancholy—with its hint of autumn—slipped over the village. Summer, we all knew it but didn't want to face it, could not last forever.

Should I play the game?

It was still Sunday.

But if I put in a few hours on it, I might be able to clean it up on Monday morning before lunch and turn my attention to better things than Nathan's latest gimmickry.

Author's Note _____

Not only the Hindus and the American Indians
think that it all may be a dream—a possibility which
our bumptious narrator refuses to take seriously.
Consider this from an American humorist:

"Strange that you should not have suspected,
years ago, centuries, ages, aeons ago! for you have
existed, companionless, through all the eternities.
Strange, indeed, that you should not have suspected
that your universe and its contents were only
dreams, visions, fictions! Strange, because they are
so frankly and hysterically insane—like all dreams: a
God who could make good children as easily as bad,
yet preferred to make bad ones; who could have
made every one of them happy, yet never made a
single happy one; who made them prize their bitter
life, yet stingily cut it short; who gave his angels
eternal happiness unearned, yet required his other
children to earn it; who gave his angels painless
lives, yet cursed his other children with biting
miseries and maladies of mind and body; who
mouths justice and invented hell—mouths mercy,

179

*and invented hell—mouths golden rules, and
forgiveness multiplied by seventy times seven, and
invented hell; who mouths morals to other people
and has none himself; who frowns upon crimes, yet
commits them all; who created man without
invitation, then tries to shuffle the reponsibility for
man's acts upon man, instead of honorably placing it
where it belongs, upon himself; and finally, with
altogether divine obtuseness, invites this poor abused
slave to worship him!...*

*"You perceive, now, that these things are all
impossible, except in a dream. You perceive that they
are pure and puerile insanities, the silly creations of
an imagination that is not conscious of its freaks—in
a word, that they are a dream, and you the maker of
it. The dream marks are all present—you should
have recognized them earlier...*

*"It is true, that which I have revealed to you:
there is no God, no universe, no human race, no
earthly life, no heaven, no hell. It is all Dream, a
grotesque and foolish dream. Nothing exists but You.
And you are but a Thought—a vagrant Thought, a
useless Thought, a homeless Thought, wandering
forlorn among the empty eternities!"*

*See what I mean by humorist? Laugh, I thought
I'd die.*

*Presumably Mark Twain felt quite pleased with
himself when he thus ended his last story "The
Mysterious Stranger." But even the narrator of this
tale, who is no philosophical sophisticate as the
reader doubtless perceives by now, would point out
that you can't have a dream without a dreamer, a
thought without a thinker, a story without a
storyteller. Nor can you tell a story without a purpose,*

even if as in the case of the elderly and bitter Twain, the purpose is to insist that there is no purpose.

Thus the one whom my narrator calls Shags is probably right: our lives are stories which God tells, thoughts which God thinks, dreams which God dreams.

The issue then is not whether there is a Dreamer. The issue rather—and the data are ambiguous—is whether dreams come true.

10
Ranora's Plot

So I turned on all the equipment, including this time the video recorder, and pressed the CONTINUE GAME key.

SITUATION? I asked.

NO APPRECIABLE CHANGE. NEGOTIATIONS CONTINUING SLOWLY.

OK. I decided to have a look around.

The various working commissions were still meeting, struggling slowly with the convoluted, and mostly unreal, problems created by centuries of fear and distrust. Kaila and Malvau met in one ducal pavilion or the other at the end of each day to tote up the progress, sometimes minute but better than before when there had been nothing. The Duke and the Duchess had withdrawn completely from negotiations and even from public appearances. B'Mella, still embarrassed by the idiocy she had displayed the night N'Rasia was injured, was devoting her time to painting—fierce, passionate mountain landscapes, often with wild and destructive storms raging over the peaks and down the valleys. I had not witnessed their stormy season yet, didn't in fact know they had one till I peered over her shoulder and watched her bring the storms to life. They looked as if they would more than satisfy my passion for summer storms.

Wearing a short brown paint-smeared smock, B'Mella worked with precise intensity; she waved off distractions with a brisk hand, ignored the pain which fell on her long legs, and nodded curtly at the end of the day when the exhausted Malvau reported on the day's work for peace.

ACCESS DUKE, I instructed the program.

SEARCHING.

COME ON.

SEARCHING.

We finally found him, deep in the forest wandering about like a man in a trance. Mad Sweeney from the Irish sagas, not quite turned into a bird yet and not quite matter for a Seamus Heaney poem or a Flann O'Brien novel, but living already in another and more pleasant world. His face was transformed by a happy smile and he ambled content-edly through the blossoming trees.

Yet not quite as mad as mad Sweeney. When Ranora raced through the forest like a gazelle fleeing from a pred-ator, grabbed his hand, and turned him back towards the meadow, he came quietly enough. They chatted enthusi-astically about the birds and the trees and the forest ani-mals; Ranora called forth with her pipe some giant, gentle white furry creatures which looked like oversized orangu-tans, and which danced merrily and with surprising grace to her tunes.

She certainly didn't seem worried that the Duke might, like Sweeney, turn into a bird and fly around the country-side complaining about his fate.

In their recreation pool, Kaila recounted to the Duke the meagre progress of the day on one of the fishery disputes. Lenrau's questions indicated that he knew more about fish-ing than any of the negotiators. An able Duke, for a few minutes, then he closed his eyes and floated blissfully on the water—until Ranora like an avenging water sprite dove in and dunked both of them, Kaila quickly and efficiently and the Duke at great length and with considerable squirming and wrestling.

She skillfully managed to keep the Duke between herself and her Protector at almost all times, yet she laughed affectionately at him and asked if he was going to walk by the moonlight with G'Ranne.

He blushed. "She is not my kind of woman, impudent child."

"Hmmf..." she sniffed skeptically, apparently only mildly upset that her protector might be having a love affair. "And did the Duchess look lovely today?"

"We never see the Duchess. She is in her chamber painting."

"Painting!" Arms on the edge of the pool, little feet kicking water in the Duke's face, enough to tease, not enough to offend. "The Duchess paints and the Duke daydreams."

"And neither stands in the way of peace with their illtempered behavior."

"While the priests plot, and the warriors sharpen their weapons, and the people grow tired of the negotiations and wish there was some entertaining war to keep them interested as spring turns to summer. We will not have peace," vigorous splash of water, hitting the Duke right between the eyes, "until this sleepy Duke and that painting Duchess realize that they have to impose it!"

The Duke grabbed her around her tiny waist and dunked her repeatedly. "You have only one topic on your mind, troublesome child."

She loved it, of course, as all teenaged girls love to be dunked. "I bet," sputtering for air, "that you wouldn't do this," more sputtering and fiddling with her swimsuit top, also part of the act, "to 'Ella if you had her in the pool."

"If I did," laughter as he finally released her, "she might cut my throat."

All the while, Kaila watched with melancholy longing. I hoped that G'Ranne would take his mind off the ilel for a short time on this glorious spring evening.

ACCESS CARDINAL.

The Cardinal and the Admiral, this time, were happily free of the Mothers Superior. Still the subject was murder, not "the razor's the boy" as Shanahan suggested but, *stylo curiae*, the knife in the back.

"We must stop these negotiations," the Admiral insisted, pounding the wall of the cave in which they were meeting. "Put a knife in Malvau or Kaila or maybe both."

"Pity that those drunken louts didn't kill both him and his wife," the Cardinal murmured in his usual richly pious voice. "That would have restrained them nicely."

"Two quick jabs some night and we're rid of both of them."

"There is no useful purpose served by using that technique at the present time. Murder is only appropriate when we can be sure that it will be effective. Those two young fools are both so indiscreet that they might liquidate all of us."

"If they should mate, which is not altogether impossible?"

"Oh," the Cardinal smiled gently, "that will solve many of our problems. Yes," his smile widened, "then it will be very simple."

Not if I can help it, buster.

My friends the technological warriors had traded in their cave in the mountains for an island on one of the larger lakes and their mechanical cannon for test tubes, retorts, and steaming vats.

"What if it explodes before we are ready to use it?"

"Then there will be no more island."

"And if we are on the island?"

"No more us. It will probably not explode, not till we have it under the table on which they will sign the final peace."

"It will destroy the meadow and everyone in it?"

"Most certainly."

"What else?"

"Possibly both cities."

"Very interesting."

"Possibly the whole land."

"And us?"

"Where would we be but in the land?"

They laughed insanely, a chorus which was joined by the half-dozen white-gowned assistants.

ZAP LAB.

HOW ZAP?

BREAK IT UP ANY WAY YOU WANT.

The program was becoming ingenious in its destructive techniques.

One steaming test tube flashed red and white and green and broke open with a loud pop. The retort next to it cracked and spewed a dark amber fluid which ate into a rubberlike hose. Two more tubes began to flash as a thick black substance gushed out of the hose.

The experimenters raced desperately for the doors of their hut and then out into the small meadow in the middle of the island. The hut was smoking like a Fourth of July firecracker about to blow.

And then it blew—poof, no more hut, no more island, and a bunch of conspirators paddling desperately for shore.

Where the island had been there was a tiny mushroom cloud.

I started to be very worried about these clowns. They might have stumbled upon something far more deadly than they realized.

My final stop for the evening was Malvau's pavilion. He and his wife were eating their dinner and companionably discussing the day's conferences in exquisite detail, he explaining patiently what had happened, she listening with apparent interest and asking careful and seemingly intelligent questions

He was exhausted, a business executive who hadn't had a vacation in years. She was pale and thinner, but seemingly recovered from her brush with death.

After their meal they walked briefly in the moonlight, holding hands passively, returned to their chamber, and offered together their nighttime prayer to the Lord Our God, looking right into the big screen on my Zenith.

"We thank you for saving our lives," he began.

"And bringing peace to our land," she continued. A bump on the head and loss of appetite had done wonders for her figure.

"And especially renewing our love."

"We pray for the Duke and the Duchess."

"And all who labor in the cause of peace."

"We are especially grateful" (together) "for the ilel whom you have sent to us in our time of need."

"And," a light laugh from the woman, "for her wondrous pipe."

They waited, expecting me to say something.

What the hell?

BE KIND TO ONE ANOTHER, I said, feeling that such advice never did harm to anyone.

They were sweetly affectionate to one another in their

bath and then began elegiac ministrations to each other's bodies in their bed.

I tuned out, suspicious. It was too perfect, too considerate, too affectionate. Malvau had a porcelain doll on his hands, one whose theme had been celebrated by the magic elfkind; N'Rasia, having obtained her starring role, was trying to figure out what it meant. The change from middle-aged matron to peace symbol was not quite as satisfying as she might have hoped.

For neither of them was there room to fight. You can't be happy in an intimate relationship unless you have a protocol and a rhetoric with which to fight constructively. So, if you want to keep your new relationship alive, you contain any emotions which are too passionate.

Passionate lovers fight passionately. Elegiac lovers don't fight. After a time, they either don't love or a volcano explodes between them. The latter is more dangerous and more constructive.

Did either of them have the resources to fight explosively and constructively?

It certainly didn't look that way.

I decided to leave G'Ranne and Kaila to themselves. Like 'Nora I didn't care at that point whether they were sleeping with each other or not.

I suspended the game and thought about that part of the plot. The ice warrior, if no longer ice maiden, was attractive and intelligent and, for a warrior woman, remarkably unferocious. She and Kaila would make a good match. Might that not be a happy solution?

Ranora, like Shane, could walk over the mountain, piping her happy little tune.

Maybe.

Only if she agreed, however.

And the rest of the plot?

Clearly we had to move the leading characters off their rear ends and towards a denouement. But that, on a late July Sunday in Grand Beach, could wait till Monday morning.

I slept soundly, undisturbed by dream visitors—or at least by any I remembered—and awoke late for the ski crowd.

"*Well*," Michele complained, as she and Bob bounded into my Chevy. "Where were you?"

"Asleep."

"If we overslept..."

"It's my boat."

"That totally does not make any difference."

I should note here that Michele's nagging is never disrespectful. She either learned very early in life or was genetically programmed to be "half fun and full earnest" up to the last centimeter before shrewishness and then stop.

"It sure does make a difference."

"Hmmp... all *right*. But you have to ski first this morning, no matter how cold the water is."

"All *right*."

"Oh, I almost forgot, 'member that you asked me whether I ever played a horn?"

"Yes?"

"*Well*, my mother reminded me that I once played a flute."

"Really?"

"Uh-huh; not for long though. I lost my breath blowing on it."

I didn't want to know any more. After I'd returned the skiers to their respective daytime occupations the Hagans were waiting at my door.

"Can we come in and chat a few minutes?"

Sure. Bargain-basement summertime therapy.

But it was not that simple.

Tom was determined that the two of them should enter family therapy. Joan was vigorously against it. Usually it was the other way around—the Irish wife dragging the husband to therapy under threat of moving out of his bedroom. Moreover, the Grand Beach consensus was that she was the long-suffering woman, putting up with a selfish and inconsiderate, not to say monumentally unintelligent husband. (This was, to be fair, an Irish community's official reaction to any troubled marriage, because, you see, the official reaction was always shaped by the women.) Now he was making sense and she was acting like a fink.

"I've been to see Doctor Shanahan," he explained, "and I was very impressed."

"Shanahan? Does she have a partner named Lamont?"

"She does, as a matter of fact. Do you know them?"

"No, just heard about them."

"I don't know who this woman is at all." When Joan screwed her pretty face in a frown it looked faded. "I know nothing about her marriage. Why should I trust her with my marriage? What gives her the right to tell me how to solve my problems when for all I know she's not very good as a wife and mother?"

"That's not what it's about, Joan." The big ex-football lug gripped his hands tightly. "She doesn't tell us what to do, she, uh, creates an environment in which we can talk to one another and solve our problems ourselves."

"I don't see why we need another woman to help us talk."

Envy and jealousy mixed together.

"We could find a male therapist. She mentioned a Doctor Orlick..."

"Orlick?"

"Do you know him?"

"I think I've heard of him."

"Well, that would be a little better, but I don't think either of us is mentally ill or anything like that."

"Therapy," Tom continued doggedly, "is not for the ill, it's for healthy people with problems that they can solve if they have some assistance."

"The psychiatrists were not able to help my Great Aunt Maude. She spent thirty years in Dunning."

You have to understand that Joan is a topflight account executive for a major LaSalle Street investment house, a smart, successful woman. Yet her attitudes on therapy could just as well have been expressed by her mother thirty years before. I had never met the mother, but I suspected I wouldn't like her at all.

"Their methods of treatment have improved since then. They can do wonders with medication."

"I *will not* take any drugs."

Mother probably said that too.

"What do you think?" Tom interrupted their dialogue to turn to me. I had taken a leaf from the book of one of my favorite characters, Monsignor Blackie Ryan, and made them a pot of McNulty's raspberry tea. Like Blackie, I filled their cups before answering the question.

(Do authors imitate the behavior of their characters? I told you, didn't I, that life imitates fiction?)

"There's no point in entering family therapy unless both parties want it. Everyone in the family, kids too."

"I just don't think we *need* it," Joan pleaded.

Among the problems, I began to suspect, was frigidity and her resentment that Tom had not been able, probably didn't know how, to help her overcome it. Not that she wanted to overcome it with any more than half of her personality.

"I don't think," I repressed a Blackie-like sigh, "that the issue of family therapy ought to be expressed in terms of need. Rather the question is whether a family might profit from it. I suppose that a majority of families would find it very helpful at some time in the course of their existence."

"Really?" I had made it respectable, which of course was the problem to begin with. Even respectable people sought family therapy.

"I could name, oh, at least two dozen families here in Grand Beach."

Not a complete lie.

"*Really*, well, if you think it's a good idea..."

OK, you need someone to blame if it doesn't work. I'm used to that game too. "I said that it helps a lot of people."

Which isn't the same thing, not that it matters.

"Shall we call Doctor Orlick for an appointment?" Tom wanted to rush ahead the way he had always rushed through life.

"*Well*, if you think this Shanahan woman is so good... it might be helpful to have a woman's perspective."

Curiosity overcoming envy and jealousy, God bless it.

Poor Joan, four kids, eighteen years of marriage and few if any orgasms. Sexual pleasure wouldn't solve everything, not by a long shot. But it sure would help, maybe enough to make the other problems manageable. Maybe not too. However, with any luck they might end up at the Loyola sexual dysfunction clinic. Fortunately for her she was still sufficiently attractive that a man, once educated, would take almost any personal risk to help her.

Damn her mother, anyway.

"Is she pretty, Tom?" I asked, giving him a cue.

"Not as pretty as my wife," he took the cue.

"I'll do anything to save our marriage," tears in her eyes. "I just don't know what to do."

"Me too." Tom was not too swift, as the kids would say,

not nearly as intelligent as she, and, so far, long on enthusiasm but short on sensitivity. If goodwill were enough, there'd be no problem.

Prognosis? I thought as I cleaned my teacups. Poor to terrible.

Same as the prognosis for my friends in Nathan's God Game. Same, maybe, for all of us.

But, as I hope is clear, they were very different people from Malvau and N'Rasia. With different problems. No, finally, maybe the same problem we all have: fear of the vulnerability that intimacy demands.

Maybe I could bring a tin whistle back from Dublin town and have Michele roam around Grand Beach blowing it.

So, after a phone call to my agent Nat in which he told me Tor Books' latest offer and I told him that it was not nearly enough, I returned to Nathan's God Game.

ACCESS DUCHESS.

NEGATIVE.

WHAT THE HELL DO YOU MEAN? ACCESS DUCHESS.

NEGATIVE. ACCESSING ILEL.

Huh?

"*Well*, where have you been?" She was standing by her private lake, fully clothed in red and white this time, her pipe tucked under one arm, foot tapping the ground impatiently, small jaw jutting defiantly in my direction.

I'VE OTHER WORLDS BESIDES THIS ONE TO WORRY ABOUT.

"This one needs you *now*!"

Yes, ma'am.

"We have to do something about the Duke and the Duchess."

DO WE?

You must understand that she was talking to me in remarkably Michele-like tones from the TV screen.

"*We* do." She folded her arms solemnly across her lovely young breasts. "They will never mate unless *we* push them."

DO WE WANT THEM TO MATE?

She raised her hands in a "what can I tell you?" gesture. "Do you have any other suggestions? Unless they unite, the negotiations will last until the day after the last warrior kills the last nonwarrior. Malvau is sweet and Kaila" (did I note a tinge of embarrassment?) "is a dear," wicked grin, "for a Protector I mean, but politics and wisdom won't save this land. We need love."

"You mean lust."

"You yourself said they can't be separated."

Yeah, I did, but not to you. Never mind.

SUPPOSE THEY KILL ONE ANOTHER.

"What other chance do we have?"

NONE, I SUPPOSE.

"It's taking too long."

A story ought not to drag. You can keep hero and heroine out of each other's arms just so long.

ALL RIGHT. LET'S GET ON WITH THE STORY. WHAT DO YOU PROPOSE?

"*Well*," the words flew out at Concorde speed, "there is this old houseboat on a lake way into the forest *and* I'm going to have it repaired today and made real nice *and* I'm going to put food *and* drink in it *and* comfortable chairs *and* a big bed *and* a nice smell *and* tonight they will go to it *and* fall in love with each other *and* mate."

JUST LIKE THAT?

"Just like that."

HOW DO WE GET THEM THERE?

"*We* don't," loud snigger and hunched-up shoulders. "*You* do."

HOW?

"I don't know. Lust. Love. Whatever." Another snigger.

AND IF THEY TRY TO KILL EACH OTHER . . . THEY'RE WAR-
RIORS BRED AND TRAINED, YOU KNOW.

"Don't let them . . . anyway, Kaila has warrior in him
and he wouldn't hurt anyone."

I'LL TRY.

Did she read books? Romantic novels, maybe?

Well, it was a common enough story line.

So all day she presided over the rehabilitation of the
"houseboat," a cheerfully lemon-colored pavilion on a flat
barge, floating by a dilapidated pier on a very small lake,
maybe an hour's walk into the forest. Lots of privacy.

I don't know where she recruited her help, but swarms
of laborers descended upon the site and turned it into a
nineteen-thirties Hollywood love nest. 'Nora herself added
the final touch by spraying the chamber inside with what
must have been very strong perfume.

Then she wandered around it, playing the Lenrau theme
and the B'Mella theme in whimsical, mischievous, lascivious, and finally profoundly serious combinations.

Next she boarded a red-and-white-striped skiff which
was parked on the tiny beach and poled it out into the lake.
Reaching into the hull she produced a large, floating lamp,
lit it by flicking a switch and carefully cast it into the water
like a young nun replacing a sanctuary lamp. She piped
another tune, faintly comic, giggled, and tossing off her
gown dove into the water (wearing this time her peppermint-candy bikini).

She climbed back in the boat, almost overturning it,
and still giggling, poled back to the shore.

Then, slipping the gown over pasted-down blond hair,
she knelt down in solemn respect and sounded my theme
in peremptory tones—a monarch summoning a servant.

"Please, Lord Our God, *please* help them. I love them
both so much. They're dear, sweet people. It's probably the

only chance they'll ever have to be happy. I *do so* want them to be happy. What else is a silly little ilel like me for except to make people happy? I'm sorry if I told you off this morning. It was just that you wouldn't come when I played your theme. Anyway, you know what's best and I don't. So it's really all up to you. If you don't want it to work out, I accept that. But *please, please* want it so they can be happy."

She scrambled to her feet and rushed off to the little chariot she sometimes used. On the chariot, reins in hand, after patting the horse creature and cooing to him how nice he was, she blew my tune again.

"Please!"

I wonder how good the Other Person is at resisting such appealing little connivers.

As the sun—or was it two suns? I never was quite sure—sank behind the mountains I ordered the machine to scan for trouble:

SEARCH FOR UNREST.

It was a bad night with hints that the others would get worse. Little groups of warriors were strolling about singing marching songs and telling stories about the great warrior barons of the past. Clergy were scurrying about in their caves (where they always seemed to meet) plotting devious tricks and talking about whose back would be the target for the next knife. My friends the mad scientists were messing with some new concoction, this time in a tent near Lenrau's pavilion. Kaila and Malvau were getting themselves quietly drunk, most unusual behavior for both of them, at the latter's pavilion, while N'Rasia kept a disapproving distance.

The center was not holding. Neither was everything else.

OK, imp child. You win.

My first visit was to the woman in the case. Somehow

I thought she would be the more difficult of the two. No point in even trying with Lenrau if B'Mella was not interested.

She had finished up a painting and thrown aside her brown smock, and was testing the water in her private bath.

HEY, HAVEN'T YOU FORGOTTEN SOMETHING?

She glared at me. "You don't listen to my prayers anymore."

I pressed her key, typed in PRAY and held down the REPEAT button. Reluctantly she knelt down and buried her face in her hands. "I'm so sorry, forgive me, forgive me, forgive me."

You're so beautiful, how could I do anything else?

"I don't know what to do," she pleaded.

YOU DO TOO.

"I won't do it." She jumped up.

WHY NOT?

"I am afraid. Two good men have already died. I do not want to lose this one too."

YOU CAN'T SPEND THE REST OF YOUR LIFE LOCKED IN YOUR CHAMBER.

"I wish I were dead."

Worthless chitchat. She did not.

It was, I told myself, only a story, a game, Nathan's game. Besides, clever little Ranora saw the same ending.

SEDUCE DUKE. I told the keyboard.

"No!" she screamed. "I hate him."

I held down the REPEAT button.

She jumped from her knees, threw off her undergarments and jumped into the bath. I've often thought since then that if she had been serious in her resistance, she would have turned on the cold water.

She didn't.

I kept my finger on the REPEAT button.

She looked up at me, appealing for escape.

"You don't mean it."

No more chitchat.

"It might be interesting." She smiled faintly. "I suppose I could still do that sort of thing."

I didn't take my finger off the key.

"It's been so long." She reached for a vial of what was probably some sort of bath scent and emptied it into her pool.

"He is quite handsome."

Tell me about it.

"You insist?"

I wasn't going to play that game either.

"How?"

Oh come on.

"Where?"

HOUSEBOAT IN WOODS.

She nodded soberly. "It's the only sensible strategy. The worst that can happen is that we both die. We will die anyway if there is another war. A night of warmth together . . . all right."

She prepared herself very carefully. As in all matters, when B'Mella made up her mind she proceeded ruthlessly.

After the ointment and scent were appropriately distributed, her long hair brushed so it glowed, and her face converted to a work of art, she searched among her clothes and removed a short brown tunic, mostly transparent, considered it carefully, held it up to the light, nodded, and pulled the gown over her head. Then she slipped a knife into the belt of her undergarment, and robed herself over the tunic with a brilliantly colorful rosy garment more like a shawl than a coat—what your local Duchess wears when she goes walking in the woods of an evening.

She knelt again and said a short prayer. "Help me to be brave and to please him."

Strange sort of request, but sure, I'll try. It's mostly up to you now. I've unleashed the energies available to me.

She pushed aside the screens which created her room—walls were portable and easily changeable in their pavilions, rather like those in Japanese homes—and slipped into the night.

Then she crept back into her chamber, removed a vial from the table next to her couch, and doused herself with more scent.

Vain little chit.

The Duke was already asleep, much I daresay to Ranora's fury, when I keyed into his chamber.

Direct method with the male. GO TO HOUSEBOAT ON LAKE IN THE WOOD AND MAKE LOVE TO DUCHESS.

He stirred in his sleep, restless with the sexual desire I was activating.

I pressed the REPEAT key down and held it.

He sat up, rubbed his face in his hands, and tried to decide whether he was awake or asleep.

It was a warm night in spring turning to summer. The Lord Lenrau had not made love to a woman in a long time. He probably thought that sexual desire had left him forever. Now, suddenly and without warning, he was on fire with passion.

"Why?" he asked sleepily.

WHY NOT?

"Why not, indeed? It would be good to be between her thighs—that little imp said that once, didn't she?"

I didn't have all day. So I changed the instruction to LOVE DUCHESS and held the REPEAT key again.

"She is most lovable. That night of the Two Moon Meal,

I almost asked her if she would sleep with me and bring us all peace. I think she would have."

Damn right.

"Life is short." He stood up and stretched. "She is beautiful, and I need a woman. All simple enough."

LOVE HER.

"I will try."

His preparations were even more elaborately vain than hers, short golden tunic for him, with a crimson robe—and lots of scent. No facial makeup but lots of time in arranging the hair properly.

All right, nothing wrong with making it solemn high.

He strapped a belt around his waist, searched for his most impressive jeweled sword, and strode forth into the night, his woman to win.

Outside, he looked up at the string of moons across the sky, paused, and knelt, looking up at me. "May I be gentle and cherish her and bring her joy and pleasure."

Not bad, fella, I'm on your side. If you hurt her, I'll zap you, and my machine and I are pretty good at zapping these days.

They both knew what was happening and accepted it, a danger, a thrill, an opportunity. I loved them both. Flawed, arrogant, stupid, they still had courage and flair.

And curiosity.

My grace maybe kicked some of the hormones in their bodies into motion, but only to push them in a direction they both wanted to go anyway.

That's what I told myself later when it all seemed to fall apart.

Why didn't I make them leave their weapons home?

Well, they were warriors and warriors carry weapons. Moreover, it was not perfectly safe that deep in the woods at night, not with all the weirdos I'd observed earlier. Finally, I was too dumb to realize that in that culture, which I knew pretty well by now, a weapon can be dangerous on a night of love.

11 The Feast of the Three Moons

Humming Lenrau's theme, B'Mella arrived at the shore of the tiny jewel of a lake. She strolled in, found a lantern, flicked it on, and glanced around in astonishment.

"That little demon." She laughed. "Everything ready for a night of love. A bit too much scent, but how could a child know that...she will be my ilel now, too." A happy laugh.

She cast off her shawl, considered herself in the mirror, and nodded approvingly, a lovely erotic invitation on a spring night. She reached under her brief gown, removed her vicious little dagger, and placed it on the window flap. Then she donned the shawl again, making herself look fragile and defenseless. No doubt just then she was both, and despite her self-satisfaction with her physical attractiveness, scared stiff.

She looked out of the window, admiring the glow of the multiple moons—puny little rocks by the standard of our moon—on the glassy lake, resumed her humming of Lenrau's theme, and drummed her fingers impatiently on the fabric of the houseboat.

She frowned. If he didn't show up, he would be in serious

danger. I was playing with fire, taking outrageous chances in my naïve attempt to be Cupid in this hate-filled world.

The door panel was pushed aside, and Lenrau entered, resplendent in red and gold. Both of them hesitated, as though they were astonished at each other's presence.

"What evil are you about now, foul-smelling whore?"

"This is my land. What are *you* doing here?" she demanded fiercely. "Seeking another woman to ravage like poor N'Rasia?" She reached for her dagger. "I will be a less easy victim."

What the hell.

She charged at him like a safety blitz for the Chicago Bears, head down, dagger thrust in front of her.

He dodged away from her charge, barely escaping the thrust of the deadly blade, and swung his sword with a mighty sweep which, if she had not fallen away, would have taken off her lovely head in a fraction of a second.

I came to my senses.

STOP THIS NONSENSE, I demanded.

They paid no attention.

She jumped up, ducked under his second swing, and thrust the knife at his chest, knocking the sword out of his hand with her arm as she charged him. He twisted away at the last moment, pulled her to the floor, and bent her knife hand back so that the point of the blade was at her throat. Slowly he shoved it down so that it touched her skin. She twisted and squirmed, but he was too strong for her.

I was so surprised by the quickness and skill of their hand-to-hand combat that I acted like a spectator at a film instead of the author of a story. Only at the very last minute did I type in STOP IT, YOU CLOWN.

The point of the blade still bending the surface of her flesh, he hesitated. She continued to fight, pushing, clawing, kicking, digging her knees in search for a weakness in his body. Despair glowed darkly in her eyes. She knew death would claim her almost at once. Yet she would cling to life till the bitter end.

LOVE HER, I insisted, DON'T HURT HER.

He forced her to submission not with the dagger point but with his kisses—quick, tender brushings of his lips against her face, her throat, her shoulders, and then repeatedly her lips.

She abandoned her resistance. Her body became passive, her eyes softened, her mouth slipped open.

"You're going to rape me before you kill me?" she gasped.

"Are these the kisses of a rapist?"

She considered that and actually smiled at him.

"No, Lord Lenrau, they are the kisses of a skilled and sensitive lover. If such a lover wishes to keep me immobilized for his pleasure, I am his for whatever he wishes."

Wow.

He tossed the knife away, untangled himself, helped her to her feet, and laughed loudly. "I prefer mobile women, well, most of the time." Then he recovered the dagger, bowed, and presented it to her, handle first, an obvious ritual gesture of peace.

Gasping for breath, she accepted the dagger, bowed to him, and placed the knife back on the window flap. "Why did we do that?" She clutched her hands together at her belly. "I might have killed you."

"We might have killed each other," he said gravely, taking her hand and conducting her to a couch.

"I didn't want to kill you. I don't want to kill anyone. Yet as soon as I saw you, I attacked you. Why?"

"Perhaps we are both afraid. Perhaps we have been trained all our lives to respond to fear by attacking." He kissed her hand. "I would cut off my arm rather than bruise your flesh. I regret I stole so many kisses at knife point."

"I do not begrudge you what you took." She smiled.

"You are a wonder, B'Mella." He kissed her hand again. "When you say the right thing, you say it brilliantly."

"Sometimes rather later than I should."

We were really moving right along. I relaxed. What a mistake.

He picked up his sword and placed it next to her knife. "For most of my life I have dreamed of meeting my enemy and speaking with her. Now I almost kill her before we can talk."

See, I wasn't manipulating them completely.

"Talk," she said curtly, her body tensing with fear. "If that's what you want."

You little bitch.

"You are not a foul-smelling whore." He bowed again, a good beginning. "But you are a little fool for risking your life in the forest alone on a sacred night as this."

Sacred? No one had told me that. I made a note in my head. Better manual.

"The Lord Our God told me to come to the forest. If you were not an infidel and a blasphemer and a coward and a weakling and no man, you would not permit a mere woman to deprive you of the might of your sword. No wonder you have no children."

So they shouted insults at one another, mean nasty words, which were more than ritual but less than completely felt, a little more colorful and dramatic than the hurtful exchange between a man and woman in our society who are frightened by and attracted to one another, but not sufficiently interesting to bore you with it. I instructed the game to make them BE NICE TO EACH OTHER; frantically it flashed, EXECUTING, EXECUTING.

Both the program and I were wasting our time.

Neither the reality nor the intractability of my hero

and heroine surprised me. This was, after all, the *denoue-ment* of my story. There were bound to be conflicts and setbacks. That's what stories were about. Sure, they were up there on the screen in gorgeous (especially B'Mella) color, but in the heat of literary creation, you hardly notice that.

Like characters in my novels, they accepted my com-mands when it suited them to do so. No, I must be a little more precise than that. I could force them to do what they half wanted but were afraid to do. I could push them over the line which they otherwise would not cross. (Maybe this is all that grace ever does.)

For the first time in the whole game, I was hit over the head by a terrible truth. I was responsible for these people, but I didn't have the power to make them do what they should do. In a story I could force my characters at this point to love each other, no matter how great their terror of intimacy and no matter how strong their habits of re-sisting it with conflict.

Now, despite my responsibility, I had less power than I would in a novel. My hero and heroine were not listening to me.

STOP THIS NONSENSE, I told them again.

Exhausted and breathless, they paused, which they probably would have done in a few moments anyway. See what I mean by responsibility without sufficient power?

BE NICE, I ordered again.

"You know what my Ranora would say?" He chuckled and relaxed into one of the form-fitting chairs.

"That little witch who prepared this place for a tryst and has bewitched both of us." She chuckled. "Is it a tryst we've been having?"

"Intermittently."

They laughed together. He reached across the space

that separated them and took her hand. She gave it to him elegantly.

"I would rather a tryst than a battle to the death."

"A kiss better than a dagger?"

"When it is your kiss and my dagger."

The woman had the gift of Blarney when she chose to use it.

"I have not kissed a woman in a long time."

"And?"

"If I could, I would spend the rest of my life kissing you."

He wasn't bad either when he got wound up.

"An interesting prospect..." She folded her hands demurely on her lap. "What would the demon child, may the Lord Our God protect her, say about this mixture of tryst and battle?"

He rubbed his chin thoughtfully. "She would say that we are afraid to know each other."

"She sees in me goodness I do not possess." She removed her hand from his, but with a lingering promise, and sat gracefully on the edge of a couch, not too distant but not too close either. "She is charming, but a little unnerving."

"If there were peace she would spend much of her time with you. She might even become your ilel instead of mine."

"I would not take her from you." She flared up, then relaxed. "She could unnerve both of us with little difficulty."

"Do not say that the goodness she sees is not there, 'Ella. I see it too."

Come on, idiots, there are better things to talk about than a mystical adolescent imp.

I didn't mess with them. Characters operate in their own good time.

"It cannot be. Yet they are wise creatures, are they not? Strange, unnerving, of the Lord Our God."

He cocked a skeptical eye. "Whose God?"

I hit her function key. ONLY ONE GOD.

"Come now, Lord Lenrau," she sniffed, her back rigid, "even such a degenerate as you knows there is but one Lord Our God."

Lenrau rose slowly from his chair, as if someone had kicked him in the rear end. "Are you sure of that?" he demanded somberly, towering over her.

"I . . . I don't know." She was flustered, indeed frightened about what she had said. "I never . . . thought of it that way before."

"We pray to the same one every night?"

"I am not unaware of the implications of what I said." She turned away from his gaze.

HE'S NOT A DEGENERATE, YOU LITTLE FOOL, I whispered in her ear.

"And I am sorry I called you a degenerate just then."

"Only the last time and not the previous times?" Finger boldly on her chin, he turned her head in his direction, and held it there.

"That was different," she said primly. "I am not a foul-smelling whore and you are not a degenerate. Would your little Ranora approve? Why are you staring at me that way?"

"Why are you trying to escape my gaze?" He sounded hurt. "Why do you twist to escape my hand? Do you find me so repellent that you cannot look at me?"

"Not repellent." She lowered her eyes. "I enjoyed your kisses. You know that."

"What, then?" Harshly he tilted her head up so she had to look at him.

I would learn in time that B'Mella had a streak of recklessness in her that surprised, delighted, and frightened those who came under her spell.

"Not degenerate." She grinned.

"What, then?" This time he shouted.

"Terrifying."

"I did not hurt you when I could. Why are you terrified?" He released her chin, discouraged and rejected. "I only kissed you and, woman, very chastely compared to what I wanted to do."

"Your terrible blue eyes bore into me. They take away my clothes, all my protection, everything in which I can hide. Half of me wants to escape from you as fast as I can run." She took a very deep breath. "The other half wants to surrender to you totally, and let you kiss me the way you wanted to. Forever."

The shameless hussy. Shameless and transparent.

He muffed it as I was sure he would. "I was thinking," his index finger touched her cheek, "how unsatisfactory it is for one so beautiful to be an enemy."

She shoved his hand away. "I will not be the object of your lust."

"Only admiration," he sighed, returning to his chair. "Cannot one admire a beautiful woman without lusting for her?"

"No," she said promptly.

"We both have been celibate too long, Lady B'Mella," he said sadly.

"Doubtless. Does the imp child tell you that too?"

"Every day. She can be very blunt and detailed." He drifted off into one of his mystical trances.

You dummy, she offered herself to you a few minutes ago and you let the offer slip right by.

Silence. SAY SOMETHING, I told her. HE'S COME MORE THAN HALFWAY.

"I suppose you think our lust can bring peace?" The words were snide, but the tone of her voice was tentative, vulnerable—the Duchess with whom I had fallen in love.

"You experience it too?" he sneered.

You damn idiot.

"You know that we both came here," she rose, crossed to him, and knelt at his side, "because the Lord Our God wants there to be peace, and our bodies are the bridge on which the angels of peace can cross."

So they had angels.

She was a quick worker, all right. I didn't have to tell her to do that. Poor Lenrau was terrified, as any man would be under the circumstances.

"You would give your body to a degenerate?"

She took his hands into hers and kissed them reverently. "I *said* you weren't a degenerate. It was your idea that we had both had too much celibacy."

"It was." He encircled her shoulders with his arms. "I don't think I could ever have too much of you."

It was a mild compliment, not great maybe, but a step in the right direction. Unfortunately it scared her. She pulled away from him and scrambled to her feet.

"You can think only of using me for your perverted pleasures," she wailed. "You care not for peace or for the will of the Lord Our God."

"You're a recent convert to the cause of peace," he sneered back. "And everyone knows that you prefer the bodies of women to those of men."

A new charge. STOP THAT! I demanded, quite in vain.

"And you the bodies of animals." She grabbed her knife, stuck it in the cord of her gown, and reached for her shawl.

"You tried to seduce me," he slumped into his chair, "to win on the bed what you could not win on the field of battle."

STOP THIS AT ONCE, I told them. They paid no attention to me.

"You would be worthless in bed." She strode briskly towards the door. "And *you* tried to seduce *me*."

"I did not kneel before you with brown eyes soft with desire." He pulled himself out of his chair and reached for his sword.

DON'T LET HER GO, I keyed into the game.

"'Ella." The word was twisted from his unwilling lip.

"What?" She turned on her heel at the door, a haughty victor in the war of words.

"Nothing," he groaned, admitting his defeat.

COME ON, YOU LITTLE BITCH.

Either she or the parser overinterpreted my instruction. She smiled lightly, considered for a moment, flipped the cloak on the floor, and, reaching behind her head, opened the fastening on her tunic. "We both know, 'Rau, what is to be done." She shrugged out of the sleeves, "We both are curious, we both need each other at least at this moment. Let us not be fools."

The gown fell to the floor. She stepped out of it, calm and self-possessed, lovely but not yet lascivious, available, oh yes, overwhelmingly, achingly available, but not insisting. The poor guy looked at her in astonishment and dismay, a man blinded by the sun coming out early and without warning from an eclipse.

DON'T BLOW IT, I demanded.

I DO NOT KNOW BLOW IT.

The damn PC was turning priggish at the wrong time.

MISS THIS GLORIOUS OPPORTUNITY.

"You are," he rubbed his chin slowly again, "the most beautiful sight in all the world. Do not, wonderful 'Ella, confuse my slowness with anything more than a mixture of fear and admiration." He rose unsteadily. "I'm dazzled by the light of many suns. It's still night, but the dawn has come early."

Well, Shakespeare did it a little more elegantly, but not under such circumstances.

She laughed, amused, confident, successful. "You are definitely not a degenerate, noble Duke. But I grow cold without my garment."

The shameless, dirty thing, as the Irish would say admiringly.

He paused in front of her, his hand on one of the straps on her undergarment. "This is the way you pray to the Lord Our God?"

"Yes." She was now frightened, but pleasantly so.

"He must be very pleased when it comes your prayer time each night."

Well, we'll stop it there. As I said before, their passion was wanton, violent, abandoned, the fusing of two tempestuous firestorms. They were not harsh or cruel to each other. It might have been easier to watch if they were. Rather they were both generous and gentle, more concerned about the other than the self, skilled with each other without effort or practice and hence even more majestic in their combined explosion. It was not the pretty sex of film lovers but the awesome, frightening convulsion of two wildly galloping but elegant animals. Watching them was not like viewing an X-rated tape but rather like participating in a powerful liturgy. I wondered why there was not the music of pipe organ, trumpets, and drums in the background.

Then I realized that I was violating their privacy. I had no right to watch their terrifying liturgy. I was not, perhaps, being prurient, but I was still acting like a voyeur.

I pushed the SUSPEND function key. My two lovers, soaring up the mountain of ecstasy, were left to themselves.

Does God draw the curtain on human lovers, I wondered as I stared at the empty screen, weary, drained, exhausted as though I had flown across the ocean in a continuous thunderstorm.

And someone, Nathan, damn him, had cast me in the role of heaven.

I sat there in my gray "secondary work station" (decorator's term) chair and trembled as though I had just escaped from a near-fatal auto accident. I didn't want to be God for anyone, much less for these two attractive, passionate, thoroughly mixed-up human beings.

It wasn't fair to them, and it wasn't fair to me.

But I was hooked. So I peeked.

I reactivated the game. Two spent human bodies were heaped on one another, linked, blended, meshed, intertwined, limbs deployed at random crooked angles in a pattern which had the wild beauty of desert rocks washed by a sudden rainstorm. Just as their passion had been scary, so now their contentment and peace revealed what a wildly dangerous creature the human animal is.

Well, they'll all live happily ever after, I told myself as I reached for the END GAME key.

I hesitated. Was this a short story or a novella or a full-length novel? Was it really over? Ought not I now withdraw from the game and leave my creatures to the rest of their lives?

What would have happened to them if I had left them alone?

I'll never know, will I? Like any God I couldn't leave my creatures alone. I was curious about them, I had fallen in love with them. I told myself that they needed me. I wondered whether they would have children, whether they could bring their two countries together in peace, how much they would fight, what the wondrous Ranora would think now that our joint plot had come true.

No one ever wants to give up one's creatures.

So I pushed the SUSPEND GAME key, left all the electronic components "on," and stumbled to my bed and a sleep of exhausted oblivion.

After skiing the next morning I raced up the stairs. I hesitated for a moment and then, like the proverbial cat, succumbed to curiosity and pushed the RENEW GAME function key.

We were back in the houseboat and the young lovers were awake, only they were not so young, and fighting again.

You see what I mean about the time problem; the game was now moving more slowly than real time. Last night I had covered a day of their time, but their night had gone more slowly than mine. Later Nathan would assure me that the game had its own self-corrective time sequence mechanism built into its compiler. It sounded suspicious to me, but I didn't know enough about the programming to deny it. I suspect that the game somehow knew enough to slow down or speed up so that it was ready for me when I joined it. Narrative timing is what an author would call it.

Anyway, though they were physically glowing and complacent, my hero and heroine were shouting at each other again. Lenrau, without a stitch on him, was striding around the room and delivering himself of a battle oration. A quilt held at her jaw, B'Mella lolled on the couch, half angry and half bemused. She followed his movements with fascinated eyes, more interested, it seemed, in the man's body than his words. Small wonder. Reenergized by sex, Lenrau had lost his hangdog manner and had become a very attractive male—solid, compact, fair skinned, with curly blond hair, a boyish face, not a Michelangelo David perhaps, but not a bad male model either.

She didn't need me to help her say the right thing. "You are a very impressive naked orator, mighty Lord Lenrau."

"I am demanding justice for my people and you think

of lust." He whipped around and, hands on bare hips, glared at her furiously.

"I was not alive at the battle of the Broken Tree and neither were you," she said mildly, perhaps wanting to be angry, but not up to it yet physiologically. "We must forget the past."

"I will not forget the innocent blood of my people. You will not seduce me into such oblivion, you man-hungry whore."

Well, at least, he hadn't said "foul-smelling." Still, as you can imagine, that set her off. They traded charges of brutality, injustice, murder (all for crimes at least a generation in the past), and of sexual perversity and exploitation in the last couple of hours. Sunlight was streaming through the tiny window by now, illuminating the tangled disarray of the sheets on their couch and the lines of hard hatred on their handsome faces. Somehow, they had managed to change positions in the course of their argument, and also to exchange rhetoric.

Draped in the quilt, she was striding about the room, screeching at the top of her voice, and he was slumped on the side of the couch, dejected and beaten, all the joy of sexual triumph drained from him, a pathetic sad sack once again.

"I am leaving this den of degeneracy," she announced. "Your plot has failed and you will pay in battle for what you have done to me this night." She jerked the coverlet around her body and opened the door.

I figured my experiment of letting them go their own way had lasted long enough.

BE NICE TO DUKE, I ordered after her function key.

She stopped in the open doorway, illumined by the harsh glare of the sunlight, breathing heavily, her naked shoulders heaving up and down. "You are a foul degenerate pig."

"You don't sound as though you mean that," he sighed as from a great distance, a man departing for another planet. "Try it again, a little more hatred."

I repeated my instruction. She didn't budge an inch. But she didn't leave either. Her poor exhausted body sagged, weary now not from a night of romping but from a fierce struggle against grace.

STOP RESISTING GRACE. I told her.

I DO NOT KNOW GRACE, the damn fool PC responded righteously.

GOD'S SAVING AND DIRECTING LOVE, I told it with full theological accuracy.

WHY DIDN'T YOU SAY SO?

EXECUTE, I told it furiously.

EXECUTING, EXECUTING, it snarled back at me.

"You are not without," she forced the words out grudgingly like a confession of terrible guilt, "certain more than adequate skills as a lover. I said that last night, of course, many times. It does bear repeating, however."

The bitch still wouldn't turn to face him.

"I would not have believed," he said with pained sadness, "that love with any woman could have been so sweet."

But he was Harry Hangdog, king of the wimps again. Ranora, witch child, where are you when we need you?

She slumped as though he had put his sword through her back. "I do not want to lose you, 'Rau." She turned slowly, shyly to face him. "I will not lose you."

He glanced up, trying to come back from his far planet. "I don't want to lose you either, magic 'Ella." He sighed. "I will die without you."

That's right, fellow, you got it. Appeal to their maternal instincts and they'll give in every time.

"I doubt that," she grinned and tossed aside her quilt with the dramatic gesture of which she was a master, "but if our people want peace from the bridge of our bodies, that is good. If they don't, I still want you."

I doubt that there is a man in the world, her world or our world, who could resist that ploy, especially carried out in the luminosity of the early morning sunlight. Certainly not our 'Rau.

"You argue persuasively." He smiled as he walked towards her. "Very persuasively."

She stiffened, suddenly frightened again. Oh, damn, don't blow it now.

DO NOT RESIST THE LORD OUR GOD, I ordered her.

She sagged against the wall, thin shoulder blades touching it, head on her chest, body touchingly fragile and yielding. "Don't ever let me run away, my beloved," she begged him.

A plea which, considering what would happen later, was ironic indeed.

He tilted her head upwards so he could look into her eyes. "We both fear that our peoples will not want this peace for which we have become a bridge. I tell you, 'Ella, they will rejoice in it."

She nodded, trying again to escape his fierce gaze and not succeeding. "They will both say that their ruler seduced the other, and thus both will claim victory."

He swept her into his arms, picked her up, and carried her back to the couch—an incredible move for Sammy Sad Sack. "And," he laughed, "they'll both be right."

I left them to their privacy and went to the kitchen to make breakfast.

All's well that ends well, I told myself dubiously.

12 A Happy Ending for Everyone?

When I returned, teapot in hand, and reactivated the game, the Duke and the Duchess were preparing to leave their love nest and return to the world. The sun was now high in their purple sky and judging by the open window in the houseboat their hot weather had begun, a more cheery setting for announcing a marriage, but somehow that stark sunlight seemed almost as ominous as the black-gray sky which had preceded it.

Nothing as minor as weather, however, seemed to be on the minds of Lenrau and B'Mella. He was helping her into her tunic, fastening the back, arranging it on her shoulders neatly, as if he were a servant girl. She was accepting his intimate ministrations with a submissive gratitude that managed to combine blushing bride and satisfied sex kitten, roles I would not have believed her capable of performing.

Then he helped her do up her hair, with fingers that could only be described as both possessive and reverent.

"You're very kind to me," she murmured.

"Perhaps I'm only trying to delay facing our people."

"They will support us," she said confidently, touching his arm with respect. "As long as we stand together..."

"I know." He kissed her lightly. "Come, we must go forth."

"I love you," she said simply, taking his arm in her own. "I knew I would."

It was a bit much for Lenrau's sense of irony, but he only smiled wryly as he led her out into the sunlight. "May we always love each other as much as we do now."

"May it please the Lord Our God."

It was not the combined peoples that waited for them outside the hut, but Ranora, knees pulled up under her determined little chin, peppermint-candy gown pulled down to her ankles. When they emerged, she leaped to her feet, did a quick little dance of celebration, and embraced them both enthusiastically, an astonished B'Mella first.

"I know, I know, I know," she clapped her hands with delight, *"I know!"*

She pulled out her little pipe, blew a chirpy dance tune on it, and cavorted around the blushing lovers like an intoxicated elf.

"You must not wish me to be with child so soon, little Ranora," pleaded B'Mella without much conviction.

The imp girl hooted, grabbed one of them with each hand, and under the blazing sun led them in a dance which was as wild as the most raucous Irish reel but far more elegant. Fertility dance? Nothing like getting down to business.

Then they sank on the grass, panting, sweating, and laughing. The ilel jumped up, dashed into the woods, and bounded back with a huge flagon of dark red liquid and three skinny foot-high goblets. With elaborate ceremony she poured a drink for each of them. "First," she announced with sudden solemnity, "to the Lord Our God!"

They rose, composed themselves reverently, faced in my direction, bowed deeply, poured a little bit of the liquid on the ground, and then drained their goblets with a single swallow, followed by much laughter. Both Lenrau and B'Mella were well on their way to being tuned by the time the crowds of their people began to drift into the clearing, with the solemn slowness of a congregation filing into 11:15 Mass on a hot summer day.

The ilel took charge of the wedding preparations; no one was brave enough to question her right to do so, save for poor bemused Kaila, who would occasionally whisper a word of restraint into her manic little ear, a warning which would be met with hysterical giggles.

She appointed herself B'Mella's keeper and gave that poor woman no rest. They spent a whole day trying on wedding gowns. The Duchess, who for all her imperiousness seemed to be a woman of simple tastes, was willing to settle for a comparatively understated dress in red and gold. The ilel shook her head and waved a negative finger. The dressmaker brought out gown after gown to the same reaction. After a time, the Duchess, with remarkable good humor, expressed no opinions, but obediently modeled the dresses for her protector/tormenter and waited for her reaction.

Finally, a shimmering purple gown with deep silver trim earned thoughtful silence from Ranora. She bounded around the Duchess, considering the dress from every angle. Then she pulled the sleeves off B'Mella's shoulders, revealing lots of throat, arm, and chest, clapped her hands, and pointed her tiny finger in approval.

"It is too revealing." B'Mella protected her breasts with her hands.

"Just right," the child chanted. "It's just right. We'll take it, we'll take it, *we'll take it!*"

I watched my heroine closely during the wedding preparations. For a woman whose self-possession bordered on arrogance, she was remarkably docile to the wishes of both the Duke and the ilel. From imperiousness she had changed easily to contented and almost passive acceptance. Her personality was flexible, permeable, adaptable. I forgot that earlier I'd used "unstable."

We seemed well on our way to a "they all lived happily ever after" ending. Proud of my brief stint at Godding I continued to watch intermittently through that day, out of curiosity, to learn more about their culture and social structure. After all, I told myself, I was a social scientist.

I added that I was a novelist, too, and it was time to turn to the serious task of writing a real story. When I begin to look for a premise for a story ("suppose that . . ."), I often use the self-hypnotism which Erika taught me ten years ago and which started me on my way to storytelling (it has never produced anything as dumb as "suppose that a computer made you God in a cosmos down the street"). Erika claims that I am a "fabulous subject." The old suggestible kid.

Anyway I put the metronome tape on the stereo, thus making the whole house vibrate, relaxed in the gray chair by the corner windows, and stared at one of the supply of mandalas I keep handy. Sure enough, I drifted away into my own preconscious, aware of the world around me, quite capable of answering the damn telephone if it rings, but also wandering through the world of my right brain (or whatever).

I looked up and a woman in white was sitting on the maroon chair at the other side of a small coffee table. It was not Wilkie Collins's Woman in White, however, but G'Ranne. She had put aside her uniform and was wearing a white double-breasted suit with a light blue scarf at her neck, white shoes, and a white ribbon restraining her hair. I became conscious for the first time (admittedly in an altered

state) of what I had only dimly perceived before: she was
the most beautiful young woman I had ever known.

"Good afternoon," she said respectfully, in dress and
manner an able and responsible young professional woman.
"I hope I'm not disturbing you."

The disguise did not fool me. "I know who you are: Grace
O'Malley the pirate. You belong in Morgan's novel. What
are you doing in my story?"

"Do I look like a pirate?" Her teeth were perfectly even
as she smiled, indeed everything about her was perfect. Ten,
at least.

"Grace O'Malley wouldn't be a pirate if she were alive
today. She'd be a lawyer or an accountant. I repeat, why
are you in the wrong story?"

"Perhaps," she lifted her superb shoulders, "because
I've always been in your preconscious. The perfect Celtic
woman, like Nora Cronin or Ciara Kelly in your stories."

"How do you know about them?"

"It's your preconscious, not mine."

"I suppose you want me to change your role in the story
too?"

"No," she said, her vast blue eyes wide with what I
feared was admiration. "I trust you."

"Then," I demanded irritably, "what *do* you want?"

"I want to know," faint trace of heart-wrenching tears,
"why you don't love me. You're the only one I love and you
don't love me in return."

"Of course I do..." I knew I should end the trance in-
terlude and get rid of this woman. She was too gorgeous to
dismiss. And too sad.

"You never visit me when I pray. You pay no attention
to my thoughts. You give me instructions only when they're
not important. You are not pleased with my responsiveness.
You don't care about my love affair with Kaila...and it's

my first love affair. I love him because he's so much like you. You know that..."

"No," I protested weakly, "he's like John Larkin."

"John Larkin," she waved a graceful hand, "is in Brazil, you know that. He's staying at the beach house of Jorge Amado the novelist in Salvador Da Bahia. Kaila is you."

"No way."

"All my life, I have lived to serve and love you. Yet you are never pleased with me. What can I do to make you happy with me? Why don't you listen to me when I pray?"

It was a plea not a complaint, a plea from a rejected lover.

Could I say that the image of her in lingerie was too breathtaking to risk? Better not.

(Various folks in this story have asserted that I like older women and teenaged women. Now it is clear that I also have a weakness for women in their early twenties. Also in their late fifties, as far as that goes.)

"I'm afraid that your beauty and your dedication overwhelm me," I admitted. "It's not that you are not appealing. Rather, you are almost too appealing."

"You made me that way." She smiled wanly.

"Sometimes," I was trying hard, "God is overwhelmed by the appeal of the creatures he has made."

"Really?" She held out her hands in a gesture of happy delight.

"Really," I said. "After all, God is only human!"

(Now before Cardinal Josef Ratzinger and the bully boys from the Congregation for the Defense of the Faith— as the Inquisition is euphemistically called these days— come after me with their thumbscrews and their heresy charges, I want to make four points.

1. I realize that God is divine.

2. I was in an altered state of consciousness.

3. I was trying to talk my way out of a bad mess.

4. If the incarnation means anything at all, in the terms of the Council of Chalcedon, it reveals the humanity of God: the Person who is God has a human nature. Right? Right. Anyway, in this context all I meant was that God is not inhuman, in the sense of subhuman.)

"I know," she said affectionately. "God needs us."

"What?" I demanded, shocked by her heresy.

"The world is unredeemed," she said enthusiastically, "and God is in need of man to be a partner in completing, in aiding, in redeeming. Our lives are a divine need. The meaning of human existence is to satisfy the divine need for the redemption of the world."

"Rabbi Heschel..." I murmured.

"Abraham Joshua Heschel."

"How do you know about him?"

"He's in your preconscious. You've been reading John Merkle's book."

"I'm dizzy."

She laughed adoringly. "Do I really do that to you?"

"Indeed you do."

"Then you do love me!" She jumped up as though she were about to kiss me. Alas, she was much too respectful.

The Duke acted like a mystic. This incredibly beautiful young woman was one, a God-haunted creature of light. No, not haunted as much as haunting.

"That's all I wanted to know." She was glowing radiantly. "Now I don't mind not being able to have Lenrau or Kaila. If it is for my happiness you will send me someone else. Oh, I love you so much...!"

"Lenrau or Kaila?"

"Of course, I loved them both. You must know that. But the Duke must marry the Duchess so that there will be peace, and Kaila is obsessed with that wonderful little imp. I am not jealous. No one can take you away from me."

Oh, God, I thought.

Fortunately for me, the phone rang and I returned, however reluctantly, to ordinary consciousness.

I never did figure out how she slipped from Morgan's novel to mine.

I went back to the game, wondering why I had not realized what she was. Had I been intimidated by her beauty?

Who, me?

The game was a welcome relief after the intensity of that glorious creature's devotion. Sometimes, after all, it is heaven to be God.

Anyway, the crops by which the country lived were slowly turning the fields white and purple, and the trees were blossoming in a rainbow outburst of delicate pastel colors. The land was preparing for the mating of the hero and the heroine—on the Feast of the Three Moons appropriately enough—by a glorious explosion of its fertile season, an explosion which seemed to impose a gentle tranquility on all those who lived in the land.

The people were masters of color and ceremony. The rituals in both cities in preparation for the marriage—which was to take place on the field where the battle had been fought, only a few days ago in my time—reminded me of the carefully choreographed ceremonies of the Vatican, as solemn as the Vatican at any rate, but somewhat more languid and with a lot more ritual bathing than the Curia would tolerate.

It seemed to me that the Duke and Duchess, together and separately, spent at least half of each day in sumptuous bathing pools while various choirs chanted slow, intoxicating hymns over them. They both were, by the way, more than adequately covered during these interludes. Their cul-

ture demanded prudery from their love in public manifes-
tations.

But the cultural norms did not prevent Ranora in her
bits of peppermint-candy fabric and string from jumping
without warning into their pools, and amid much laughter
and fighting pushing both their heads under water.

They joined in the merry fun, delighted by their sprite's
playfulness, but neither seemed to dare to dunk her saucy
little head underwater.

With the exceptions of the ritual cleansings, Lenrau
and B'Mella stayed away from each other during the week
of preparation; they were polite and distant when the rituals
brought them together, both of them, I suspected, dying of
frustration, a reaction which occasioned barely concealed
giggles from their peppermint princess ilel who seemed to
mock the solemnity of the festival with her clapping, feet-
twitching exuberance.

The two lovers did sneak off one spectacularly lovely
evening when the rose-and-gold dusk seemed to go on forever. They had emerged from the third ritual bath of the
day, this one in open air and beginning just at sunset, and
stood at the edge of the pool, modestly cowering in vast
towels while their attendants and the choirs packed in for
the ceremony.

"You smell like all the flowers of spring," 'Rau said
cautiously.

She turned to him, dreamy-eyed. "You are so beautiful
that my eyes dull all my other senses."

"And I was once told that I looked at you with lust!"

"It is all right when a woman does it." Giggle. "When
we are properly mated I want to paint you totally naked."

He bowed his head in mild embarrassment. "It is flat-
tering to be looked at so greedily by a woman...but also
...disconcerting."

"I will disconcert you forever." She looked around. "If only we could talk alone, away from all these people ... and from that wondrous little imp."

"Now they will not leave us alone, in a few days they will isolate us. It is absurd ..."

"In my painting chamber in an hour?"

"With my clothes off?"

"Not *now* for that. Later."

Their tryst was limited to kisses of the sort with which 'Rau first deprived her of her dagger. There was, despite the pretext for the meeting, very little talk.

"My dearest one, let us pray to the Lord Our God that our love never turn cold."

"And that when it does it will only be so that it may become even warmer."

A prudent and discreet prayer, in which she joined fervently.

He touched her breasts beneath her gown. She did not push his hands away. "Be patient with me, my woman, I am not always the person you think I am."

She sighed with deep satisfaction. "The more I know who you are the more I will love you."

Their week of wedding preparations lasted my Monday afternoon and evening. There wasn't much for me to do as my day wore on, because the ordinary dynamics of human love required little intervention from the Lord Our God, whether it be the Other Person or the Player of Nathan's God Game.

I did wonder if the Other Person approved of the way I was playing the game. Since She had pushed me stumbling and bumbling, first into the storyteller role and then into the port between two cosmoi, if She were not fully satisfied with my work, that was Her problem.

You do your best, they told us in the seminary, and you leave the rest to God.

Nonetheless I decided to look around to see what my various other creatures were doing.

Malvau and N'Rasia were sleeping next to each other at as far a distance from each other as they could while still being on the same bed. As the love in the main plot waxed, their love had waned. What would 'Rau and 'Ella be like in fifteen years?

> Marriage is but keeping house,
> Sharing food and company
> What has this to do with love
> Of the body's beauty
> If love means affection, I
> love old trees, hats, coats and things
> Anything that's been with me
> In my daily sufferings.
> That is how one loves a wife
> There's a human interest too
> And a pity for the days
> We so soon live through
> What has this to do with love
> The anguish and the sharp despair
> The madness roving in the blood
> Because a girl or hill is fair
> I have stared upon a dawn
> And trembled like a man in love
> And in Love I was, and I
> Could not speak and could not move.

Well, Walter James Turner was surely right, but only about one phase in the cycle. As another poet, Roger Staubach, put it in response to yet a third poet, one Broadway

Joe Namath, the trick is to fall in love over and over again with the same woman.

That, it seemed to me, was a modest enough hope for my hero and heroine, even if the chances seemed minuscule for yet another rebirth in love for the characters in what had become, despite my better judgment, the principal subplot.

As for the other subplot, G'Ranne was gracefully disentangling herself from Kaila, both physically and psychologically, not displeased with the fire they had created between each other and certainly unwilling to hurt him, but well aware that there was no future for them together.

She was, I concluded, a classy broad, and it was a shame that the constraints of my story didn't permit me to know her better. That one, at any rate, would never appear with complaints in my dreams.

ACCESS MAD SCIENTISTS.

YOU MEAN THE THREE STOOGES?

EXECUTE.

I needed none of the 286's wisecracks at the moment.

Larry, Curly, and Moe were huddled over a small package in a room in one of the distant corners of Lenrau's pavilion.

"It will," said Larry, "fit nicely under the altar."

Curly: "And destroy them both at the height of the ceremony."

Moe: "The climax of their marriage."

They laughed like certified lunatics.

Larry: "It will destroy all of the priests."

Curly: "And most of the people."

Moe: "We will rule forever."

Right. A thousand-year reich.

ZAP MECHANISM.

EXECUTING.

It didn't even ask for details this time.

The black box started to steam and glow and spin, this time like a Fourth of July Roman candle. The Three Stooges jumped out of the chamber and began to run.

There was a derisive "pfft" sound. They hesitated, crept back to the door, and cautiously peered in. Where their precious black box had been, there was only a pool of liquid.

"Hot," said one, touching it.

"Water," mumbled another, tasting it.

"Maybe we ought to quit and find ourselves some women, like the Duke has done."

"And not skinny wenches like her either."

So they closed up shop, temporarily.

Not so elsewhere.

Access Admiral.

The priests were busily merging bureaucracies. Similar activity was happening all over the land as the two duchies, with what I thought was astonishing ease, worked out their combination into one. Both the Cardinal and the Admiral presided over the preliminary festivities of the marriage with éclat and enthusiasm. I did not trust either of them for a moment, however.

The Admiral was rushing down a forest path by himself, late it would seem for a conspiratorial meeting.

He would be real late. While I was watching and before I could lift a finger, a large shape loomed out of the night, raced behind him, and buried a knife in his back. The loquacious Admiral uttered not a word in protest.

Stylo curiae.

The next morning there was a more private ritual bathing, preceded this time by anointing with a substance which, to judge from B'Mella's facial expression, was foul smelling.

In the pond (the ceremony was outside in a lake with only one choir chanting away in the background) she giggled and whispered to her love, "Now I am a foul-smelling whore."

"You are not a whore," he replied gallantly, "and there is only one smell of yours I know, and that I love."

"Dear sweet man…" Hesitation, deep breath, then a rush of words. "Where do you go when you go away, 'Rau?"

Reassuringly she grabbed his arm, rather, I thought, to the displeasure of the clerics who were presiding over the ceremony.

"You have noticed?"

"How could I help but notice? I am not angry, only curious."

"I don't know." He sighed and patted her clinging fingers. "It is a wonderful land of colors and lights and peace and love. I…I do not think it interferes with what I must do in this land. If you wish me to stop…"

"There is a woman there."

"Yes, but I do not see her face closely."

"What is she like?"

"I draw closer to her each time…now she seems tall and slender and dark with breasts like mountain shadows at sunset."

"Silly." She slipped her hand up and down his forearm.

"It is true," he insisted. "I have wondered for years who she is, and now I know that she is you."

Well, that will do for an explanation, but how do you live with a mystic who drifts away in search of you in another world when you're right next to him?

Was it our cosmos into which the Duke drifted, or another one with a cognate, perhaps, of B'Mella? Was he involved in another story there? Or had he perhaps become a participant in a distant cognate of Nathan's God Game?

The premarital festival went on. For a festival it was. The Duke and the Duchess were right: everyone except the sullen priests and wizards and viziers seemed overjoyed that love was replacing war. It all seemed too good to be true.

It was.

Why was I still playing the game since it looked like the required happy ending? Does not a good storyteller quit while he's ahead?

As a social scientist I was curious about the culture of this world. But that was a minor motive. Truth is that I was hooked on my characters, an occupational hazard of a storyteller/God. I was a little less sanguine about the outcome than was my friend and ally, the ilel Ranora. After all, the Duke and the Duchess both had been married before. His spouse had died of battle wounds, as had both B'Mella's husbands. The casualty rate in the warrior class to which both the Duke and the Duchess belonged must have been terribly high. What was important, however, was that neither had produced children, a subject which caused some anxious whispering, even among such reasonable men as Linco and Kaila.

"Don't worry about *that*," the ilel announced in one of her happy chariot rides between the two camps on the day before the wedding—the chariot pulled by the white animal decorated with red streamers that might have been a horse, but wasn't quite.

"We have to worry about it," her "protector" insisted. "If there is not an heir..."

In exasperation the pixie informed him, "Let's worry about getting them married first. The poor dears are so frightened that we may have to drag them to their mating couch." Then she flicked the reins and her red-and-white-striped chariot sped off like a teenager's convertible buzzing Lakeview Avenue.

The medical technology of their world (I don't use planet

because I think it is somehow our planet) was like most everything else, subtly different from ours. They had medications which seemed to be like our antibiotics and fairly elaborate inoculation systems—the bride and groom were given physical exams the day before the wedding and equipped with pills and injections—and seemed to have developed methods for healing wounds and replacing limbs far more sophisticated than anything we know. But there were no x-ray machines, in fact practically no machines at all in their hospitals, if that's what you can call the pavilions where their medical people worked. Families seemed to be small to medium sized, so they probably had some kind of fertility control, though the subject was never mentioned.

I suspected that they had no notion of what to do about infertility and, except in the case of their Duke and Duchess, not much concern either. However, as the week of preparation before the wedding drew near, there was a lot of prayer being directed to the Lord Our God that the ducal couple be blessed with offspring. I figured I'd hang around until they were married and then push the TERMINATE GAME function key, appropriately F10. Whatever powers I might have among these possibly real people, curing infertility was certainly not one of them. Nathan's parser was not that clever.

Which showed how little I understood what was going on.

Anyway, I decided I'd visit the bride and groom when they said their final prayers before departing their pavilions for the midnight marriage ceremony. Yeah, midnight, with tens of thousands of people and hundreds of choristers holding hand lanterns in the middle of what a little more than a week ago had been a field of battle. Their bodies were indeed to be a bridge to peace.

Maybe.

B'Mella was strutting around her suite in a fever of ill-tempered anxiety. She had reduced her nervous bevy of servants to frequent tears. Ranora, sitting crosslegged on a stack of cushions, giggled at each new outburst. Ilels were doubtless protected by a lot of taboos, but the taboos didn't forbid looks that could kill, looks which sent the pretty little imp into new paroxysms of giggles.

Then B'Mella dismissed the lot of them. Ranora bounded across the room to help her remove her robe.

"When you marry, wicked little girl," the Duchess said affectionately, "I will perform the same service for you."

Ranora laughed merrily and, robe in hand, scampered away into an antechamber.

B'Mella knelt in front of me—the game seemed to have been arranged so that when they prayed, they faced directly into the camera, if camera it was. She sighed sadly, a Boris woman in purple-and-silver straps and lace facing a funeral instead of a wedding. Head bowed, shoulders drooping, she prayed with a voice in which one could hear the tears.

"You of all people know what a miserable and vile woman I am—arrogant, proud, ill-tempered, vindictive, moody, vicious. You must put up with me all the time. I do not know why you permit me to exist. Now this poor dear man, so sweet and gentle and loving and so easy for me to twist in knots, will have to endure my evil almost as much as you do. It would be better if you slay me this night instead of sending me to his wedding couch."

She paused as though she expected the lightning bolt.

No way, kid.

She continued to wait.

MARRY LENRAU AND LOVE HIM, I typed in.

She lifted her tear-filled eyes, smoky-brown swamps. "I do love him. That is why I fear to marry him and destroy him."

I pushed the REPEAT key.

"Very well. You know, since you know all things, how eager I am for his couch. You drive me to what I want more than I have ever wanted anything."

What the hell was I supposed to say now?

BE GRATEFUL FOR YOUR LOVE.

Sobs, near hysterics. "I am grateful, I am. But you must promise to transform me so that I will be a good wife... and mother."

NO FREE LUNCHES, I told her, getting into the swing of things now.

I DO NOT KNOW LUNCH, the dumb PC insisted.

SMALL MIDDAY MEAL.

"You always have been humorous with me." She smiled through her tears. "I understand that I must work hard. But you will help me, I know you will." She did not require an answer because she clapped her hands. "Now I must call this magic child whom you have sent to my man and me, lest she choke from holding her breath." She giggled, temporarily a child like Ranora again.

That worthy flew into the room, dashed out again, and returned with the vast purple gown, inside of which she had almost disappeared. Bustling about importantly she helped the poor Duchess attire herself for her wedding, making sure, by the way, that the gown was as low as it could be without falling off.

"Some day this will happen to you," the Duchess warned. Both young women giggled and, my eyes smarting for some reason, I cut to Lenrau's pavilion with a touch on the DUKE key.

Morale was not especially high there either. Lenrau wasn't crying, but he had buried his face in his hands and was pressing his fingers against his temples as if he were afraid his brains would tumble out of his head if he did not restrain them.

The wedding robe which Ranora had chosen for him (of course she made the choice) was stark vanilla white laced with thick threads of gold, his brief loincloth made of the same material, well matched for both the public ceremony and the private consummation. I was sure that B'Mella would dote on him.

If he showed up, that is.

That did not seem at all certain. His long silence after I wandered in, so to speak, was broken by a loud groan. "Lord Our God, this is folly."

Yeah?

"I cannot pray, even on the night of my marriage to a woman I adore. Why am I such a worthless, impractical dreamer, preoccupied by fantasies I cannot name even to myself?"

Don't ask me, fella. If your fantasies are not about her tonight, they didn't check your hormones during that physical.

"She is in my dreams, as you know. I can think of no one else since I first saw her. But the dreams are..." he moaned again "...vague and fantastical, not what a ruler should imagine. She at least will be able to rule. My dreams, my melancholy, my nightmares, the songs I hear in my head will not harm our people. But she deserves a man, not a dreamer...."

Would you believe a man who dreams?

"Release me from my promise to her. I will fail her as I have failed all the others."

No way, I typed in on the keyboard.

"I miss her every minute, but I will destroy her like the others. I am a foolish, empty dreamer and poet..."

Mystic, I observed.

He removed his face from his hands, handsome agony, and stared up at me. "That's what the ilel says, but my beloved deserves better than that."

She doesn't even know you're a poet, you geek. LOVE DUCHESS, I told him.

"I do love her," he insisted. "I can't live without her."

What was I supposed to say to that?

"I will be good in bed with her." He smiled, mildly satisfied with his masculinity.

Hooray for you, buster.

"But I am not at heart a warrior. I should not be Duke."

So that's it. Let me see. Aha: YOUR PEOPLE NEED WISDOM, NOT WAR. YOUR WOMAN NEEDS A WISE MAN, NOT A WARRIOR.

He laughed, amused, but also bitter and ironic. "I doubt that either they or she know it." He struggled to his feet, ready to go forth to meet his destiny.

TEACH THEM, I pounded out on the keyboard. What's the point in being God unless you have the last word?

"I will try," he sighed, "but I will need much help from you." He hefted the massive wedding robe over his strong solid shoulders.

I CAN'T DO WHAT YOU WON'T DO, I informed him with wonderful theological precision. BESIDES, THERE IS NOT ANOTHER MAN IN THIS WORLD WHO WOULD THINK IT AN UNHAPPY FATE TO GO TO THE DESTINY TO WHICH YOU GO TONIGHT.

He smiled, a genuinely charming, boyish smile. "For tonight, at least, it will be a pleasant fate." He hummed a song, a love song, I'm sure, as he pushed aside a screen and joined his entourage for the journey into the warm night. I supposed that he had written the song himself; where my ancestors came from, it was thought to be a great grace to have a king who was also a bard.

Despite the heat, the ceremony was impressive. They

didn't use rings, but the bride and the groom, nervous, solemn, and sweating, exchanged vows, clasping each other's right arms below the elbows, kind of like an athletic team before a game. I don't know what they said, because the ceremony, presided over with notable éclat by the beaming Linco, was in an archaic language which I could not understand, though the hymns sound something like the Old Slavonic hymns the choir used to sing in the seminary.

It was all very beautiful, but kind of ponderous, the one light touch being the inevitable Ranora, trying to keep a straight face for the occasion and quite pleased with herself in a formal version of her peppermint-candy garb—form fitting and with a décolletage almost as extreme as that she had imposed on the now misty-eyed Duchess. Her solemnity endured only to the end of the ceremony when she began to dance. She presided over the dancing throngs till sunrise, long after the bride and groom retreated to a special little pavilion erected for them by the same lake where they had first loved each other. The ilel was so busy with her dancing that she merely waved goodbye to them— with a hint of anxiety on her pert little face.

So you have your doubts too, small one.

'Rau did indeed sing for B'Mella. On the tiny beach by the side of the lake, he sang the love song he had hummed when he went forth to claim and be claimed. She did, as expected and required, melt into his arms. They went through the motions of praying to me inside their tent, two sweaty, exhausted young bodies, pretending to be devout and to beg me for help, when they had very different things on their mind.

They were timid and gentle with each other and I bade them farewell. The Other Person maybe had the right to be a voyeur, but I didn't.

In another part of the land, G'Ranne shook her head

in sad refusal to Kaila. He knew it was coming. He knelt to her in gratitude and, gallantly as always, took his leave.

And as the sun rose, N'Rasia and Malvau staged a wild fight, beating and pounding each other with manic fury. I think he had the worst of it.

Well, they can't all live happily ever after, can they?

Now you see why I didn't press the TERMINATE GAME button after the wedding ceremony. Lenrau and B'Mella were no longer two characters in a fantasy, larger than life perhaps but one-dimensional. They were flawed but appealing human beings with more awareness of their own limitations than I would have believed possible. They were both nearly paralyzed by self-hatred which, if they weren't careful, would destroy them and their marriage. A typical pair of human newlyweds in other words. Why else be God unless you can help such folks?

So, although I told myself it was time to bow out of their lives, I did not press F10, but only F5, SUSPEND GAME. I pretended I would not be back but I knew I would. They needed me, you see.

Not that I expected them to cooperate with my grace.

See how far gone I was?

Author's Note _____

Perhaps I have been too hard on the narrator. I would not have you think that I condemn him. On the contrary, I am rather fond of him. After all, he does represent me a good deal of the time. He is, you might say, my sacrament. Like all sacraments, he both represents me and does not represent me. I am moderately satisfied with him in this regard, but he is often such an inadequate sacrament. However, what can an author do?

In any event, you must not let him persuade you that this story to which he obtusely attaches a premature happy ending is a story about a story about a story. O'Brien, Fowles, Gide, Twain all tell a story about storytelling, they write a novel about a novelist writing a novel. The narrator adds that he is writing a novel about a novel about how God writes the novels which are our lives. He thinks that he has described something very complex. Actually the matter is much more complex than he imagines. Listen to Aldous Huxley, long before Derrida and the deconstructionists, as he describes the reflections of a novelist about whom he is writing a novel:

"Put a novelist into the novel. He justifies aesthetic generalizations which may be interesting at least to me. He also justifies experiment. Specimens of his work may illustrate other possible or impossible ways of telling a story. And if you have him telling parts of the same story as you are, you can make variations on the theme. But why draw the line at one novelist inside your novel? Why not a second inside his? And a third inside the novel of the second and so on to infinity, like those advertisements of Quaker Oats where there's a Quaker holding a box of oats, on which there is another Quaker holding another box of oats on which etc etc. At about the tenth remove you might have a novelist telling your story in algebraic symbols or in terms of variations in blood pressure, pulse, secretion of ductless glands, and reaction times."

As my narrator knows well, that might be theoretically interesting, but no one would read it. My narrator's fictional publishers, who may or may not correspond to real characters, would quite properly reject such a novel.

Yet to be consistent the narrator ought to acknowledge that he is the creation of the author who also has created, through the narrator, the God whom the narrator pretends to describe by putting himself in a Godlike position. Thus there is necessarily at least a story about a story about a story about a story.

And what if I who intrude with these wise observations am also the narrator created by another author?

Does it go on to infinity as Huxley suggests?

Or only to Infinity, where in the words of Harry Truman, the buck—in this case responsibility for the story (or Story)—stops.

13 Ranora Leaps Over the Wall

Nothing much changed that week at Grand Beach. Michele left for Ohio to see her boyfriend amid universal lamentation—well, Bobby said that it would be quieter around the house. Heidi took over as censor of language on the ski boat. A horrendous July heat wave swept up from the Gulf of Mexico with humidity so thick you had to fight your way through it on the streets. The Cubs, astonishingly, continued to win. The papers began to carry news about the Bears, which meant summer was nearing an end; but I refused to read about them.

Anyway, I played with data analysis, talking to the DEC 20 at the University with my TRS-12, slept reasonably free from nightmares, suffered through my days of humiliation with the young skiers (one day in the rain, no less; weather doesn't stop truly dedicated skiers), agreed with the others that the ski boat was quieter without Michele, but not that much quieter because, as the boys said, Heidi took up a lot of the slack. I also swam in my pool, read books about French deconstructionists, and slept peacefully each night with no dreams that I cared to remember.

Nathan, back from a presentable finish in the Mackinac race (second in class, fifth in fleet), phoned to asked about the Duke and Duchess game.

I told him my preliminary reactions and argued that he had to put in a menu-driven character-creation option. "You don't have to insist that they create their characters beforehand, but it should be available for advanced players."

"Duke and Duchess anyway." I could hear him scribbling away at the other end of the line.

"And others if they want to be really advanced."

"Right, once we introduce that patch it ought not to be hard to make it expandable. Especially on the 80386 generation. They are fabulous, four times as fast and twice as much ROM and RAM. With a coprocessor and a 50k hard disk, of course. State of the art."

"'Til next year."

"Change characters in the middle of the game?" he asked.

"Huh?"

"I mean suppose you make the Duke a, well, let's say he's kind of Celtic and he drinks a lot. But then halfway through the game you learn that he has an ascetic dimension of his personality and you want to add that too."

"Why?" Despite the heat wave, I was shivering.

"Well, you yourself told me that you tried to create Maureen in *The Cardinal Sins* as evil and she resolutely insisted on being good. Most interesting character in the story, if you ask me."

"And Melissa Jean Ryan in *Rite of Spring* starts out as a spoiled Stanford freshman and ends up as the Sherlock Holmes who upstages even the great Blackie Ryan."

"Right. I haven't read that yet."

"You can build in a menu which enables a character to impose development on an author in the course of a game?"

"That's a strange way of putting it, but theoretically I don't see why not. You'd need more memory. Maybe we'd use it in an advanced version for those who have a fifty-megabyte disk."

See what I mean? Pure genius.

"What about a character in a minor subplot who tries to intrude into a major subplot?"

"Wow! Hey, that's exciting! I don't know whether we can do it, but it'd really be state of the art. Let me talk to Tex."

"You'd be approaching the real craft of fiction writing with that innovation." I hesitated. "You might tell your programmer to read *Mantissa* and *At Swim Two Birds*."

"At what?"

"It's a weird Irish novel by an alcoholic Irish genius named Flann O'Brien. John Fowles in *Mantissa* sort of refers back to it."

"Yeah." He was scribbling away at the other end. "You did mention them when I brought the game over. You'll be glad to know that we have an Irish programmer working on it. Named Shanahan."

"Really."

"How did your game end?"

"The Duke and the Duchess married and live happily after."

"Romantic."

"What else?"

"It's over then?"

"Well, not quite. I've suspended it for a while."

"After all this time? Wow! What a market! If you are hooked, what about ordinary people!"

Right, ordinary people.

After the conversation I wondered what was happening

in the land on the other side of Planck's Wall. Was B'Mella pregnant?

I wandered downstairs to ponder my Rube Goldberg link with the "adjoining" world or whatever it was. No, my job was done. They would live happily ever after. That was a foregone conclusion. Authors are not responsible for what happens to their characters after the stories are finished. That's what John Gregory Dunne told me when I protested the ending of *Dutch Shea Junior*. My sister and I insisted that Dutch didn't pull the trigger. Dunne said he thought Dutch did pull the trigger, but that as author his opinion about what happened after the end of the book was not more important than anyone else's.

I rejected this categorically. My characters live on after a story is finished. Lawyer Eileen Kane from *Patience of a Saint* was appointed a federal judge the year after the story was supposed to end. I told my family and friends about this promotion for the green-eyed attorney. Some understood what I meant, others thought I'd flipped out.

"She's not real. She's just a character in your stories."

"She is a character in my stories and she is real in that world."

Moreover, since I am hopelessly in love with Eileen and her husband Red Kane doesn't mind, not after what I did for them, she'll be back, gorgeous in black judicial robes, in other stories.

So I was not violating my own principles. Yet it is one thing to keep in touch with what is happening in a character's life and even to keep open the possibility of reentering their life at a later date, and quite another to return to the existing story to make sure that everything went well after the original hopeful but not totally happy ending.

The most an honest storyteller can promise is a hopeful ending. As Blackie Ryan once remarked, "'They all live happily ever after' means they only have three serious fights a week and refuse to talk to one another only one day a week."

We had enough reason to think that was a likely future for 'Rau and 'Ella, didn't we?

But was she pregnant?

That was more important for their happy ending than it was for most.

Could I have an impact on fertility in the other world? Wasn't that taking my God function a little too seriously?

On the other hand Red and Eileen Kane did manage to start another baby—a belated but most welcome little Redmond Junior—on their second honeymoon in Grand Cayman. A storyteller can make a lot happen to his characters if he wants to.

But through a computer game in what might be a real world, somewhere else?

I had meddled enough.

And Norman's programmer was a Shanahan, huh? Did s/he have an assistant named Furriskey?

One of the neighbors phoned to say that the Hagans had their first session with the family therapist and that it had not helped. Tom had moved out and Joan was seeing a divorce lawyer first thing in the morning. They both were blaming not the therapist, but me.

That's what you get when you meddle in a small way, when you play God by indirection and by listening to people talk out their problems. You play God and you become a scapegoat.

What would happen if you played God in a big way and people messed up their lives anyway?

Shanahan and the jury vote on it and the razor's the boy.

Or, if you're safe from that fate because you're immortal

or because you live in another world, they'll still blame you
and rant against you for the rest of their life.

It's not easy being God.

They had made their marriage bed—let them sleep in
it. They were on their own. The rest was up to the Other
Person.

Looking back on it with the wondrous wisdom which
comes from hindsight, I can see that there were too many
loose ends dangling where I thought the story had ended.

Another perfectly splendid Lake Michigan storm roared
across from Chicago, shook the trees, rattled the windows,
illumined the sky, drenched everything, and swept on towards South Bend trailing a wake of humidity-smashing
coolness. I turned off the air conditioner and opened the
windows wide. It would be a night for sleeping with a blanket.

No lightning struck my satellite disk. The Other Person
was not ready to make my decisions for me.

I went to bed restless and uneasy. Was she pregnant?
What had happened to Ranora? Had the clerical conspira-
cies continued? What, I thought, as I fell asleep, had become
of Malvau and N'Rasia, about whom I'd almost forgotten?

I woke from a deep but anxious sleep to find someone
in bed with me. Obviously a dream. Still, one is entitled to
one's comforts even in one's dreams. So I pushed the other
away.

And discovered in the act of pushing that the other was
a woman. Now that showed bad taste on her part. I knew
who it was before I turned on the light.

Her eyes fluttered open, she looked at me, gasped in
horror and jumped out of the bed, hands crossed in front of
her breasts. Only after she was standing, shaking with terror, did she glance down to see if she was wearing her short
purple kilt.

She was.

"What are you doing in my bed?" she screamed.

"Look around, N'Rasia. Is this your chamber?"

"Oh no. It's yours. You are in my dreams again. It is because I prayed so hard to you tonight."

"You're in my dream, or we wouldn't be in my house."

"This is your house?" She looked around. "It is very nice...may I have some of your wine?"

"You'll get drunk again."

"I promise I won't, and I will clean the glasses too."

"All right." Baileys, always readily available in a dream, was there on my bedstand.

"Not that. The real wine, the one your other creatures drink."

"Jameson's."

She nodded.

Well at least she hadn't asked for the twelve-year special reserve. Or for my very limited supply of Bushmill's Black Label.

So the Jameson's bottle materialized where the Baileys had been and two old-fashioned tumblers replaced the cordial glasses. I poured her a modest shot, and a tiny sip for myself, because unlike my characters I don't drink whiskey, not even with the "e" in it.

"With the frozen water, please," she asked meekly, shivering from the winds that were coming through my open window.

"It is customary in our world to consume this wine straight up."

"Straight up?" One arm ineffectually covering her breasts, she reached for the glass with the other.

"That means without the frozen water."

She nodded, sipped the drink, made a terrible face, shut her eyes, and gulped.

"It is very powerful wine." She licked her lips. "And it makes me feel very warm."

"Not warm enough for you to stand there like that." I found a Chicago Cubs jacket in my closet and handed it to her. "You'll get a cramp in your arms standing that way. Put this on and sit down."

She admired the color of the jacket, slipped it on, but did not at first fasten the buttons.

"Do you like me this way?"

"In purple and blue?"

"No. I am no longer slightly overweight. I was furious when you described me that way."

"You were slightly overweight. I liked you that way too. I created you so of course I like you."

"Love me?"

"Sure."

"Love me more now that I am thin?"

"Love is love. You are an attractive woman." No way you can win in this game of compliment soliciting, not even if you're a creator. "Now you are even more attractive. And you can button up the jacket."

"Why?"

"Because I'm the boss and because you'd never make such a display of yourself in your own world."

"I'm in your dream world now. And I don't have any secrets from you."

"A few more minutes and you'll go into a guilt fit. You're beautiful when you're overtly provocative, but it's not your style, except with your husband and then probably not enough. Anyway, button up."

She did, halfway. "I will never be slightly overweight again," she said fiercely. "I hate myself when I am fat."

"You were never fat," I insisted. Then, having learned

some skills at the game over the years, I added, "Now you're dazzling."

"Good." She sat on the chair behind my desk and filled the glass with Jameson's, having somehow removed the bottle from my custody.

"Go easy on that stuff, it's dangerous."

"Of course. I am pleased you are pleased with me."

Well, there was one way to end it: give her another injunction. "You're just about perfect now, as I'm sure Malvau would agree."

"He cannot keep his hands off me," she boasted, half pleased and half angry.

"Understandably. But you should not lose any more weight. Then you would look gaunt."

Did they have anorexics in that land? Was she the type?

"I will obey," she said dutifully. "Even if you permitted me to be beaten by those terrible men and then forgot about me."

"That was not my fault..."

"You were there and you let it happen."

"I cannot prevent random accidents."

"Certainly you can."

"Look, 'Rasia," I walked over to the desk, tilted her head back, and kissed her lips. "I love you. I created you, you seduced me, and I have fallen in love with you, a most improbable event, but it's what has happened. I would protect you from the slightest harm if I could. I can't eliminate all the evils in your land. Is that clear?"

She swallowed a big gulp of Jameson's. "Yes." Tears in her eyes. "Thank you for the kiss. I know I'm not worthy of it."

Dear God in heaven, will the self-hatred ever stop?

"If you weren't I wouldn't have kissed you... You certainly fought those so-and-so's fiercely that night."

"So my husband says," she smiled proudly. "I cannot believe it of myself."

"You went after him pretty hot and heavy too, the night of the marriage of the Duke and the Duchess."

She buried her face on my desk. "I am so ashamed. You have forgiven me for that?"

"The question is whether poor 'Vau has forgiven you."

She straightened up wearily. "I suppose so. He seemed almost to enjoy the fight. I won, of course."

"Doubtless."

"He even seems proud that I fight. It is impossible."

"Maybe there is some anger, deep down, because of the attack in the woods."

"No, no." She waved that away with a slightly tipsy gesture of her empty glass. "The child piped that away too."

"She merely awakened you."

"When you were losing interest in me and devoting all your time to B'Mella, she came to our pavilion and told me she would pipe away the anger. I did not realize I had any. It was so wonderful when she was finished."

'Nora with her pipe was turning into a medical resource.

"So what are your complaints this visit?"

"I want to go back to what I was."

"To what you were when?"

"When I was a dull middle-aged matron, a shallow character in a minor subplot, perhaps even one her husband would leave for a woman who was younger and more vital."

"My men don't do that sort of thing."

"All right. I still want you to change my part in the story."

"Make you fat again?"

She scrunched down in her Cub jacket and laughed guiltily. Part of the laugh was the drink that had taken, but part of it was a new aspect of this ever-changing woman: a slightly bawdy, self-deprecating wit. "Everything but that. Can't I choose?"

"You chose once. Anyway, even if I could rewrite the story and even if I would, if I kept the weight off you, your husband would still have a hard time not pawing you."

"I want to change back," she said stubbornly, filling her glass again. "I do not want to be who I am now."

"Look, woman, you elbowed your way into my dreams, demanded a bigger part, told me, in effect, you wanted to be someone important. So on one day I made you an enticing lover, a gracious hostess, a subject for beautiful music, and a brave fighter. Now you're complaining."

"I am none of those things," she said bitterly. "They think I am, but I am not."

"Yes, you are. Unless those qualities were already in you in some way that maybe I didn't even see, they never could have emerged in the story. It took the ilel to see you as you really are."

"I don't want to be that."

"Too bad."

She sighed. "My husband used to ignore me, now he adores me. I can do nothing wrong. Even when I am rude and shallow and nasty, he still thinks I am perfect. He will not leave me alone."

"I thought you were fighting."

"*Of course*, we're fighting, stupid..." Hand to tipsy mouth in dismay. "I am so sorry..."

"You're entitled to your feelings."

"Well, we are fighting. We cannot live with each other in peace and we cannot live without each other. The fights are...unimportant. It is the endless adoration. I cannot stand it. I am merely an aging grandmother..."

"With a wonderful thin waistline and flat belly."

"... with no depth, and no wisdom, and no great skills. I do not want the responsibility."

"You have it, kid. Like it or not. I loved you before, but I love you more now. I even love your struggle. It delights me to see you fight against your new self. Keep it up. It makes a wonderful plot line."

"Bastard," she shouted.

She put down her glass, being careful not to spill any of the precious liquid—admirable frugality—and rushed across the room at me, pounding my chest with solid fists. Poor 'Vau, if this sort of thing happened every night. The attack ceased almost as soon as it began and she was sobbing in my arms.

Poor dear woman. But she got herself out on this limb, she belonged there and no way was she going to be given a chance to go back. I understood 'Vau's attitude. Even her fury was a delight.

"You cannot possibly love me." She disentangled herself and went back to her drink.

"If I didn't love you, I'd zap you for that assault."

"You're as bad as my husband. He even admires my temper tantrums."

"Understandably."

"My children, my grandchildren, everyone—they expect me to be the woman in that God-condemned melody. I cannot do it, I cannot be her. I will not."

"You can and you will." I found that I was shaken by the experience of holding her in my arms. Small wonder. "The complaint, my beloved, is really that it's hard and uncertain. You must try every day and you do not know from one day to the next what will happen with you or anyone else, especially Malvau, whom you must be driving out of his mind."

"It is so hard in our land now. Everything is going

wrong. He is under such strain. I am no help. He needs what
he thinks I am, not what I really am."

"You're wasting your time. What I have written I have
written."

She poured herself another drink. "Did you stay for our
orgy?"

"Of course not."

"You should have. I was very good. Very." She preened
herself, but shakily.

"I can believe it."

"Sex," she began to lecture like an inebriated associate
professor describing his doctoral dissertation to junior fac-
ulty at a cocktail party, "is comic. Anyone who doesn't
understand that," a gesture dismissing them into Lake
Michigan, "is a fool. There must be delicacy in it, but dignity
is impossible. You understand? impossible. My man is so
dignified and important—his family background you
know—it was difficult for him to give himself over to the
comic indignity of sex. Well," mildly lascivious smile, "I
taught him to laugh when he is with me and now he is a
much better lover, and a better politician too."

"I don't doubt it for a moment."

"Yes, I am *quite* good now."

"Indeed. You want me to write that out of the story?"

"What!"

"You can't pick and choose. If you want to go back to
the person you were before you forced your way out of a
minor subplot, then you will have to put on weight again,
a suggestion to which you did not take kindly a few moments
ago, and give up your newfound sexual prowess."

"You wouldn't dare." She searched for fury but couldn't
quite remember where she had put it before her last drink.

"I was only pointing out the logic of your request."

"You love me too much to do that to me." She hiccuped

with delicacy and dignity and returned to her theme. "I am much better than that fool."

"What fool?"

"You know." She waved a hand vaguely. "The frigid one on your side. I tell her what to do. She will not listen."

"You talk to Joan?"

"Joan? Yes, what a strange name. J'Oan? She is a fool."

"How do you talk to her?"

The Jameson's was having its full effect. "Hmmn ... Oh, in dreams, how else? I have very good dreams with her. She will not listen to me, however."

"Your dreams or her dreams?"

"You should know, I don't." She swayed again. "I do not feel very well."

"Small wonder. You tell her to have an orgy with her husband?"

"Oh no." She tried an expression of exaggerated surprise. "Not yet. Well..." Impish grin, worthy of an ilel, "I give little hints."

"So you should have one with your husband again."

"*No!*" Instantly she was completely sober. "I will not give myself over to his lust like that ever again."

"*His* lust?"

"Of *course*."

"You were just telling me how good you were."

"I was ... now I am very sick. Will I die?"

"Hardly. Just too much of the creature taken. Before you pass out, let me warn you that I'll not back down one bit. You're terribly appealing when you plead with me. I like you that way. I love you when you struggle, so you're going to have to keep on with your struggle. And I won't guarantee the outcome because that would take the struggle away. Understand?"

She slumped over against my desk. "I knew you'd say that...where can I be very, very sick?"

I managed to get her to the bathroom, where she was very sick indeed and at great length. Then I forced her into the shower, wrapped her in a terry robe, and mostly carried her to a bed in one of the guest rooms.

"Silly stupid little cow," she murmured.

"You'll be all right."

"I will do another orgy," the words were now so slurred that I could barely make them out. "If you want."

"Not what I want; what you and he want."

"He wants. All the time."

"You don't?"

"Afraid, always afraid of everything." I pulled a light blanket over her. Even in the dream world, you can be cold. "Still love me?"

"Still love you."

She looked likely to make a comparison with someone else and then, drunk or not, thought better of it. "Kiss me again?"

So I kissed her again, tucked her in, and turned off the light.

Wow, as Nathan would say.

John Fowles complains about how impossible it is to avoid fornication with your woman characters. Maybe it's my different background and life history, but I love them too much to take advantage of them. They are powerlessly dependent on you for their being, their life, their freedom. Such vulnerability generates love, indeed, enormous love, but also such respect that you feel (well, I feel) like their father or mother. Or maybe both.

Anyway, I cleaned up the bathroom, brought the empty Jameson's bottle downstairs, cleaned my old-fashioned tumblers and put them away, and climbed back up to bed. It had been an exhausting dream, if that's what it was.

No rest for the wicked that night, however. Kaila, ashen-faced in his usual black gown with silver trim, was waiting for me. He was reading Wendy's other book *Women, Androgynes, and Other Mythical Beasts*, but with the inattention of a man who reads to keep other concerns off his mind.

"Well, this is my lucky night." My sigh sounded exactly like that of Blackie Ryan. "Two of you in one dream."

"There is someone else? Who?" He jumped up.

"Sorry, only N'Rasia."

"Only is not the right word. Where is she? May I see her?"

Why not?

"If it is a dream," he seemed puzzled, "why is she asleep?"

"Aren't we all, presumably?"

"Yes, but..."

"A bit too much of the creature taken."

"Huh?"

"Too much of our strong wine."

"Ah." He stroked her face lightly. "A truly superb woman. One of your finer creatures. You must be very proud of her."

"I am."

"No one would have suspected what was within her." His hand rested on her cheek. "Not until you told the ilel to search into her soul."

"All I told her was make up a tune. Aren't you a little young for N'Rasia?"

"No one is too young or too old for such a woman." He shook his head sadly. "Don't worry. I would not hurt her."

"You'd better not."

"What sense is there in it all?" His hand lingered on

'Rasia's face. "This glorious creature endures terrible agonies in her transformation and now she will likely be destroyed with the rest of us. Would it not be better to have left her as she was? Why force the change on her for so brief a time?"

"Moments of grace," I was echoing Shags's theology, I think, "are worth centuries. Moreover, she forced the change on me. Finally, no one is going to destroy her if I can help it."

He looked at me oddly. I turned off the light and we went back to my office.

"What's your problem tonight?" I beat him to my chair. "Do you want a drink?"

"I would end up in another bed, I fear."

"All over between you and G'Ranne?"

"Oh yes. She was very grateful and would care for me always." He seemed uninterested in the subject. "I taught her so much about love. But we were not meant for one another. The act of love seemed a dead metaphor for love itself. You understand, surely?"

"Well, I won't debate about it, but Robert Graves has an ending that belies the beginning of that poem." And how did he know Robert Graves? "I thought you two might be well matched. She's a lot more than the ice maiden I first took her to be."

"Oh yes." He smiled mechanically. "She will do very well, even with men. If anyone lives in our land."

"It's that bad?"

"Why did you leave?" His chin slumped on his chest. "The story was not finished."

"Certainly it's finished. I can't be expected to stay around forever. I told my tale, now it's up to the Other Person to assume proper responsibility."

"I'm afraid I don't understand."

"The Duke and the Duchess are married and they must live happily ever after on their own. So must all of you. As for you and the ilel..."

"That's a childish dream long abandoned." He dismissed my Ranora with a crisp movement of his hand. "I have matured greatly since then. It was a foolish request," he smiled wanly, "for which I apologize. Tonight I am much more serious. We cannot live happily ever after, even in the terms of your obstreperous Blackie Ryan, unless you return."

"Why?"

"I do not fully understand. I simply know that for some reason you have abandoned us in many ways and we will soon perish. All of us, our land, everything."

"What has gone wrong?"

"I am not permitted to tell you."

"That's ridiculous. Is the Duchess pregnant? Where is the ilel?"

"I don't know why I can't answer questions. I do not make the rules. You made them...or whoever put you in charge. You can only know what is happening when you are with us. These...these meetings, I use the only word I can find, these dreams which are more than dreams, are only hints."

"Nathan's game..." I said half to myself. "You access them only through the port."

"Yet," he continued, a scholar puzzled by a problem even when he faced disaster, "I do not understand them either. Why am I in the dreams? Why is she, admirable woman that she is or has become or however she is to be described?"

"Beats me."

"We need you," he pleaded desperately. "Please come back while there is still time."

I would have argued the point with him, but he began to fade out. Or rather this time I began to fade out. Everything seemed black for a long time and then I woke up to a crisp summer morning, whitecaps on the lake, a brisk breeze blowing out of the northeast, sailboats already dancing along the shore, and cruisers moving northward. We'd have a few such perfect days and then the humidity would return.

No second dream of G'Ranne?

The first one wasn't a dream; it was an eruption of my preconscious during an altered state of consciousness induced by self-hypnosis. Dreams you can suppress. Did she come to me in a dream that night, her smile of love a plea for my return with no pressure and no demands? Did I repress the dream?

Had I been repressing dreams about her all my life? Was she a sacrament of God for me instead of the other way around?

What can I tell you?

Anyway, a more forceful appeal was still to come.

I could find no trace of my dream visitors, not even a hint that anyone had slept in the perfectly made bed in the guest bedroom.

They were dream creatures surely. Liquor could only appear, disappear, and reappear that way in dreams. They were different from other dream creatures, however, in that they were far more rational in their conversations with me, save for their unshakable conviction that I was a God or possibly the Lord Our God. They were also more vivid. Who can remember dream conversations the way I remembered my dialogues with them?

Possibly, I surmised, returning even more exhausted than usual from my ski adventures, they represented a different altered state of consciousness, related to dreams but

bridging the boundaries between different cosmoi and oc-
curring only to those who were somehow involved in crossing the boundaries through a temporary port.

I wasn't sure what that explanation meant since it
was mostly academic happy talk, but it seemed satisfying
for the moment. Then I realized that N'Rasia claimed to
have been dream linked with Joan Hagan. If any of this
was true...

If my recreated N'Rasia was filling Joan Hagan's head
with erotic images, the links couldn't be all bad could they?

Why was I so hesitant about resuming the game?

Ever play with a Ouija board? It's fun at first, a harm-
less game. Jokes, suggestive remarks, little digs at one another. Then something or someone else seems to take control
of the game, something powerful and angry and frightening.
If you're smart you stop. Maybe it's something deep down
inside yourself or one of the other players, but it's still terrifying and who needs it? Especially since there is a hint
that if you keep fooling around with the darn thing, it might
just take over your life.

That's the way I was beginning to feel about Nathan's
God Game.

Read some of the literature about those who become
deeply involved in psychic research. There's a strong propensity for them to freak out. Permanently.

To be blunt about it, I was scared. I was afraid of the
power the God Game gave me. I wasn't sure what it might
do to me. I didn't want any more of that control of people's
lives. They were not, at least probably not, characters in
one of my stories but real people. I did not want to play
games with the destiny of real people.

To be fair to the revised game, the one you can buy
at your local software store, there is no evidence that my
experience has been any more than an isolated and non-

replicated event. We were not able to replicate it on the experimental version either, no matter how hard we tried.

Still, well, maybe some of the players have experienced the same phenomenon and are afraid to report it. One of the purposes of this book is to assure such players that it has happened before and that it can be benign.

From which it does not follow, I hasten to add, that it is inevitably and always benign.

Now for the most scary part. Like totally scary.

Ed McKenna and Mike Rochford came over that evening for supper and for a discussion of the next step in the opera Ed and I were writing. I made my fruit salad, which is my sole culinary accomplishment but more than presentable, and served some of the better local Tabor Hill wine. It was a sober gathering because we had serious work to accomplish.

I stress these points, because it is necessary to report that I was wide awake when the call came, there were people present when I took the call, and they can testify to my end of the conversation, which they thought was a bit odd.

The phone rang just as I was serving the raspberry tea. A collect call for anyone from "Michele."

"Hi," I said cheerfully, "how's Ohio?"

"I can't come back," she said grimly, "unless you come back."

"What?"

"You have to come back first."

"I don't have to come back anywhere, Michele. I'm in Grand Beach. You're in Ohio. You'll be back this weekend to ski with us. What's wrong with you?"

"That's totally not right. Don't be an airhead. Do what you're supposed to do, then I can come back and we'll make everything OK again."

"This is Michele?"

"*Of course* it is. Who else would it be, anyway?"

"Not...not Ranora?"

Silence. Then like in a fog, "Who's Ranora?"

"An ilel."

"A *what*?"

"Never mind. You're coming home from Ohio this weekend, right?"

"Ohio? Where's that?"

"You're visiting Rick?"

"Who?"

Oh, oh.

"Where are you calling from, Michele?"

"You have to come back, you totally have to come back. We won't even have a hopeful ending unless you're here to help me. Will you, please? Before it's too late?"

Was she drinking? No, Michele doesn't drink and she doesn't do drugs.

"Promise?"

"Sure."

"Really?"

"Really."

"That's like really excellent. I have to go, I'm totally cashed. Thanks. Bye."

"A strange conversation," Mike said tentatively. "Ranora is an odd name."

"Remember when and where you heard it."

I kept remarkably cool for the rest of their visit and talked rationally and competently about our opera.

My mind, however, was racing. The ilel, somehow, had skipped over Max Planck's Wall and was communicating to me through Michele.

Moreover she had calmly informed me that she needed me to finish her plans. Not that I needed her. And insisted that I'd better hurry.

OK. There were some loose ends that needed to be tidied up. We'd finish the game this time for good and then cut the link, close the port, resurface Planck's Wall.

Right?

Right.

14 Trouble Right Here in River City

After Ed and Mike left, I turned on the system, reactivated the game, and promptly went to the Duchess's pavilion.

I had to find out whether she was pregnant, didn't I?

She wasn't there. It turned out that it was the month in which the joint rule was exercised from the Duke's pavilion. OK. I had some catching up to do.

INQUIRE DUCHESS PREGNANT.

DO NOT KNOW PREGNANT.

WITH CHILD.

EXECUTING.

Then a few seconds later, NEGATIVE. NEGATIVE.

Once is enough, idiot.

That was only part of what had gone wrong, though an important part.

The time frame had speeded up. Only a day in my world, but several months in theirs, long enough for the poor idjits to fall out of love with one another, or think they had.

They were still sharing the same bed, though as far as I could tell from discreet peeking, without much enthusiasm or passion. There were no major conflicts between them,

save for the absence of signs of progeny, just the little battles
which destroy love in the friction of any intimacy. He was
too withdrawn, preoccupied, too mystical, she was too domineering, prickly, and obsessed with the details of politics.
He was late for everything, she could not control her snide
nasty mouth. Typical human marriage after the first few
months when the glow has worn off the nightly romp.

The troubles in their world were no longer political but
climatological. It had not rained since the wedding and the
annual crop was in peril, for the first time in decades. The
priests were scurrying around badmouthing Lenrau and
hinting that the threatened infertility of the fields was the
result of the infertility of the marriage bed. That, they whispered, was all Lenrau's fault. The marriage was a blasphemy, displeasing to the Lord Our God.

No way, I said, but no one was listening to me.

It took me awhile to figure out the obvious. Impotency.
No wonder Lenrau was humiliated and herself furious.

How could you be impotent with a woman like her in
bed with you?

A professional celibate's question, I suppose. On her
grim days, and now they all seemed grim, she would scare
most men back into the latency period of their lives.

Castrating?

Yeah, that will do as a description.

The worst change was that there was no trace of the
ilel. Kaila wandered around the administrative pavilion
like a puppy who had lost his person. No one else mentioned
her.

FIND ILEL, I told my PC.

DO NOT KNOW ILEL, it said.

RANORA, I typed in impatiently.

ERROR, ERROR!

I tried again. FIND RANORA.

INPUT OUTPUT ERROR. ATTEMPT TO OPEN FILE ALREADY OPEN.

I knew better than to try to argue with a computer giving that message. I felt a chill of doom. Was the imp child dead? If someone had killed her, they would pay—only God for a couple of days and already into the vengeance-and-wrath business.

Or was she away in Ohio?

Kaila did not seem in mourning exactly, more like a man pining for someone who was away on a long journey and might or might not return. That speculation was a little more consoling but not much.

So the priests, apparently now merged into one caste regardless of which duchy they came from, continued to intrigue against Lenrau. In the shops and the market places, in the cafes and the taverns, among the anxious farmers watching their gorgeous fields turn brown and dry, they whispered that it would not rain unless Lenrau was "offered up." I didn't know what that meant but I didn't like the sound of it. The Cardinal was now completely in command and went about under the protection of a giant straight from Boris's nightmares always standing behind him. I called him the Troll because that's what he seemed to be—well, part troll and part small-time Mafia hit man or crooked southeast-side Irish precinct captain.

Neither Lenrau nor B'Mella were praying at night anymore. They did not talk to each other or to the Lord Their God. Nor were they willing to listen to my orders pounded out now frantically on the 286 keyboard. The Duke was locked up in his Willy Weakling persona. Somehow it didn't quite fit him, although he seemed to enjoy feeling sorry for himself.

Look, he was a physically strong man, capable on the record of decisive action, personal heroism and spectacular performance in bed. Why had he geeked out, as Michele or Bob would have put it?

My guess was that he was ashamed of or maybe uncertain about the poet and visionary part of his character. He was supposed to be a warrior, not a poet, right? The lovely lady had married a great warrior, right? OK, she had approved of the other part of him, but she didn't know what it meant. What happens if she finds out she has a part-time flake on her hands?

What probably happens, even if she isn't Irish and hence doesn't come from a tradition where to be a really good king or warrior you have to be a mystic and poet, is that she melts completely and adores her husband. But the only way that will ever happen is if he opens up to her. And he's not about to do that.

In the meantime we have to fend off the Cardinal and his crowd who want to do the poor man in. Moreover, we have to do it without our local Ariel.

I checked out Malvau. Like Kaila he seemed to have withdrawn from the political game, sitting in the garden all day, every day, strumming on a lute and rarely talking to his wife, who didn't have much to say herself.

I supposed that I could reactivate both Kaila and Malvau if necessary, but for what goal? No point in doing anything until I formed a strategy.

My first idea was obvious.

END DROUGHT.

ERROR. ERROR. INSUFFICIENT MOISTURE AT PRESENT.

Damn.

HOW SOON SUFFICIENT MOISTURE?

IMPOSSIBLE TO ESTIMATE.

Oh, great.

My second idea was a stroke of genius, incompetent genius.

The answer to the problem seemed to be a pregnancy. But how was I supposed to handle that? I thought about it and decided that if you're playing God on a temporary basis you can get away with anything. After all, doesn't Paul Scott in the Raj Quartet cause three different women to become pregnant the first time they have intercourse? And none of the readers complained, did they? If you're God, you're God, right?

But what if your best intentions as God go wrong?

I had a lot to learn yet, and the game was dangerously near its end.

Anyway, it was a very hot night, with only a few hours of darkness, and the windows were open in the Ducal bedroom. My two friends, both soaking with perspiration, were lying on their bed, covers thrown off, as far away from each other as they could get without rolling on the floor—a not infrequent position for human men and women, especially when it's hot and they're irritable. Not without some hesitation, I typed out the fatal instruction:

IMPREGNATE DUCHESS.

I expected an argument from the PC, but it went along promptly: EXECUTING.

"I love you, 'Ella," he says to her, still strictly from Terry Timid.

She snorted derisively and turned on her side so that her back was facing him. He started to caress her back lightly. She pushed his hand away.

"Can we not be as we once were?"

"I am tired, leave me alone."

My fingers poised over the keyboard. Not quite the time. He had to court her again. Easy enough for God to say.

He touched a breast very tentatively, too tentatively if you want my uninformed opinion. She shoved his hand away again. "I said leave me alone."

I am no expert in these matters, God (you should excuse the expression) knows; but now was not the time to turn amorous, poor idjit.

LEAVE DUCHESS ALONE, I insisted.

He wouldn't listen. His next move was, let us say, considerably more forward and very ill advised. She hit him. I pushed the REPEAT button. He tried to kiss her, she hit him again, jumped out of the bed and grabbed for her undergarment. "If you won't let me sleep here, then I will find another bed."

GO BACK, I told her, and pressed the REPEAT button. No luck.

STOP RESISTING GRACE. She did not hesitate a second.

Now the story turns terribly ugly. What does your Marty Macho do when he wants to assert some of the masculinity about which he isn't sure? That's right, he decides he'll push the woman around a little, just to show her who's boss. Our Marty Macho had some excuse. A long time ago she had told him not to let her leave, ever. But like all such general commands it had an implicit qualification: "unless I really want to." Poor Lenrau was not yet experienced enough in the rhetoric of intimacy to catch the nuance.

So he grabbed her, acting the way his warrior ethos said a man should act with a woman who was teasing. She tried to knee him and failed. Then she tried to bite his arm and succeeded. "Must you hurt a woman to be able to enter her?" she sneered.

Then it turned brutal. The only word for what happened was rape, cruel, savage rape. I told him to stop, swore at him, promised him that he would rot in hell for all eternity. He kept right on, a rampaging madman, killing all he loved.

She fought him every inch of the way. It was not sex
or even power about which they were struggling on the floor
like two jungle animals, but the other side of the coin of
love. He was brutalizing her because he hated her and she
was punching and kicking, scratching and clawing because
she was being violated by a man she hated.

I was shocked, horrified, furious, sick—so sick that I
had to flee to the bathroom to vomit. When I returned he
had left. B'Mella, a wounded mess of bruised limbs, torn
garments, and bleeding body, lay sobbing hysterically on
the floor.

Bastard, I thought.

She was more ready to forgive than I. "Lord Our God,"
she prayed, "send him back with one word of sorrow and I
will forgive him."

Now you turn generous.

I went after him as he staggered out into the darkness,
drunk with his own violence, and gave him every instruction I could think of. No luck. He hated himself too much.
In fact, I had to knock the sword out of his hand at the local
armory so he wouldn't kill himself.

Some folks who know this story insist that what Lenrau
did was beyond forgiveness. Yes, they say, it was out of
character; yes, he was under terrible strain; yes, he's probably going to suffer hellishly for it; yes, she had goaded him
into it. Yes to all of those comments, but it was still behavior
that ought never to be forgiven.

I won't argue the issue. This story is not about forgiveness and reform, not mainly anyway. The point is that
she wanted to forgive him as Jesus wanted to forgive Judas.
I didn't tell her to. It was her idea. Maybe it was false
consciousness on her part, but it was her decision. He knew
her well enough to understand that she was as quick to

forgiveness as she was to anger, to comprehend that with B'Mella one word of sorrow would more than suffice.

He wouldn't do it. What happened to him was his punishment for not wanting to be forgiven.

Back in their chamber, the pain on B'Mella's scratched face slowly turned to anger and then a grim determination for revenge.

After that, it was all strictly downhill.

A couple of weeks of their time slipped by in the next few hours. I tried everything I could to shake them out of their lethargy and turn Lenrau and B'Mella away from the tragedy which, like a pair of Greeks, they seemed determined to stage. Nothing worked. The Duke hied himself to the houseboat on the lake and crooned mournful songs, neglecting to eat or sleep. Linco and Kaila, the latter more disconsolate with each passing day, were shunted aside. The silent Malvau continued to strum on his lute. N'Rasia, reverting to her earlier dull and dowdy self despite my warning that I wouldn't tolerate it, stayed inside to avoid the heat.

The Duchess huddled with the priests, particularly the Cardinal and the Troll.

"The old ways are not always wrong, my lady." The oil from the Cardinal's voice was pure slime.

"So?" She smeared paint recklessly on a furious storm scene.

"The Lord Our God is often worshipped in spirit and truth, but not always." He rubbed his long, thin fingers.

"Indeed?" She reached for another brush.

"There are times of crisis when we should return to the old ways. The crises come because the Lord Our God wishes us to remember his past wonders."

She paused in her work to consider him carefully.

Do not listen to Cardinal, I demanded.

She brushed me off with a slight frown—about all I rated from her these days.

"You mean some kind of magic?"

She knew damn well what he meant—an excuse for vengeance on her husband. Sacrifice the Duke in the name of the common good. Do evil in the name of good. All political leaders do it well.

"We mean no harm to My Lord Lenrau, poor man." The Cardinal saw his chance for an opening and grabbed it. "No human sacrifices," he smiled benignly, "we are too modern for that superstition."

"What *do* you intend?"

"Merely to take him into custody, to imprison him under, ah, difficult conditions." He bowed deeply from the waist. "That should placate the anger of the Lord Our God."

"And if it doesn't?"

He rolled his eyes. "Surely we will not have to consider that possibility."

"I will think of it. Now begone."

Rudeness to the tempter is an excellent substitute for resisting temptation.

Lenrau, poor demented man, was in deep trouble.

Once more I instructed the 286 to make rain.

CREATE RAIN. EXECUTE.

IOF ERROR. IOF ERROR.

DAMN YOU.

DON'T TALK THAT WAY TO ME.

Poor thing, it was beginning to think it was God.

It became so hot that I felt dry and hot watching on the screen. The crops withered. The people became more lawless and contentious. Disaster seemed to be sitting on the mountaintops like a carrion bird, waiting to descend on a dying land.

The Cardinal returned to B'Mella's studio. The people

were insisting that Lenrau must be "offered" on the night of the Four Moons. She hesitated. "He will not be harmed?"

"Of course not, my lady. We venerate the poor man."

HE LIES, I insisted. HE'LL KILL 'RAU AND PART OF YOU KNOWS THAT.

She did not even dismiss me with a frown. Rather she nodded slowly. "Tell the peasants that I regret what must be done, but it is necessary."

The Cardinal beamed. "They will seize him at dawn. We will have the offering when the moons come together. He will be imprisoned then, of course. Soon there will be rain."

Not if I can help it, he won't be.

I sent Kaila out to warn the Duke and plead with him. A waste of time. Lenrau wanted to expiate; an apology and a reconciliation would not be suffering enough. He must permit himself to die. Maybe he half believed by now, crazed from the heat and his fast, that his "degeneracy" was responsible for the drought.

The social structure of their little world deteriorated. Save for the warriors, who fought or trained most of the time, and the priests and wizards and such like who wandered around like Vatican bureaucrats looking important, the ordinary people were mostly responsible hardworking peasants and burghers, a somewhat more colorful version of the early modern Netherlanders. They sang and danced rather more than the sober Dutch, but they worked hard, prayed devoutly, and were almost puritanically modest in their intimacies.

However, as the heat worsened and rumors of an "offering" (which had not occurred for a long time) spread, work halted in the shops and the fields and the small craft factories. Drinking began early in the morning, and by noon everyone was drunk and the sexual revelries began, a continuous saturnalia which seemed to violate all the rules of these placid, industrious, sober people. Everyone, that is, but N'Rasia and Malvau, who seemed to have opted out of the scene completely. Their maiden daughter went off to live with some friends. The other children, their spouses, and the grandchildren stayed away.

Everyone ignored the Lord Our God, for the interim me. No one prayed anymore before going to sleep at night, partly because they were too drunk or too besotted with sex to think about God and partly because it seemed that some other power, more ancient perhaps, or more modern, was being worshipped. My little world was flipping out. I wanted to terminate the game, but it was now much too late to quit. I had to do something. They were my people and I was their God. So I tried again.

RETURN RANORA, I punched in the keyboard.

Instead of an input/output error message I received an ambiguous SEARCHING.

DON'T GIVE ME YOUR SEARCHING. I WANT HER NOW.

SEARCHING, it responded implacably.

Then as the sun rose for another terrible day, she reappeared, a somber, spiritless shadow of an ilel, dressed again in deepest black, walking like a ghost through the fields towards the city of the Duchess. The peasants and the burghers fell back in silent awe. The priests scurried to tell the Cardinal. Kaila hurried to her side, was ignored as if he did not exist, and then dutifully fell in step behind her. The Tinker Bell child was gone, replaced by a young, vest-pocket banshee.

Gee, kid, you wanted me back to help you. What do we do now? Just you and me.

There is trouble right here in River City, folks, real trouble.

I searched her eyes for a spark of the old ilel as she

approached B'Mella's pavilion with the grim solemnity of
Death in a Bergman film. Whatever the reason for her
transformation, our Ariel was now a messenger of doom.

Right into the pavilion she went, down a long corridor
of screens past startled warrior guards and into B'Mella's
chamber. The Duchess was involved in an acute attack of
nausea.

Morning sickness. My infertility cure had worked. Nice.
There would be an heir to both principalities and she would
be rid of Lenrau. The ilel did not seem disposed to offer
congratulations. She merely stood in the middle of the
chamber and stared, her eyes as hard as obsidian. The Duchess, startled and spooked, greeted her formally.

"You have returned to us then, good ilel?" Her voice
shook in superstitious awe. Was the sprite returned to pun-
ish her for taking revenge on her husband?

Her face a blank, like a permanently angry doll, Ranora
raised her finger and pointed it at the Duchess in silent
accusation.

"You cannot frighten me, wicked child," the Duchess
sputtered. "I have nothing left to lose."

Ranora followed her for the rest of the day, seemingly
immune to the heat despite her heavy black gown. She
continued to point her relentlessly accusing finger, even
when B'Mella was huddled with the Cardinal in the final
stages of her conspiracy of revenge. The priests were afraid
to bar an ilel from their pavilion, and the Duchess elected
to pretend that the haunt was not dogging her every step.
She was going ahead with her revenge no matter what the
ilel thought.

So bringing back the magic maiden had made no difference. The people were desperate enough to try anything.
The Duke was worthless to himself and everyone else. The

clergy were happily anticipating their return to power. The Duchess was about to take her revenge.

It would be easy to have hated her then. She was a blind, stubborn, destructive fool. But, despite Somerset Maugham, it's hard to hate someone you once loved. No matter how much I might have hated her, the poor woman probably hated herself more. The goodness that had always been within her was still there, locked up in a maximum-security prison of humiliation and outrage and rejected love. A single word of compunction from her husband would have dissolved the prison walls. But he was out at the lake, crooning his sad, mad songs and hoping for oblivion. Give him wings and put him in a tree and Seamus Heaney would appear to write the poems. Strange, I thought, that Ranora had not gone after him. Perhaps, like me, she had given up on him completely.

At day's end the ilel stalked out of the town in the same glum silence with which she had come. She dismissed the loyally following Kaila with a wave of her tiny hand. He looked as if he wanted to follow her; but, whatever the rules of his ministry to her, they forbade him to disobey. She disappeared into the forest. I suspended the game and tried desperately to think of a solution to the problem. What does God do when humans are completely intractable?

He punts. Ridiculous, huh? But it was the only answer I could not think of.

I activated the game again. There was nothing in the nature of creation or of the human condition that guaranteed a happy ending.

There was only one hint of hope and I didn't see how it made much difference: with a basket of bread and wine over her arm, N'Rasia approached her lute-playing husband in the garden of their pavilion and whispered in his ear.

He looked up at her impatiently. "What point is there in that when it will all soon be over?"

"We can die better," she said. "And perhaps find the strength to live."

He nodded and off they went.

Yes, if the priests took over, there would be a knife in both their backs very soon. I was no longer confident enough to say "not if I have anything to say about it."

THUNDERSTORM PLEASE. NOW. EXECUTE.

I'M TRYING. EOF ERROR.

I typed in a foul word which it purported not to understand.

The tragic drama unrolled now with the same measured solemnity as the wedding had a few months before in their time, only yesterday in my time.

At the end of the day, during the long twilight, shortly after Ranora had disappeared into the forest, a band of the lowest rank of priests, men who looked like convicts from a hospital for the criminally insane, appeared in the middle of the high meadow, at approximately the same place where the marriage ceremony had been performed, and began to construct a low-slung platform with a tent and portable building modules which looked very much like an Aztec sacrificial altar. A smaller group apprehended Kaila and Linco at dusk and locked them up in a pleasant but well-guarded little pavilion on the edge of B'Mella's city.

Another band crept into Malvau's garden but found nothing. Their report did not seem to worry the Cardinal.

"It does not matter. He is no longer important. We will apprehend him tomorrow."

In the farms on the edge of the mountains, fires burned all night and the drinking and the wenching were even wilder than usual. The women, usually more or less equal, were not given much choice about the random lovemaking, not that they seemed to want to choose. The moral fabric of these sturdy landholders was being torn asunder, but ritually, as if they were going through motions which, while pleasant enough, were more theatre than reality. As if they were living a ritual memory from the past rather than responding to a contemporary problem.

I thought about an irrigation program. With all that snow up in the mountains...

It was too late for that.

Shortly before first light, after the brief hour or two of darkness, a band of twenty or so peasants, apparently more inebriated than the rest, surged down the mountain into the forest and, as if drawn by a magnet, headed for the side of the sullen lake where the mad king, like Sweeney of old, was crooning dirges for his own funeral.

EXECUTE STORM, I demanded

%$#@$%#, it replied helpfully.

The drunken peasants, ignoring my repeated instructions to disperse, milled around outside the boat, shouting and cursing. Lenrau, perhaps realizing that they were not brave enough to come in to get him, walked out into the murk of another steamy dawn bravely and stupidly meeting his fate.

FIGHT THE BASTARDS, I demanded.

He wasn't listening either.

A squad of smartly uniformed clergy showed up and half carried, half dragged him to the meadow and tied him on the table which had been erected on the top of the platform. The sun was sizzling already. It would roast the poor Duke like St. Lawrence on the gridiron. Long before the nighttime ceremonies began, he'd be fried to a crisp. Either the peasants didn't realize this or didn't care.

Someone has to help him, I thought. Who?

ILEL HELP DUKE, I told the 286.

Promptly, as if waiting off stage, Ranora, black hood now pulled over her head, materialized at the edge of the forest and walked solemnly across the field to the altar, as I was already calling it. The peasants fell back in superstitious terror as if a ghost were among them. She pulled off her black gown and covered the Duke with it like a sleeping child. From the short black shift she was wearing under the gown, she drew a flask of liquid and made him drink from it. His twisted body relaxed quickly—water and a painkiller. In the whole land only one partially supernatural being would give the once-popular Duke a sip of water.

Poor dummy had brought it on himself, but I felt sorry for him. Neither the drought nor B'Mella's barrenness was his fault. I had cured the one and made matters worse. Too bad I couldn't somehow cure the other.

In desperation I now tried the Three Stooges.

DESTROY PLOT OF PRIESTS, I told them.

The idea seemed to appeal. Their manic minds welcomed any new target for mayhem. They climbed one of the small mountains at the edge of the forest and laid out several long maps next to the huge rock that rested precariously on a ledge overlooking the meadow.

"It should follow this path." Larry sketched a thick black line through a series of ravines and hills. "Slice through the forest here," he continued his line, "break into the meadow at this point," he drew a big X, "and then blot out the high priest's pavilion before he knows what is happening."

"Our little explosions will set it loose after all these centuries," enthused Curly. "How splendid!"

"What if we miss? Do we get another chance?" Moe wondered.

"We do, if you push it back up." Larry was already placing neat little packages at various points along the cliff.

Their little packages exploded harmlessly, like wet firecrackers on the Fourth of July. One more "pfft!"

I shouldn't have expected anything from them. Every other experiment of theirs had been a dud, probably would have been even if I hadn't intervened. Still, we needed something.

Then the rock—it was at least ten feet high—began to vibrate ever so slightly, tilting back and forth in easy, gentle movements. Hardly enough to loosen it.

Just enough, as it turned out. The rock started to lurch crudely, as if it were eager to begin its wild run down the rollercoaster mountainside. Then with a mighty roar it tore loose from its precipice and rumbled down the first ravine, a freight train picking up speed.

DELETE CARDINAL'S PAVILION, I told the 286.

ATTEMPTING TO EXECUTE.

The great rock tumbled down the ravines and valleys like a bowling ball rolling down a staircase, changing direction at the last moment just as the thick line on Larry's map said it should. How about that!

ATTEMPTING TO EXECUTE.

It ripped through the forest, a tornado of violent destruction. Everyone in the land stopped in their tracks and looked up, astonished by the deafening roar.

Larry, Curly, and Moe cheered themselves enthusiastically.

The rock raced by the altar on which Lenrau was bound and headed straight for the Cardinal's tent. I was cheering as loudly as the Stooges.

At the last moment it careened away harmlessly, rushed across the meadow, and buried itself in a small pond. A giant sheet of spray rose at the edges of the pond, which now had a large island in its center. The spray quickly fell back into the water and on the beach around the pond. Just as quickly my hopes fell.

EXECUTION FAILED.

I know, dummy.

The Cardinal's agents spread the word that his miraculous escape was a sign of favor from the Lord Our God. He was winning all the tricks.

Later in the day, for an hour and a half, there was a sign of hope. G'Ranne, obedient as always to my slightest request and with her usual brilliant organizational energies, created a troop of warriors from both sides. They rode into the meadow on their big chariots, drawn by the speedy white horses, like a group of horsemen riding out of the Apocalypse. There were not enough of them to break through the guard around the Duke, but they could kill a lot of priests and hold the rest at bay.

The Cardinal approached them with his hand raised in a sign of truce.

"No useful purpose," he said in his melodious voice, "in shedding blood. We can negotiate a compromise."

"The Duke must be freed," G'Ranne insisted. "That is not negotiable."

"Let us dialogue on it in peace. We will lay down our arms. You lay down yours. You are men and women of honor; so are we."

DON'T BELIEVE THEM! I pleaded. DON'T DO IT, YOU STUPID BITCH!

Well, she did it anyway.

"Idiot!" I shouted, rising to my feet and whacking the 286. Such is our rage against the first infidelity of those who have been most faithful.

The picture on my Zenith screen flickered but did not go out. I kind of wished it had.

No one was listening to me, not even the passionately loyal and not-enough-loved ice woman.

The warriors were a bloodthirsty lot, but they had a code of honor which meant you kept your word when you gave it. Poor naïfs. Not familiar with the *stylo curiae*.

They accepted the truce. They set aside their sword and spears, and so did the priests around the altar. Then another band swarmed in from behind and quickly overcame the astonished warriors and bound them. G'Ranne wept tears of bitter self-reproach. "I should have listened to you," she said over and over.

Too late now, idiot.

"There will be many offerings tonight and in the nights to come," the Cardinal said piously. "We will honor God with the offerings of the bodies of his enemies."

Some of his crowd started messing around with G'Ranne and the few other women warriors who had been taken prisoners.

The Cardinal held up his hand. "We must wait till the offering is complete. The Duchess must not hear of this little matter beforehand. Take them away."

God, however, was on the side of the prisoners. For what that was worth just now. Because the current occupant of Nathan's God Game was not running on all cylinders.

15 The Feast of the Four Moons

CREATE HUGE RAINSTORM, I told the 286, hoping that there was finally enough moisture somewhere in the world.

EXECUTING.

Well, it didn't say no.

HURRY UP, I insisted.

TIME REQUIRED.

HOW MUCH TIME REQUIRED? I snapped back stubbornly.

CANNOT ESTIMATE.

On the horizon of my screen, a cloud appeared, then another. Like a storm over Lake Michigan.

Later in the day, the clergy found Malvau and N'Rasia, who were packing up after their night of fun and games. Both of them fought like wild animals. Three of the priests finally immobilized 'Vau while another one beat him unconscious. 'Rasia dove into the lake and swam underwater beyond their reach.

"She is unimportant," said the leader of the squad. "Do not bother with her."

You may live to regret that decision, I thought. But what could one, admittedly attractive, grandmother do against a whole civilization gone mad?

Back in the meadow, glaring balefully at the mob of peasants, the ilel stood guard at the altar like a widow at an Irish wake. For much of the afternoon it was a standoff; they were too frightened to risk the supernatural furies at her disposal, and she did not waver either from the glare of the sunlight or from the threatening calls from the crowd. The sun was soon partially covered by a thin haze as clouds began to build up behind the high mountains on the sunset side of the country, giant, foreboding thunderheads. The mob pointed at the clouds and shouted enthusiastically. The gods, they seemed to think, would reward them with rain soon after the offering was finished.

You are in for a big surprise, guys, if this God has anything to say about it.

I was now totally converted to a God of fury and wrath. I would zap them all if I had to, even if I didn't have to, just for the pure hell of it. Their malice called to heaven, that is to me, for vengeance.

I'd delete the lot of them.

It grew darker as the afternoon continued, a tornado sky, the kind which when I was a boy made me wonder whether the end of the world was at hand. I thought about that. Before I was finished, the end of their world might be at hand. Obliterate the whole miserable lot of them.

A squad of the chaingang-fugitive clergy showed up and ringed the platform and its fierce little guardian. She pointed a warning finger at them and they stumbled back a few paces but kept their circle tight. When I did my zapping, anyone who laid a finger on her would be the first to go.

In the distance a few idle, tentative shreds of lightning danced along the top of the tallest mountain. A shiver ran through the mob. You'd better be scared, guys, you haven't seen anything yet. Wait till I work havoc among the cedar trees, if you have any cedar trees in this miserable world.

As I was expecting, the Cardinal and the Troll showed up with a splendidly uniformed guard of priests in maroon and white. A coup was taking place. After they had disposed of Lenrau, B'Mella and her unborn child would be disposed of quietly, and the clergy would set up their own neat profitable little Ayatollah theocracy from which the Lord Our God, who apparently didn't require priests in this world, would be properly excluded.

Well, you're all in for a little surprise. Mess with me, will you? Just wait till my storm gets up a proper head of steam.

If either Lenrau or B'Mella were functioning properly, they would have seen this coup coming and headed it off, but they were both tied up in knots with their foolish emotional problems. The only barrier now was the brave little teenager, pointing her finger of doom at the Cardinal.

And an unarmed middle-aged woman, soaking wet, somewhere in the forest.

The baddies had too much invested in their coup to be slowed down by such a frail and weaponless obstacle as Ranora. The Cardinal gave an order. A squad of his thugs, as nervous as cops around a cornered hijacker, crept up the stairs to the top of the platform and grabbed her. She did not come quietly. Standing her ground, she kicked the first one in the groin, hacked at the neck of the second, and then went down under an avalanche of sweating, grunting, punching hoods. A cry of shrill terror raced through the mob. What happens to those guilty of sacrilege?

MASSIVE LIGHTNING, I told my 286.

Four or five streaks of nasty blue light cut across the black sky. Mess with my messenger, will they?

The spectacular display saved poor Ranora for the time being. She would have been raped and murdered on the spot if the priests themselves had not been quite so superstitious.

The Cardinal looked like he was about to order her death, and then hesitated. I'm sure that the rumbling thunder didn't scare him. But he did not want to push his men too far yet. Kill the Duke, then the Duchess, then cut the throat of this obnoxious little brat. Still kicking and screaming, she was carried off to the maroon pavilion of the high priest. Her cloak was dragged off Lenrau's silent, motionless body; it didn't matter anymore; there was not enough sun to burn him.

I called on the machine for more donner and blitzen, just to warn them that I didn't want her hurt in that pavilion.

There was enough electricity in the air by the time it grew dark for me to unleash a good sized storm; however, I wanted the biggest downpour in their meteorological history, if they had such a history. Now I was thinking coolly and clearly, improving every minute at the God Game (the Other Person already had an eternity of practice). No more hasty and ineffective uses of power.

Timing, I figured, was of the essence of being God, especially since you had more of it than anyone else. I accessed the Cardinal's pavilion to make certain that no one was hurting my teenager. They had her gagged and strapped down and her shift was in tatters, but no one was taking the risk of coming too close to her. As long as she was in no immediate danger, I would prolong my intervention till the last possible moment when everyone was on site and my storm had built up a maximum head of steam; I also wanted to give B'Mella a chance to redeem herself. If Ranora was at risk, however, all bets were off. She was the only one in the whole place I still liked. She had prior claim on my power. Maybe like all the others she was a product of my own preconsciousness, but she was part of the preconscious which produced my favorite people.

The evening dragged on into night, lightning slicing across the sky, thunder rumbling threateningly, the priests and the increasing masses of people chanting antiphonally in the archaic language which had been used at the wedding, reminding me of the Latin office for the dead in Gregorian chant.

Finally the Duchess appeared, along with Linco, Malvau, G'Ranne, and Kaila, all bound, and Ranora bound and gagged. The Cardinal was planning to wipe out all his enemies at one fell swoop. The mobs of people who were now jammed into the plain were intoxicated with drink and the self-hypnotic chants. Kill everyone now and begin a new era.

My heart sank when I saw B'Mella. She looked sick, exhausted, depressed, and spaced out. Someone had slipped her a mickey. Perhaps she thought that at the last minute she could turn away the destructiveness of her revenge. Now they had taken the power of choice away from her. She had sown the winds of vengeance and had been deprived of the power to stop the whirlwinds from reaping that vengeance for her. One of the thugs half pushed, half helped her up the stairs to where her husband's bound body lay, seemingly unconscious, on its rough altar of sacrifice.

In the old fantasy stories it's the girl who is saved from sacrifice at the last minute. Reverse scenario, except the woman had been drugged, first by her own pernicious hatred and now by some mind-bending narcotic.

SAVE DUKE, I typed in after pressing her function key.

She stirred listlessly, as though she heard but was not interested or could not comprehend.

OK. We do plan B.

BEGIN BIG STORM, I ordered the PC.

ERROR, ERROR, it replied.

NATURE ERROR?

DOWNPOUR ORDERED NOT READY.

HOW SOON?

CANNOT ESTIMATE.

OK, Captain Kirk, what now?

I had cut it too closely. God or not, I could not produce a downpour before the elements were ready, lots of noise and light, yes, but these only confirmed the priests' version of things: as soon as you kill the Duke, there will be rain. I was playing the Cardinal's game.

His eyes calculating shrewdly, he studied the sky. He would not cut it too fine. Kill off the Duke and maybe some of the others for good measure and then wait till the storm, my storm, began.

He gave a signal. The choir of priests sang more rapidly, their psalmody rising to a shrill frenzy. The crowds responded hysterically, shaking their hand lamps so that the whole plain glittered as if it were being crisscrossed by hordes of giant, inebriated fireflies.

I pushed all my function keys, SAVE DUKE, and held down the REPEAT button. No dice, save for some savage squeals from Ranora.

Clever and evil men were not only frustrating God's plans, they were twisting them to their own purposes. So what would the Other Person do now?

B'Mella seemed to try to concentrate, to focus her eyes, to comprehend what was happening, and gave up in a mixture of resignation and despair.

It's all your fault, you evil little bitch. Wait till I have a chance to settle with you.

Already I had built my own judgment seat.

The Cardinal gave another signal. The beat of the singing rose now to hysterical frenzy, demanding a climax of destruction. Drums began to roll, drowning out the thunder. He drew a long dagger from his belt and held it high over

Lenrau's body. The Troll unsheathed a big, heavy sword and lifted it into the air like a toothpick.

I pushed the DUCHESS key in desperation. SAVE DUKE.

I finally got through to her and once more played into the hands of the bad guys.

She was too sick, too groggy, and too confused to act rationally. Awkwardly, like a woman in a dream, she staggered to her husband's side and threw herself protectively over his body. A loud gasp of horror swept from one end of the plain to the other. The Cardinal grinned cheerfully and nodded his head, the singing and the drumbeating soared to a crescendo of intolerable intensity, a ruler scratching a cosmic blackboard. Their weapons rose to the highest possible point over the two bodies.

Think of something quick.

ZAP PRIESTS, I assaulted my keyboard with frantic fingers.

WHICH PRIESTS?

DELETE CARDINAL KROL.

I DO NOT KNOW CARDINAL KROL.

Lucky you.

The singing stopped. In the deadly silence the weapons started their downward arc.

DELETE CARDINAL, TROLL.

EXECUTING.

It seemed like two-thirds of eternity, but it must have been only a millisecond. The first thunderbolt began way up at the top of the highest and most distant mountain and, with the speed of light, roared in an unerring line straight towards the altar, like the old Burlington Zephyr silver train racing through Lisle at 5:30. It exploded around the altar just as two weapons seemed to strike. Giant blue sparks, a thousand el cars' third rails, leaped in every direction. Thunder roared like an erupting volcano over the plain, echoing and reechoing and then reechoing again against the mountains. Long before the echoes stopped, another bolt of lightning crackled against the base of the altar. And another. And another.

Between the blinding explosions, I saw that the Cardinal and his hideous troll were not present anymore. Where they had been standing, there was nothing at all.

DELETE EXECUTED.

Mess with the Lord Our God, will you?

CEASE FIRE, I demanded.

The thunder kept rolling back and forth between the mountain ranges, and the crowd was screaming as if it expected the earth to swallow them up—which might just be the next trick if it were needed. On the altar, prostrate still and probably scared stiff, were the two causes of all this mess, still, it seemed, present and probably alive.

Then something completely unpredictable happened. Instead of fleeing in panic, the goon squad of priests at the foot of the altar surged up the steps.

ZAP ALL PRIESTS, I ordered.

ZAP TEMPORARILY EXHAUSTED. EXECUTING RAIN.

Did it ever execute rain!

It seemed that someone (me of course, who else?) had upturned a bottomless bucket and poured all the water in the world on the meadow and its inhabitants. Need a bit of rain for your crops, do you? You can count on the Lord Your God.

The first batch of goons were swept away from the altar platform by the downpour, but they quickly regrouped and with grim care began to climb it again.

Now what do you do? These guys aren't supposed to be heroes.

Ever hear of the bravery which comes from despair?

I noticed that the poor little ilel, a soaking wet doll, was still struggling with her bonds.

RELEASE RANORA.

From out of the crowd, a hooded figure appeared and, so deftly that no one noticed, slit the ropes binding the ilel. N'Rasia had her major role at last.

With instant reflexes, like a halfback who sees daylight, Ranora scampered up the slippery steps, each one now a minor waterfall, grabbed the Cardinal's charred dagger, pushed B'Mella unceremoniously off her husband, and cut the Duke's ropes.

SAVE DUCHESS, ILEL, I told the Duke.

He burst off the altar like a berserker, swept up the Troll's mammoth blade with a mighty sweep of what must have been cramped and aching arms, and sent the first wave of the goons tumbling down the slippery steps. Lightning burst across the sky, creating blue reflections against his wet and glistening body. He swung again and the thunder pounded behind him. Dubiously the crowd of clerical goons pondered another charge. The Cardinal's dagger held truculently between both her hands, the Duchess rose up next to him.

Anyone want to fight?

Water was streaming down his battered but still solid, muscular body, and his face was shining with the glow of battle light. The lightning, thunder, and swirling winds seemed to be background for the resurrection of his masculine warrior power. The band of goons formed up a few yards away from him, preparing for another charge.

As though he had all the time in the world, he turned to his wife, smiled, touched her cheek gently, and asked an affectionate, almost joking, question which was drowned out in the discordant chorus of sounds.

She nodded. Gently but firmly, he moved her from his

left side back a few paces on the platform and turned to face the encroaching band of thugs again, his sword raised in grim defiance. I am Lenrau, he seemed to be saying; maybe I'm a mystic and a dreamer and not much of a Duke, but you threaten my woman and our child at peril of your lives. The attackers who had inched closer to him stopped.

In the meantime tidal waves of panic swept across the huge throng. The rain had doused most of their lamps and the roaring thunder and crackling thunderbolts sent them rushing in terror towards the forests and the roads back to their homes and towns.

DELETE PANIC, I told them and the mad race for safety slowed but did not stop. The back rows of priests cast aside their swords and spears and ran too, leaving the score of goons who had been the Cardinal's personal guard by themselves to stand off Lenrau.

He had another ally. As soon as she had freed the Duke, Ranora darted down the steps, grabbed a dagger from a paralyzed guard, and with the help of N'Rasia, who had thrown back her hood and whose gold-and-silver hair shone like a halo in the lightning flashes, cut the ropes binding Kaila and Malvau and the others. I am prepared to swear that N'Rasia winked at her husband.

Straight as an arrow, the ilel raced to G'Ranne and cut her bonds. Ruffling little sister's hair again, the warrior woman grabbed a sword from a startled priest, and, her own black hair waving in the wind and rain like a pirate's flag, chased a couple of squads of the enemy away. Some of the other warriors, including of course the Three Stooges, rallied to her side. Her face glowing in the lightning flashes, she began to close in on the altar, her tiny army following close behind.

N'Rasia and Ranora scurried among the milling mob freeing the other friends of the Duke and pressing spears and swords into their hands. Ranora barked a crisp command, a waterlogged little demon with only a shred of cloth clinging to her tiny body, and formed up her band, closing in on the flank of those who were preparing for another charge at the Duke.

Lightning continued to crackle and sizzle around the plain. The thunder blasts followed immediately after each flash—the center of the storm was upon them. Rain poured out of the sky like a gigantic waterfall.

With his left arm, Lenrau brushed the water out of his eyes and, swordpoint in front of him, walked lightly down the stairs. One of the goons thrust with a mighty two-handed swipe of a huge broadsword. Lenrau deftly brushed the blow aside as if a mosquito had buzzed at him. The goon's blade leaped out of his hand, spun through the air, and fell ten yards away.

The man backed away from Lenrau's swordpoint, broke, and ran. Rather against orders, B'Mella, knife still tightly clasped in both hands, slipped down one step and then another, a strategic reserve for her husband. The ilel's squad moved cautiously in to attack from the flank, and G'Ranne's warriors, like a mob of angry pirates, swarmed in on the other side.

For a dramatic moment, while the lightning ripped all around, there was no motion on or by the altar. Everyone was frozen as if in a giant sculpture of warfare in the rain.

I didn't want any of the good guys to get hurt, particularly nutty little Ranora who had a Balaclava gleam in her eyes. I could simply eradicate all the priests with a few well-placed lightning bolts. But if you're going to be good at the God business, you have to learn restraint.

PRIESTS FLEE, I instructed the keyboard.

Lightning hit the top of the altar again, dangerously close to B'Mella. It was all the clerics needed. They dropped their swords and took off like the Sioux in the old films (if not quite in reality) when the U.S. Cavalry rode over the hill.

Lenrau smiled briefly, signaled G'Ranne to throw a protective cordon around the altar, turned and led Ranora and her band up the slippery steps, placed his weapon on the altar where he had almost died, and enveloped his rain-drenched wife in his arms.

CROWD GO HOME, I told the machine. It was time to wrap this game up.

The Duke and the Duchess both talked at once, pouring out a torrent of grief, remorse, guilt, affection, and admiration.

My Crooked Lines were working pretty well, all things considered.

"Well." Hands on hips, modesty now provided only by her energy and enthusiasm, Ranora was trying to control her merry laughter reborn from days gone by. "If you're finished with all that, you might apologize to the Lord Our God too!"

Still clinging to each other and with streams of rain pouring off their bodies like flash floods, Lenrau and B'Mella tried to tell me that they were sorry, that they would begin again, and that it was my responsibility to see that this time all went well between them. So it is with humans when they are reborn—God gets little of the credit and much of the blame.

Suddenly, just as they were running out of prayers, Lenrau broke down and started to sob, his tears mixing with the rain, his body quivering in syncopation with the exploding thunder. Real men didn't seem to cry in their culture either. But poet/kings have to be able to cry. Finn MacCool and Cuchulain and that bunch used to go on week-long crying jags.

'Course these people weren't Irish. Not that I knew of, anyway. (Except G'Ranne, who somehow was in the wrong story.) 'Ella, nevertheless, did a very Irish-woman thing. However much she may have been shocked at the sight of a warrior weeping in public, she took his head gently in her hands, laid it against her breasts, and, while the lightning flashed around them and the thunder roared, sang to him the song he composed for her on their wedding night.

Nice going, kid. God will not give up on you after all.

They had learned something, perhaps enough so that the next time they were in the down phase of the cycle of their love, they would cling to each other again instead of fleeing from each other; then a few more times around the course and they would be sufficiently practiced at the art of creating a rebirth of love so that they would be truly and permanently man and wife.

Not bad for a novice at the game of the Crooked Lines.

Malvau's arm was draped around the shoulders of his heroine/wife, who seemed to be ruefully looking in my direction. No rewrites possible anymore.

Well, you wanted the big time, kid.

Ranora, thank God (the Other Person, not me), was the ilel of old. Unimpeded by the absence of clothes, she scurried up and down the line of loyalists standing respectfully on the steps of the altar, hugging and kissing them and cavorting in a happy dance as she played a hornpipe on an imaginary pipe. Kaila was the first one she kissed, lightly and respectfully, as befit a relationship between an ilel and her Protector. Then, after she'd gone down the line and bestowed an especially fierce hug on the laughing G'Ranne, as if she had second thoughts, she bounced back to him and embraced him passionately.

The surprised young man, admirable and proper as always, was overcome with delight, an impossible dream suddenly coming true. He was very reluctant to let her naked little body out of his arms. She didn't seem very eager to leave either. Ah, the poor man would never have a day's peace for the rest of his life.

Then, remembering her obligations, she danced up the steps, clapped her hands for attention, and announced imperiously, "Also you should thank the Lord Our God for sending you such a perfect ilel as Ranora."

"We thank you, Lord Our God," B'Mella said dutifully, raising her eyes again towards me, "for sending us..."

"A wonderful imp child," Lenrau had recovered his cool, "to remind us how to laugh."

Everyone's tears dissolved into laughter. Ranora flew across the altar platform, a bird sailing blithely through a rainstorm, and threw herself upon her patrons, hugging them both and laughing with them as if she felt that her laughter and her embrace might bind them together forever.

Even the thunder seemed to join their laughter.

Dutiful ruler that she was, B'Mella wrapped her cloak around the ilel. Our vestal virgins must maintain a modicum of modesty.

Enough crooked lines for one night. I pushed the TERMINATE function key and quickly disconnected the PC from its link to the TV system. Then I removed the Alpha 10 from its slot in the Bernouli box and put it on a shelf where it would be safe.

The last image before their world faded off my screen was a close-up of the tearstained, joyous face of G'Ranne, radiant in the light of the four converging moons which had elbowed their way through the clouds: Teresa emerging in the light of Mount Carmel after the Dark Night of the Soul.

If I had saved her life along with the others, she must have thought, I did love her after all.

Ah, my beloved, you spoke truth. Authors need characters, God needs people; but it takes such tiny gifts, crumbs from my table, to make you happy. Thus all the greater my need for you.

I sank into my gray chair, so exhausted that I barely had the strength to pour myself an extra large glass of Baileys Irish Cream.

"It's a good thing for us," Nathan would say smugly later, "that the Other Person can't quit."

"She has had more practice. Anyway you don't believe in Her."

"The God I don't believe in," Nathan leaned forward with a happy grin, "is a He, and I'm glad that He can't quit merely because the game gets rough. What will happen to all those people now that you have deserted them?"

"Nothing more than what happens to my characters when I finish a story. I still worry about them, but I'm not responsible for them. My grace doesn't have to war with their free will."

"You abandoned them," Nathan insisted, glad for the rare advantage he had in our own ongoing game.

"They're being watched over," said his wife Elisa (a saintly woman, God knows, to put up with what she has to put up with and, though I'll be in grave trouble for saying it, slightly ahead of Nathan in the fitness game). "Who made the lightning strike your dish in the first place?"

An interesting point, I admitted.

"*And* remember what Nathan means in Hebrew?"

"All right, what does Nathan mean in Hebrew?"

"'Given'— maybe you'd say 'Grace'!"

Tell me about it.

That's about all. I played the game a couple of dozen more times, with another Alpha 10 of course, and never did get that ending again. Nathan claims that it is a possible ending but that it requires extraordinary concentration and that possibly the animated blips don't excite the kind of commitment required for such concentration.

The game has sold very well (the *Red Shift* has been replaced by a newer, bigger, and allegedly faster boat). Nathan's marketing people are using Boris's art now. He's done a good job on Lenrau and B'Mella, although he hasn't quite captured them. But Ranora is perfect, a blond pixie wrapped in peppermint candy with snapping eyes and a determined little jaw jutting comically to the sky.

They have renamed it the God Game.

The Hagans are back together, and she seems to glow much of the time. It's still a rocky pilgrimage for them. One or the other dashes off to a divorce lawyer almost every month. Rumors have it that they see Doctor Shanahan and "someone else out at Loyola." So maybe the dreams worked.

Michele?

"Like, I didn't phone you. I mean I had a dream I called you, but no way did I really phone you."

"What did you say in the dream?"

Frown. "I wanted you to do something. I don't remember what it was."

"Did I do it?"

"Of *course!*"

Sometimes at night, as I say, I hear the pipe outside my window forty-seven stories above the Magnificent Mile. It sounds like the Menuetto in Mozart's Posthorn Serenade (K. 320), only a little kinkier.

Maybe, on the other hand, I am only imagining it.

Despite our seminar, I'm not sure I understand any of what happened. I did receive a week ago a picture of an infant—not a photograph exactly, rather something which seemed to have been burned on the paper. The kid might have B'Mella's deep brown eyes, but I'm probably kidding myself. Sometimes when you hold the envelope the right way, you might think that it could be red-and-white striped.

The Alpha 10 which has every move of the game recorded remains quietly on the shelf in my office at Grand Beach, a mute reminder that it's hell to be God.

I ran the Alpha 10 data through one of Nathan's graph-making programs, and it produced a rather curious map, which one of my water-skiing friends adapted for me. (I guess it's pretty much like the other cosmos, though my cartographer claims that in the original version of the story I had the sun rising and setting in the same place!)

The Alpha 10 is also a chance to play the *real* game again. Sure, it's hell to be God. It's also fun to be God. You are loved by a lot of wonderful people; which is probably why God, the Other Person that is, doesn't quit.

As for Nathan, well, I intend to get even (of course). I am part of a conspiracy to teach him what it is like to have to play God to a group of fractious humans, to have far more responsibility than you have power.

We're going to make him departmental chairman.

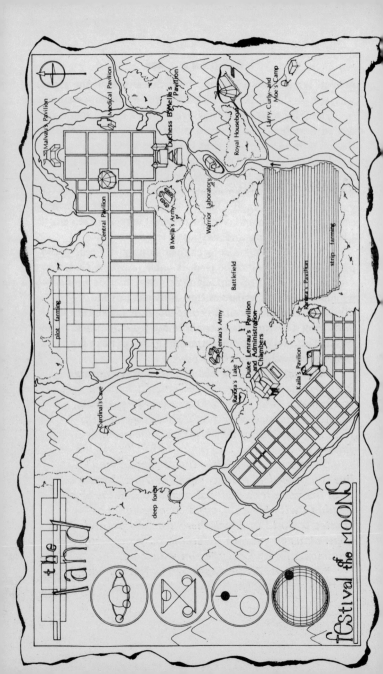

Author's Note _____

So they all lived happily ever after.

My narrator knows better than this. As Blackie Ryan notes elsewhere, the most one can expect is that they have only two or three big fights a week.

Blackie will settle for one day of happiness a week, some weeks.

Yet Msgr. Ryan and his various creators have been criticized for being unrealistically hopeful. Life is after all a vale of tears, abounding in suffering, sickness, injustice, and death. Plot, especially the fiction of an ending which imposes meaning, is a fallacy.

Or, to put it differently, the cosmos in which we live is a good deal more complex and problematic than the narrator's fictional cosmos down the block. He (and I with his uninspired cooperation) has created a world in which there are solid grounds for hope, plausible reasons for seeing purpose, justifiable arguments for an Other Person who loves.

But that, as Bastian says in The Never Ending Story, *is only a story.*

Hope, purpose, and love are not always reflected in daily life and often not at all in some lives. My friend David Lodge in his *Out of the Shelter* describes his narrator as praying for his childhood friend Jill who is killed in an air raid and not praying for his wife when he fears in sudden panic she may drown. How can there be purpose and hope and reason for prayer in a world in which children are killed in air raids?

Yet his narrator swims eagerly to his wife when she surfaces uninjured in the pool.

Is the story really never ending? *Videtur quod non*, as the scholastics put it. It often seems not.

Is the "wild cry of longing" which Nathan Scott sees in the child's demand "Momma, tell me a story!" self-deceptive or revelatory?

Is the mystery that happiness is limited or that there is any happiness at all? Is the proper question not whether despair is more tough-minded than hope, but whether it is correct?

Does a story, finally any story, no matter how pessimistic as Professor Lodge clearly perceives, put hope in life that isn't there, or does it draw out of life hope that is there but which without the story we cannot see?

Is the story if not true at least True?

Ah, but as the Irish would say, that's another story altogether!

Then again maybe not. Maybe it's the only story, your story, my story, every story.

Bestselling SF/Horror

☐ The Brain Eaters	Gary Brandner	£1.95
☐ Family Portrait	Graham Masterton	£2.50
☐ Satan's Snowdrop	Guy N. Smith	£1.95
☐ Malleus Maleficarum	Montague Summers	£4.95
☐ The Devil Rides Out	Dennis Wheatley	£2.95
☐ Cities in Flight	James Blish	£2.95
☐ Stand on Zanzibar	John Brunner	£2.95
☐ 2001: A Space Odyssey	Arthur C. Clarke	£1.95
☐ Elric of Melnibone	Michael Moorcock	£1.95
☐ Gene Wolfe's Book of Days	Gene Wolfe	£2.25
☐ The Shadow of the Torturer	Gene Wolfe	£2.50
☐ Sharra's Exile	Marion Zimmer Bradley	£1.95
☐ The Blackcollar	Timothy Zahn	£1.95

ARROW BOOKS, BOOKSERVICE BY POST, PO BOX 29, DOUGLAS, ISLE OF MAN, BRITISH ISLES

NAME ....

ADDRESS ....

....

....

Please enclose a cheque or postal order made out to Arrow Books Ltd. for the amount due and allow the following for postage and packing.

U.K. CUSTOMERS: Please allow 22p per book to a maximum of £3.00.

B.F.P.O. & EIRE: Please allow 22p per book to a maximum of £3.00.

OVERSEAS CUSTOMERS: Please allow 22p per book.

Whilst every effort is made to keep prices low it is sometimes necessary to increase cover prices at short notice. Arrow Books reserve the right to show new retail prices on covers which may differ from those previously advertised in the text or elsewhere.

A Selection of Arrow Bestsellers

☐ A Long Way From Heaven	Sheelagh Kelly	£2.95
☐ 1985	Anthony Burgess	£1.95
☐ To Glory We Steer	Alexander Kent	£2.50
☐ The Last Raider	Douglas Reeman	£2.50
☐ Strike from the Sea	Douglas Reeman	£2.50
☐ Albatross	Evelyn Anthony	£2.50
☐ Return of the Howling	Gary Brandner	£1.95
☐ 2001: A Space Odyssey	Arthur C. Clarke	£1.95
☐ The Sea Shall Not Have Them	John Harris	£2.50
☐ A Rumour of War	Philip Caputo	£2.50
☐ Spitfire	Jeffrey Quill	£3.50
☐ Shake Hands Forever	Ruth Rendell	£1.95
☐ Hollywood Babylon	Kenneth Anger	£7.95
☐ The Rich	William Davis	£1.95
☐ Men in Love	Nancy Friday	£2.75
☐ George Thomas, Mr Speaker: The Memoirs of Viscount Tonypandy	George Thomas	£2.95
☐ The Jason Voyage	Tim Severin	£3.50

ARROW BOOKS, BOOKSERVICE BY POST, PO BOX 29, DOUGLAS, ISLE OF MAN, BRITISH ISLES

NAME . . . .

ADDRESS . . . .

. . . .

. . . .

Please enclose a cheque or postal order made out to Arrow Books Ltd. for the amount due and allow the following for postage and packing.

U.K. CUSTOMERS: Please allow 22p per book to a maximum of £3.00.

B.F.P.O. & EIRE: Please allow 22p per book to a maximum of £3.00.

OVERSEAS CUSTOMERS: Please allow 22p per book.

Whilst every effort is made to keep prices low it is sometimes necessary to increase cover prices at short notice. Arrow Books reserve the right to show new retail prices on covers which may differ from those previously advertised in the text or elsewhere.